The Click

by

Steve Shear

The Click

Cover Art by *Kim Mendoza*

The Wild Rose Press, Inc.
PO Box 708
Adams Basin, NY 14410-0708
Visit us at www.thewildrosepress.com

Publishing History
First Sci-Fi Rose Edition, 2018
Print ISBN 978-1-5092-2276-6
Digital ISBN 978-1-5092-2277-3

Published in the United States of America

"I'm afraid I'll need some blood work from you, Oliver," Hitch heard Dr. Delahunt say.

He swung around. "Me?"

"You're a Beater. And, well you know, first OJ, now…"

Hitch held both hands up, as if to surrender, and shortly thereafter was in the lab area having his blood drawn. Two days later, in the afternoon, he and Edna were back in the doctor's office, without Kathy and Christopher this time. Ralph Delahunt sat across from them studying the lab report, nodding his head and shrugging.

"Well," he said as he handed them the report. "Two Preemies in one family does not appear to be coincidental."

"Are you saying it's because of…" Edna started to say without looking at the report.

Delahunt nodded at the report, as if the answers were there, and he didn't want to compound the pain by repeating the reasons aloud. All the time Hitch was studying the report and knew exactly what Ralph didn't want to verbalize. He was a carrier of the virus, of the plague.

Praise for Steve Shear

"I enjoy mysteries, political intrigue and international intrigue. I was taken in by the first 6 pages… I am looking forward to purchasing the finished product. Please let me know as soon as it is published."

~ Gladys L

"I couldn't put The Click down! I continued to read it at home, at the public library, and at Starbucks. The novel held my attention, even with noise around. Not many books do that for me! … I really liked The Trials of Adrian Wheeler, yet this one is better. I found myself anxious throughout the book, wondering what would happen next."

~ Cass M

"I really enjoyed the read. I think you incorporated all the elements of a great story—mystery, complexity, political intrigue, sex, and of course limited but effective violence."

~ Jack G

Dedication

To my son Mike who clicked me on to the idea and to Erik Wolter, a great screenwriter and collaborator on The Click screenplay.

Prologue
In The Future

It began slowly, according to all the articles appearing on television and the Net, like the upward seepage of water from a small crack in a pipe below ground. And then without warning, like a total failure in the pipe, an explosion of illness, then death, spread from city to city, from village to village, across the Earth; citizens of the world on the streets coughing, vomiting, dying. Many of the more fortunate who needed to venture out wore masks as they weaved around deceased bodies yet to be picked up by the caravan of mortuary trucks that carried with them bright orange body bags. The citizens still living but too weak to move from the streets, sidewalks, and even the gutters were attended to by medics and paramedics who also knocked door to door hoping to help those who couldn't help themselves.

Before the Plague, people lived longer and died of old age, most of them in their late nineties and older. Humanity had cured cancer, heart disease, most infectious ailments, and many old age catastrophes like dementia. By then the religious fanatics making up the *Coalition United for Theocratic Oversight*, the Cūtocracy, had successfully infiltrated the legislative bodies of much of the world, including the United States, institutionalizing many of its theocratic policies within what were once secular democracies. They prohibited the highly successful use of stem cell reproduction to correct birth defects and dismantled all the international programs scientifically regulating weather. Indeed, any technological advancement that placed man above God, at least according to the Cūtocracy, was considered sacrilegious. The most dramatic of those policies were the absolute banning of abortions and birth control, and the insistence on large families. The combination was synergistic, devastating, and inevitable—severe overpopulation.

The left-wing populists had no miracles, the right-wing Cūtocrats no cures, and the politicians no talking points. Eventually, all the nations of the world raced for the little bits of land and resources that remained and began staking their claims. First the Chinese, then India, two of the four economic superpowers, followed by the other two, the United States and Neuropa, both fighting polarizing internal political battles focused mainly on border control, keeping out the riffraff, and escalating budgets. They all had nuclear warheads rusting away in readily accessible silos. A touch of the button could have easily solved the problem of overpopulation. A gigantic boom here, a mushroom cloud there, and presto, no more problem. But alas, world order was restored, sensitive trigger fingers anesthetized, and overpopulation was at least temporarily curbed by the plague's deadly virus, quickly dubbed the ERAM virus, *Earth's Revenge Against Mankind*, or sometimes merely ERAM-V. The water in most places carried the deadly virus, but sometimes it was the air. The righteous, encouraged by the Cūtocrats, branded it the hand of Heaven avenging all the malignant murderers of the innocent and their renunciation of the Good Books. The Godless ones repudiated such demagoguery, insisting that the great lady of nature recoiled against a worldwide population boom playing havoc with her creation. And so it went—in churches, on street corners, barbershops, salons, and on the Net.

With time and deliberate action on the part of all nations, the plague relinquished its hold on humanity but not before a startling twenty percent of the world population fell within its grip.

Well before that devastating plague was more than a bothersome influenza in areas around the world, a small segment of the scientific community examined the virus, the likes of which had never been seen before. They recognized its virulent nature right away, that it could and more than likely would rear its ugly head on a large scale and continuously replicate itself if not eradicated once and for all. A super vaccine had to be developed.

Chapter One

On a sunny day in spring, the Cūtocracy headquarters in Rome became the destination for a string of solar powered hydro-pneumatic limousines hovering inches above the ground. Each carried one or more members of the all-powerful Cūtocratic council, including High Minister Charles Sheen, Emissary to the Supreme Minister of the Ecclesian Church, Smotec Innocent II. Trying to avoid the others arriving at the same time, the High Minister had his Limo glide around the corner and drop him off at the side entrance. From there he entered the headquarters carrying a large purse.

By the time he worked his way up six flights of stone stairs, out of breath even though he rested at each landing, Minister Sheen, now eighty-six years old, entered the reception area on the Council floor. The receptionist, a young woman conservatively dressed in grays and blacks and wearing weighty looking black-rimmed glasses, waved him into the conference room where it was clear he was the last to arrive. Everyone else had already taken their places around a large, elongated, mahogany table. Along the center edge at the far side sat the Council Chair from the United States, a young fat man in a three-piece suit. To his left sat India, then Canada, and so on. There were fourteen members in total representing the entire world. Minister Sheen's seat to the right of the Chair awaited his arrival.

He nodded to the others as he limped around the table and took his seat, carefully holding on to his purse. He knew why he was there and didn't like what was coming. The agenda for this emergency meeting merely set forth the meeting time and the requirement that all attend and cast a vote. Days earlier, each representative was contacted individually, in secret, and apprised of the details, or so the minister was informed. They were also told how to cast their votes.

The Council Chair called the meeting to order and declared it was time to vote. No discussion was allowed. He started with India to his left and went around the table. India voted *Yes*, Canada voted *Yes*, South America voted *Yes*… And so it went. High Minister Sheen heard China's *Yes* vote two chairs to his right, then Neuropa, the same, as if the word *Yes* was a mere echo within the room, as if it indicated how the chair expected him to vote. It was his turn, the last to vote, given the chairman only voted to break a tie. All eyes were on him, clearly assuming he would make the decision unanimous. The high minister bit his lower lip, slowly opened the purse in front of him and took out a document. He stared at it for a moment, as did the others, then held it up.

"Gentlemen, I have here a Smotecal Decretum executed by Smotec Innocent instructing me to vote *No*. I am sorry but we cannot make the Council's decision unanimous."

The stares from the others turned to disbelief, then anger. The room echoed those sentiments like all the yes votes that preceded them until the chairman from the United States *banged* his gavel insisting on silence. He glared at Minister Sheen for a moment, then *banged* his gavel a second time. "Nevertheless, the measure passes. Thank you all for attending," he announced and shooed everyone out, but not before eyeing the high minister as if he had committed a dastardly deed.

****

Meanwhile, in a Chinese village only accessible by air and rail stood a complex of concrete buildings the color of sandstone, located deep within the shadows of the Great Wall of China. Prestigious medical doctors, scientists, and politicians, all loyal to the Cūtocracy, presided over the complex and understood the high technology grandeur operating within its 300,000 square feet of laboratories, offices and manufacturing facilities.

Regardless of the time of day, under the supervision of those loyal to the long arm of the Cūtocracy, the workers within labored to develop and produce a vaccine, and all the time the Great Wall's shadow and surrounding landscape hid their effort from the skies above. Over a period of two years and well after the ERAM-V plague had done significant damage, but long before it had completed its task, the Cūtocratic alliance concluded its development of the ERAM-V vaccine and began manufacturing it at their Chinese hideaway.

Within the compound, Jonathan DeCarlo, tall, thin and black with Ethiopian blood running through his veins, took large strides across the complex grounds, studying a clip chart of the previous week's vaccine production. He entered the Manufacturing Building A2 that housed all types of processing equipment, conveyers, tubes, computation shells, and control panels, then practically danced from one station to another talking to operators over the noise of equipment that ran day and night. His name and *Cūtocracy* had been threaded into the shirt pocket of his uniform. It was sandstone in color with light and dark greens and browns scattered about in order to make him less visible from the Protolytes whizzing through space. Those floating brains made instant communication and computation possible while at the same time searching for anomalies on the ground like forest fires, earthquakes, and invading armies. All the nations on Earth had them, as did the United Nations, as did the Cūtocracy.

Jonathan climbed the opened staircase and finally reached his office door with a large sign printed across it—*J. DeCarlo, Director of Vaccine Production.* Exhausted and desperately in need of a break, he fell into his desk chair and closed his eyes, only to open them wide upon hearing a tap on the door. A blur across his vision caused him to squint. Commander Ginger Fly, around thirty years old, short and stocky, poked her head in, seemingly agitated. She too wore a similar camouflage uniform with her name and *Cūtocracy* on the pocket.

"Ginger?"

"Shut everything down…now!"

"What?"

"That's an order. And destroy the stockpile."

"But I've spent the last six weeks, twenty-four-seven, building it up."

By the time Jonathan finished his declaratory rant, Ginger was gone. He could hear her all the way down the hall. "Orders are orders. Do it now!"

For a moment he stared at the empty open door as

if she were still there, as if he could talk reason into her. He shook his head and looked for his scud, a device he was fascinated with. It was a hand-held best friend that just about everyone on the planet took for granted. While 'scud' was an acronym for *Satellite Communication Utility Device* and did just about everything except reproduce, most people were not aware of what it stood for, especially since the term *satellite* was an archaic reference to the earlier version of the protolytes of present day. They only knew it could communicate with anyone on Earth both visually and audibly, even holographically, and could access dozens of search engines with the tap of a finger or the sound of one's voice. Jonathan had to have the latest and greatest scud available and was the first in line to purchase the most recent version.

After finding it, he called his foreman and barked out the bad news. The foreman knew better than to question his instructions.

Later that night, having slept restlessly for at most an hour, he shook himself out of a dream he couldn't remember and jumped up from his chair. Jonathan raced down the open staircase painted a high gloss steel gray, taking two steps at a time, and through a presently silent processing facility void of operators. He left the building and practically jogged across campus under a moonless sky. He entered Administration Building A6 and bounded up several flights of similar opened stairs before approaching Ginger Fly's office. Surely she would be there. She was a workaholic. Across her partially opened door was printed *Ginger Fly—Chief Operations Attorney*. Her office lights were on.

Just as he poked his head in, a clerk walked by. "If

you're looking for Ginger, she was rushed to the hospital with a burst appendix."

Appendix? Jonathan didn't know anyone who still had one these days. Taken aback by the news, he watched the clerk walk away without thinking to ask for details. Instead, he stepped into Ginger's office and reached for the light switch when he saw her safe ajar. He went to close it but a red bound diary entitled "Top Secret" practically fell out. He hesitated, looked back into the hall, then rushed over to close the door.

After returning to the safe, he pulled out the diary and opened it. A document entitled *Smotecal Decretum* fell to the floor. He looked around, read it, first slowly, then again even more carefully. His teeth began to chatter. His shoulders tightened. He could feel his temples pulsating. His fingers seemed to graze the gold seal—real gold, he was sure. He swallowed hard then read through the diary.

"Jesus!"

He looked at the wall clock. It was one-thirty. He could practically hear the second-hand ticking. After indecisively kneeling at the opened safe for a while, he finally shut it with the diary and Smotecal Decretum clutched within his fingers.

"Jesus!" he repeated as if somehow a call to the Ecclesian savior was going to do something to help a black Jew from Ethiopia—actually, from Mumbai and parts unknown.

One thing was for sure—he couldn't stay where he was, and he had to get those documents to his sister, Juliette, somehow. Hopefully, he had at least a couple days before they were missed. Draped in a shroud of urgency, he turned off the lights in Ginger's office and scurried onto campus with the consequences of his thievery held tightly under his shirt, against his belly, as if they might otherwise be seen by the protolytes thousands of miles above.

His apartment was only ten minutes away. He would pack some essentials and think about how he planned to get the hell out of there, especially since no one could leave the village without permission and an authorization pass. The only thing he could think of at the moment was to jump a supply train on its return to Beijing and buy a throwaway scud. He had to reach Juliette and make arrangements—papers, cash, a scud, a new identity. DanSheba had to have people in Beijing and she would know how to contact them.

He hurried back to his office and checked the supply train schedule. One was due in at six in the morning. That meant it would be out by seven, giving him less than an hour to sneak on. How was he going to do that?

Less than fifteen minutes later he was back at the apartment trying to think it through while rummaging through drawers looking for the most important things he could carry in a backpack. Time was running out and he knew he wouldn't be back. They could trace him to his scud if he used it. He left it on the nightstand, which meant leaving his credit-app, his only source of ready cash. He would have to get new papers, a new scud with a credit app tied to the new papers, and a line of credit. He would for sure need Juliette for all that.

By the time he packed, the lack of sleep dominated his thoughts. He faced a long day and still hadn't figured out how to steal his way onto the supply train. He looked at his alarm clock. It was now almost three o'clock. He set the alarm and closed his eyes.

Seconds later, it seemed, the alarm woke him out of a pleasant dream, his sister's wedding day at the Rose Garden in DanSheba. That's where most DanSheban weddings took place. As comforting as the dream was, he had to shrug it off, quickly. How was he going to get onto that train? He'd have to wait and see.

As he reached the service yard carrying a bulging backpack, the train was just floating in on a stream of compressed gases. Hidden behind a low fence, he counted six cars quietly drop to the ground on wheels that were rarely used. He remained hidden within the shadows of the fence watching only the last three being unloaded. Both local staff and train people from Beijing surrounded the cars making it impossible to get close without being seen. Just when his stomach became hostile, he noticed the rusty orange crane behind him. A huge dark green metal bin of trash dangled from its long arm at least thirty feet from the ground, and no one was around it. While constantly keeping an eye on the activity around the train just over the fence line, he backed up slowly, jumped onto the crane, and looked for some type of release mechanism. It had to be the shift to the driver's right. He pushed it forward and jumped from the crane as the bin fell. *Crash.* A billow of smoky dust filled the yard, allowing him to return to the fence without being seen. At the same time, everyone from the train hurried to the crane.

Jonathan raced the other way, reaching the last car while the dust settled. He climbed in and rushed to one end, where he found large empty containers stacked on top of one another, hopefully left there for the return trip. After working his way through and behind them, he crouched down and waited. He could only imagine sneaking out from the car when it reached Beijing and into the hands of the Cūtocracy. They would shut him up for good, and generations of people to follow would… He couldn't go there. It was too frightening.

From behind thick layers of cardboard he could hear the final call, then the door *slamming* closed and locks sliding in place. All those days and nights, the sweat, the highs and lows. Just when he began feeling sorry for himself, he realized what he had done—had been part of—and he did everything to keep from vomiting into the boxes that held him captive. Fortunately, the need to sleep calmed his stomach and overwhelmed his sense of guilt.

Once the train arrived in Beijing, the downward thump of its wheels onto the tracks below woke him from a momentary snooze. He easily escaped without being detected through the crowds at every platform. He had changed his clothes on the way and blended nicely with the civilian population. With the little bit of paper money he scrounged up in his apartment, he purchased a scud. Minutes later, he made his way toward the seedier part of the city and found a cheap hotel near the Beijing Amusement Park. For the next couple of hours, he talked several times with Juliette and another DanSheban living in Beijing, a professor of Far Eastern Studies at the Hebrew University in Jerusalem on sabbatical at the Beijing Institute.

Three days later, Jonathan DeCarlo and the professor sat across from one another in Jonathan's hotel room. He hadn't left there since talking to his sister. The professor gave him a passport in the name of British businessman Raymond James, an airline ticket to New Delhi and then Mumbai, credit issued by a bank owned by the DanShebans, and additional paper cash. The flight was leaving the next morning and the professor would pick him up at seven sharp. In the meantime, the professor took the Top Secret Diary and Smotecal Decretum Jonathan had stolen from the safe and passed them on to another DanSheban with instructions to make sure they reached Juliette. The next morning, right after Jonathan was safely in the professor's automobile heading to the airport, he called Juliette to let her know.

****

Beautiful Juliette Shiffler was tall, thin, and not quite as black as Jonathan. She was also seven months pregnant. On a cold dreary afternoon in Firenze, sick with worry, she stepped into the Banco Monte dei Firenze holding a leather valise and hurried to the vault doors. She hadn't heard from her brother since the call he made from the automobile heading to the airport and tried calling him and the professor continuously but to no avail. Heartsick or not she knew the valise and its contents had to be locked up for safe keeping. What was to become of the information Jonathan stumbled upon would have to play out later.

She approached the vault door, dialed in a code, and looked into a dual eye scanner while pressing her right hand against a palm reader. A green light beam flashed past her pupils followed by the lock *clicking* open. She hesitated, studied her surroundings wondering who might be watching, then entered and quickly went to her safe deposit box. Again, she looked around. She was alone near the back of the vault. No one seemed to be paying any attention. She withdrew from the valise the red diary containing the Smotecal Decretum and placed it in the box. Once she made sure the box was locked in place, she left the vault and passed through the bank lobby trying her best to avoid eye contact with the bank manager who now stood nearby staring at her.

"Thank you, Ms. Shiffler," she heard him say as the main doors automatically opened. After stepping around dying bodies on the sidewalks and streets and making sure she wasn't run over by paramedics speeding from one emergency to another on cushions of air, she managed to reach her own vehicle. During that ordeal she passed window after window containing large screen displays reminding people that a vaccine was coming. Pamphlets with the same message littered the streets. On one corner in front of a government building she practically walked through a hologram the size of an elephant declaring that the Coalition United for Theocratic Oversight was beginning to manufacture the vaccine.

Less than an hour later, Juliette Shiffler found herself at home in Greve, around thirty kilometers south of Florence, staring down at nothing in particular, Jonathan's favorite book clenched tight against her chest as she stood on a cold stoop leading up to the stone house. She glanced toward the rooftops in the town square, barely visible beyond the trees, although impossible to see through the wetness that filled her eyes. "Water, water, everywhere, and all the boards did shrink. Water, water, everywhere, nor any drop to drink," she mumbled, loosening her grip on Coleridge, dropping it from her hands onto the pavement below. She sobbed. Many of her dear, dear friends gone, as if whisked away by the hand of a vengeful magician. And her brother, where was he? The plague swooped in and took few prisoners. Juliette, one of the lucky ones residing in Greve, managed to survive. Other towns and cities throughout the world may have fared better, especially the larger cities, but none escaped the touch of death—none escaped the albatross.

Juliette Shiffler thought about all the publicity on the upcoming vaccine and then about dear Jonathan's discovery. She had reason not to be immunized. The next morning, she packed her things and went into hiding, back to DanSheba, praying she would soon hear from her brother.

****

It was summer in Italy which meant Smotec Innocent, the Supreme Minister of the Ecclesian Church, was vacationing in in the Smotecal Palace of Castel Gandolfo. That meant High Minister Charles Sheen would be there also, even though he hated the place. He also hated this whole business having to do with the Smotecal Decretum. He wished he had been allowed to vote yes at the last Cūtocractic meeting in Rome, but Smotec Innocent could only be pushed so far by the Cūtocracy.

Minister Sheen knew that the conservative agenda of Smotec Innocent, and the Cūtocracy that the Ecclesian Church bankrolled, limited and reversed most of the technological advances made in the last several centuries. After all, he came into office as Smotec Innocent's first lieutenant fifty years earlier. At the moment Sheen happened to be in town sitting on the patio of an outdoor café overlooking Lake Albano. With a cup of coffee in one hand and his scud in the other hand, he listened with tight jaws, then abruptly barked out his demands.

"Enough excuses! I need to know how it happened. You already told me it was the Cūtocracy, but who, damn it? Well just get back to me with something positive."

The Minister disconnected and called his server over for another cup of coffee and some sweets. He was procrastinating. The smotec said he was available all morning and the morning was almost gone. After drinking a third cup of coffee and leaving most of the sweets, he paid the check and hailed a taxi. Within fifteen minutes he stood in the palace drawing room waiting for His Sacredness to appear. Hopefully the smotec would be in a good mood he thought as he tapped on the golden chest covered with rubies and emeralds he used as a crutch to help him stand straight and remain confident.

"So?" the smotec snarled after entering the room, even before the door behind him could close. Clearly, he was not in a good mood.

Sheen hesitated and before he could respond, the smotec held up his hand in a gesture of silence. "I know, stolen by the Cūtocracy, but that's not enough. Why would they?" Innocent was referring to the Smotecal Decretum he had executed to make it clear he was not going along with the Cūtocracy's insane measure they passed at the last council meeting.

"To hold it over you. At least that's what my informants tell me."

"And now some people took it from them. Do you realize what this could do to the Church, to me?" Merely uttering those words caused Innocent to swipe a tightened fist across the closest vase. The priceless relic *crashed* to the floor.

"Apparently, one person. A Jonathan DeCarlo. We could go public with the Cūtocracy's plan?"

"Are you crazy? We were part of that plan, or at least we financed it. No! Find the Decretum and do whatever it takes. This Jonathan DeCarlo and anyone else who's seen it must go. Is that clear?" Without another word, Innocent stormed out of the drawing room. He left his top minister shaking as he picked up the broken pieces of vase. Sheen knew in his heart that the smotec was thrilled with the plan they had voted against but didn't want his fingerprints on it.

****

Jonathan DeCarlo did not make it to the airport with the professor. Just before arriving, and after each one disposed of his scud, they were picked up and thrown into an icy dungeon deep within the heart of Beijing. Through days of brutal interrogation, he maintained his innocence, insisting he didn't know what they were talking about. He had no knowledge of a missing diary. Then, suddenly, the interrogation stopped. He was left alone for what seemed like days, in the dark, with only a pitcher of water and cracker crumbs that became magnets for rats the size of cats. Throughout the ordeal he thought about the professor and prayed he didn't talk. What could he say? They didn't have the diary or the Smotecal Decretum. Juliette did. Then it hit him far worse than all the pin pricks, water-soaked rags, and chain marks across his back he managed to survive. If the professor told them about Juliette, she was in danger!

"Christ, what did I do?" he blurted out. Hopefully

she had the sense to get the hell out of Italy and return to DanSheba. Hopefully!

The next thing he knew, several of his captors dragged him up hundreds of crumbling steps past cells reeking with the rancid prophesy of death. After being passed off several times, he found himself on a super transport flying several inches above its tracks at well over three-hundred kilometers an hour heading toward…where? He wasn't sure. The two soldiers who never left his side carried nano-wave cadmium blue super-laser guns hidden within the breast pockets of their maroon and gold uniforms. Normally, such hideous firearms were reserved for much higher-level officials in the military and only on a need to have basis. In the case of the two soldiers, they carried them legally, or so he was warned, due to the importance of their mission.

After transferring trains three times, they arrived in Italy, then into the Rome station during the early morning rush. A General Somebody had joined him on the last leg, and both were greeted on Platform 23 by a civilian official the general clearly didn't like. He was there to pick up the prisoner for the Cūtocracy, the official exclaimed harshly as a man who thought he knew how to take charge might.

The official then turned to the prisoner. "Jonathan DeCarlo?" he barked in a high-pitched voice that contradicted his large frame and heavy beard, a voice that gave Jonathan confidence.

"You know who I am, you bastard." Jonathan stepped toward the official with his cuffed hands raised, causing the general to step between them. Rather than wait for a reprimand, the prisoner spit in the general's face, something he had been waiting to do to someone ever since they dragged him from the dungeon.

The general stepped back, slammed Jonathan across the jaw with the butt of his super-laser gun and wiped the spit from his face. The next thing Jonathan knew, a long, narrow barrel pressed tight against his temple.

At twenty-four years old he stood six feet three inches, extremely tall for his people, and like many claiming an Ethiopian ancestry he had dark eyes and dark hair that seemed to blend seamlessly with his coal black skin. What he didn't have was a red bound diary of sorts and a certain document the authorities desperately wanted.

The civilian official pushed the general away. "Are you crazy? We need him alive." The general shoved the official back and raised the butt of his gun threatening to use it once again. The two soldiers stepped in to keep them apart.

Seeing his opportunity, Jonathan slithered down the platform like a lizard on flat ground dodging crowds of passengers stepping off and on recently arrived and departing trains. *Zing, zing, zing,* he could practically feel the rays of blue light shoot past him as both soldiers took aim. *Poof, poof, poof,* passengers on his left practically disintegrated. He had often wondered why those C-B super-laser guns were outlawed. Now he knew. And that made him race even faster into one of the standing cars after wedging between exiting passengers. Once inside the train, he plowed through standing humanity to reach the last car and escape out the back. By then, the two soldiers were in a good place to take aim and began firing once again. By the time the official reached them, a side wall of the caboose dripped with melted metal. More people died, including the train's conductor.

Jonathan jumped onto the stairs of a bridge draped across the tracks between adjacent platforms and raced over it. He could hear the two soldiers close behind, but with his hands cuffed, it was hard to run much faster. They were closing the gap, but no longer shooting. Just when he thought they were going to reach him, he leaped onto the far track ahead of a train that he didn't see coming. *Wham.*

Chapter Two
More than a century later

Meta was cleaning the dinner dishes from the night before. Yennie had driven down to Greve during his visit to Florence. They spent the evening talking about family and friends, and home. Both were black Jews of Ethiopian heritage living far from DanSheba. Yennie wasn't one to boast but rather downplayed his accomplishments. Later that night, after a bottle of wine or more, Meta understood fully the powerful position he held in the American government. But then it wasn't until around three in the morning, well after he had returned to Florence, that she realized how opportune that could be for the plan she had been hatching over the past dozen years. The problem had always been how she would start, who she would need, and how anyone could believe such an outlandish story, especially considering the world didn't even know her people existed. In the middle of the night it occurred to her. She was about to give birth to a plan and hoped the elders would approve it.

By eight in the morning, she carefully placed the evening dishes in the dishwasher, then stopped what she was doing and looked for her scud. Within minutes she heard Yennie at the other end greeting her, then raised him onto a holographic screen that projected from her scud.

"Yennie, are you leaving today or tomorrow? I forgot what you said."

"Actually, on Thursday. Why?"

"Do you remember our discussion last night about my great granduncle, Jonathan?"

"Meta, you didn't get me drunk. Of course, I remember it. But you never explained exactly what got him killed other than he stole some sensitive documents."

"Do you have a minute, right now?"

"As you can tell, I am in a very long line waiting to see Michelangelo's David. I'd say I have more than a minute. What's on your mind that we didn't discuss last night? Wait. Let me call you back on a secure line. When the call comes in it will ask for a code. Type in the name of the high school I attended back home."

He called her back; she entered the name of the high school, then proceeded to tell him exactly what got Jonathan DeCarlo killed and her plan in fair detail. She saw on her holographic screen he was skeptical at first, but warmed up to the idea after overwhelming her with question after question.

"This is our chance, Yennie, finally. Can you help?

"Truthfully I can't say. It won't be up to me. However, I think the president and her press secretary may be willing to listen if I catch them at the right time. Why don't you come into Florence tomorrow and we can continue this conversation here?"

"The bank closes at five. How about we meet for a late lunch, say around three. There's a wonderful café in the Piazza Santo Spirito."

The next day ticked by slowly for Meta, but eventually presented itself as a stream of excitement flowing through her veins as fast as the towns passing between Greve and Florence—Chiocchio, Strada in Chianti, and eventually the Stazione di Santa Maria Novella in Firenze. At the same time, she wondered if this was really the right thing to do and whether the American president could be trusted. It has been almost thirteen years since their scientists confirmed the truth so outrageously outlined in those ancient documents Juliette hid away back then, a truth that DanShebans knew well before the indisputable evidence was in. Nevertheless, knowing the truth, even having indisputable scientific evidence, was one thing; convincing the rest of the world, especially the president of the United States, was another. But mostly, up until then the village elders insisted that DanSheba had to keep a low profile. Too much was at stake. They were slowly softening to the idea that maybe, just maybe, her people had a greater obligation to their fellow man than protecting a race of people that lived in the shadows for thousands of years.

Meta and Yennie lunched under a blue canopy on one edge of the piazza, just steps from the Basilica di Santo Spirito, which during the Renaissance served as a morgue for the destitute. It was there that Michelangelo secretly dissected cadavers in order to learn his trade. And it was there that the beautiful city of Florence stored the unfortunate victims of the great ERAM plague. Most important, it was there that Meta explained in even more detail her plan. Yennie appeared to still be taking it all in when they left together and walked across the Arno River along the scenic Ponte Vecchio Bridge and doubled back on the other side of the river to the Banco di Firenze on Via de

Tornabuoni.

"So this Smotecal Decretum is like an important order or law that a smotec executes. And what does it look like again?" Yennie asked as the bank came into view.

"You will see shortly."

Yennie followed Meta across the bank lobby to a series of gadgets protecting the vault containing customer deposit boxes. She first took her right hand and placed it on a Palm/Finger reader. Once it was firmly in place, a green light lit up indicating she should place her two eyes in a binocular-like device that was designed to scan her pupils. Once she did that, a lid popped up allowing her to punch in a pass code, causing an impervious steel door to unlock. Meta led Yennie in, allowing him his first look at a real Smotecal Decretum and a red hardback diary entitled *Top Secret*. He put both in his briefcase and they quietly left the way they came.

****

It took several weeks for Yennie to get the ear of his boss, Press Secretary Dillon Burber, and several more weeks for the two of them to get President Andrea Wainwright's attention. To say she was thunderstruck by the documents being handed over to her would be an understatement. She was horrified, especially considering she had just celebrated her seventieth birthday. Nevertheless, months went by without the subject being raised again. Yennie knew better than to raise it himself even though he promised Meta he would when the time seemed right. Just when he had summoned the courage to remind Dillon of their earlier conversation, the Press Secretary popped into his office and handed him a three-page confidential document as well as the Smotecal Decretum and red diary.

"The president wants you to implement this," Dillon said without more discussion.

Before Yennie could focus on the document, Dillon was gone. He quickly read through all three pages and sighed. He was conflicted. What had he started? What had they started? Then, with another sigh and a great deal of ambivalence, he pulled out his scud and called Meta.

After putting the president's plan into action, one political and policy disaster after another seemed to put it out of everyone's mind, except Meta's, and Yennie was reminded of that often. Finally, things quieted down long enough for the plan, blessed by the president, to unfold—which seemed to take place mostly after the sun went down. The White House always appeared that much brighter to Yennie as he came and went during the late evening hours, as they plotted against the Cūtocracy. While he remained focused, every once in a while he caught himself dreaming of an extended vacation at home, far away from the insanity that consumed Washington, DC. But not now, he thought as he looked at the restroom mirror and stared at the dark red circles around his black eyes. Fortunately, his short-cropped hair never needed combing and deodorant often took the place of a shower.

Yennie took a deep breath, left the restroom, and walked down the hall to the third office on the right. The magnetic triadic arcs under translucent domes lit up the room in a way only the noon sun could, and it seemed more extreme given the time, almost midnight.

Dillon Burber was born and raised in Seattle. He hated overcast skies and dimly lit rooms, or so he told Yennie on many occasions. President Wainwright's press secretary hugged the back of his chair with his spine erect and his eyes focused on his aide, now sitting across the desk from him. Dillon's physical appearance, his short, thin frame, and thick head of uncombed hair, may have matched his public demeanor, E-flat according to most reporters, but it didn't match his ferocious private demeanor. Yennie learned that quickly after they met. Dillon attended college with the president, Louisiana State University, and was more protective of her than the president's entire security team. Few people reached the president's ear without first beating on Dillon's eardrum.

No one knew that better than Yennie, whose black skin made its own statement under Dillon's MTA dome-shaped fixtures. He graduated from Princeton University with honors, and after interning on the Wainwright vice presidential bid, Dillon hired him. Eventually he became the Press Secretary's primary aide. At the moment, he had in his hand the lab results they both had been anxiously waiting for.

"Well?" Dillon sat even more erect waiting for the verdict.

"It's authentic. There's no doubt about it."

"How could they tell?" Clearly Dillon wanted to cover all his bases. The president's reputation depended on it.

"They analyzed the paper, the toner particles forming the print, the ink making up the signature, and the watermarks. The seal itself turned out to be gold. They all go back to the period we are interested in.

What we have is a secret Smotecal Decretum, and there is no doubt about its authenticity."

"And the signature itself? How do we know it's the signature of Innocent II?"

Yennie smiled. "First, because our best handwriting expert, probably the best in the world, says so as do the others. Second, we've managed to lift a fading fingerprint off the paper that seems to match his. Third, we were able to lift a partial print off the seal, a crisp print, that our people are confident is his."

"In that case, my young friend, I believe we have our smoking gun. I will give this information to the president." Dillon Burber sat further down in his chair and was now smiling. "One more thing—does everyone in the loop understand…"

"Yes. The Smotecal Decretum and the diary have been classified Top Secret."

"All right. Then you take the lead, Yennie. I don't even trust the NSA. Make it a very subtle leak."

"Then what?"

"We will see where it takes us, who we're dealing with. We can't afford a screw up. We need the public on our side if we are to succeed."

Chapter Three

Oliver Hitchcock, six foot four and thin, looked and felt more than twenty years younger than his seventy-eight years. That had something to do with the fact he was a Beater, and good genes, he thought, bounding up the old brick steps to the front door. Dressed in baseball gear with a big "M" on the cap that covered his bald head, he *knocked* at the door and immediately let himself in. Hitch's daughter, Kathy, waited at the bottom of the stairs with a stern expression and folded arms.

"Dad, what's wrong with you?"

"Where is he? OJ."

"Four times just this morning he heard it."

Hitch stepped to one side of Kathy and yelled up the stairs. "OJ! Game time!"

Oliver Junior, Hitch's eleven-year-old grandson and namesake, raced down the stairs in his Mudrakers baseball uniform. Kathy stretched her arms out to block him.

"No! You are not…"

OJ ducked under her arms, grabbed his baseball glove off a table, and charged out the door.

"See, OJ wants to play. He's…"

Just then, meek and fragile Christopher, Hitch's younger grandson, appeared at the top of the stairs.

Kathy looked up and barked at him. "Christopher,

stay in your room." He disappeared without a word. She turned back to her father with venom in her eyes.

"No. You want him to play. We both know what he's hearing."

"What's he supposed to do? Stay in his room until… He isn't even sick yet."

"I guess throwing up in the middle of the night doesn't count."

Hitch raced for the door. "For God's sake, the Mudrakers are playing for the championship. What do you expect?" He really couldn't understand his own daughter. Why wouldn't she want what could be his last weeks to be memorable?

Just as he and OJ arrived and raced into the crowd of parents and fans, the players on the opposing team, the Possums, were taking the field and Hitch's tiff with his daughter no longer occupied his thoughts. He remained focused on the game through all six and a half innings. It was the bottom of the seventh, the Mudrakers were up by one—three to two—but the Possums had bases loaded. OJ stood on the mound, distressed and grim-faced. The count was two balls and one strike. His eyes darted from the batter to his grandfather in the dugout. He stepped off the mound and dropped his glove. The palms of his hands moved up to his temples as his eyes closed, as he grimaced, a grimace obvious enough for Hitch to see and ignore even though he could imagine the *Click, Click, Click* filling OJ's head.

OJ opened his eyes, looked back at the scoreboard in left field, to a hologram projecting twenty feet up. He turned back to the batter and picked up his glove, slowly and with a great deal of effort. Hitch stepped out from the dugout. "Come on, OJ, finish this kid."

OJ returned to the mound, looked at the base runner on third, then wound up and pitched. "Strike two," the umpire behind the plate called. The count was two balls and two strikes. Again, OJ grimaced and again Hitch could imagine the *Click, Click* but ignored it once again. He could even see the sweat dripping down OJ's cheeks. "One more strike OJ, that's all."

OJ acknowledged his grandfather with a nod, wiped the beads from his cheeks, wound up and pitched—way outside, causing the catcher to fall to his right with his mitt extended to make the save. Hitch was so focused on the save; he didn't notice his grandson fall to his knees until he heard the umpire call timeout. "Get another pitcher, Hitchcock," he snapped.

Hitch waved him off, jogged out to the mound, and helped OJ up.

"It's so loud. I…"

"Son, you're no quitter."

"I'm trying. It's… It's that sound."

"Forget that. Forget the crowd. Just concentrate on the strike zone. Just one more pitch." Hitch patted him on the back and headed for the dugout.

The umpire jumped into his path. "Are you crazy?"

Hitch snapped back. "Just do your job."

Play resumed. All eyes were on OJ who wiped the sweat from his brow and fixed on the batter. The Crowd *cheered*, players on both sides *hooted* and *hollered*. OJ glanced at his grandfather. Hitch nodded and *clapped* his hands.

The count was full, three balls and two strikes. OJ wound up and delivered the ball right down the middle. The base runners took off, and the batter swung, strike three. The Mudrakers beat the Possums, three to two. Hitch could see his grandson at the mound with his hands up and a victory grin across his face. The Mudrakers fans swarmed the field in celebration, hiding OJ from view. Suddenly, Hitch heard the umpire's voice. "Hitchcock! Get out here."

Hitch wedged his way through the celebration, spotted the umpire, then his grandson on the ground. He crouched over OJ, who was on his back, stiff, motionless. For a moment he froze, then looked up at the umpire who glared back.

****

In an uncharacteristic fit of anger, Christopher insisted he wanted to see his brother play ball. Kathy was just as adamant that they not go, that is, until her mother showed up at the front door. Edna Hitchcock, whose matronly appearance contrasted sharply with Oliver's youthful exuberance, had no intention of denying her favorite grandson his wish, and she made that quite clear to her daughter.

Kathy navigated the typical Saturday afternoon traffic through the Virginia suburbs of Washington DC on a cushion of air, allowing her scud to take control and negotiate side streets it found were clear. She pulled into the parking lot as one car after another streamed past her. "The game must be over," she said after pulling into a space and dropping to the ground.

"Mom, look!" Christopher pointed to flashing red lights.

Kathy jumped from the car allowing her to see the paramedic truck, then dashed off knowing exactly what she would find. She felt her heart racing faster than her feet could pedal, as she approached a crowd surrounding the flashing lights. Needing someone to hold on to, she slowed down and allowed her mother and Christopher to catch up. Two paramedics carried a stretcher with a body covered over, causing her to let go of her mother's hand, and Christopher's. After pushing through parents and kids, she flung herself onto the stretcher, closed her eyes, and *wailed*. By then, Hitch and the umpire were at her side. She looked up, filled with the anguish only a parent knows, and saw her father looking limp and woozy. The umpire stepped between them and spoke the very thoughts that echoed across her temples. "A Preemie in the throes of the Click and you let him play?" The umpire walked off shaking his head as the remaining crowd was shocked into silence. Only sobs and moans from the dead boy's mother could be heard.

Kathy turned away from the stretcher as it was lifted into the paramedic truck and grabbed onto her younger son, purposely blocking his view, while quietly glaring at her father.

"He died a champion, not in bed. At least I gave him that," he whispered loud enough for his daughter and the others to hear. He marched on to the empty field and fell to his knees at the pitcher's mound. Kathy could hear him sob but remained where she was, frozen in time, praying she would blink her eyes and discover there was no such thing as the Click or Preemies.

While everyone seemed to have a difficult time at the funeral, Kathy was devastated. OJ had been her first miracle, Christopher her second. She and her parents and Christopher, as well as the others, sat on wooden folding chairs at the burial site. They listened to the minister from their Liberal Church of Spirituality when she noticed her father standing to one side staring off in the distance. She followed his gaze and saw across the road a lone woman leaning against a tree staring back in her direction. The woman was wearing a black leather jacket with VAMA in yellow along one sleeve. Kathy knew the jacket and VAMA, the Vaccine Assurance and Management Agency, but didn't have the slightest idea why she was there or why her father even noticed—except for the fact that the woman seemed quite attractive.

Chapter Four

More than three weeks passed, and Oliver Hitchcock's sleep had been pummeled with nightmares of guilt and regret, emotions he successfully avoided in the light of day. On this particular morning, the bedroom was still dark when he shook himself out of one of those nightmares. He glanced to his right, toward the wrinkled sheets next to him, then looked around the room. He was alone but could hear rustling sounds from the kitchen. He started to rise, but the pain of reality flashed through his head as quickly as the nightmare receded. At that moment, all he could think about was how difficult it was for his daughter to have children, how she now only had one. No! He wasn't going there. The past was the past. Learn from it but don't dwell on it—the CIA code. Easier said than done this time.

Before starting a fight with his buried emotions—those feelings he refused to acknowledge much of his life—he heard footsteps. Janine Rousseau, Detective Janine Rousseau, forty-five years of age, tiptoed into the opened doorway wearing a thin robe. Hitch watched her smile then drop her robe, exposing the body of a twenty-year-old. She approached, licking her lips, and crawled back into bed. With her bare hands reaching under the covers, she managed to draw him into the present, into her. For the next twenty minutes they made love for the fourth time in twelve hours. Before he could catch his breath, Janine was in her robe once again, strolling back to the kitchen.

He rose from the bed and yawned, then jumped into his trousers and shoes and walked after her carrying his shirt. "Have you seen my cap?" he asked.

"Where you left it, on the couch in the living room," Janine answered standing at the kitchen stove with her back to him.

It was there as she said, along with her black leather jacket with VAMA in yellow down one sleeve. Next to both were a Phoenix-classic black leather shoulder holster and matching pearl handled laser handgun, an empty bottle of vodka, two glasses, and a half empty pitcher of orange juice. Hitch picked up his Mudrakers cap, which he constantly wore as a reminder of better times, and stood there buttoning his shirt. All the while, he noticed for the first time a framed photo of Janine standing with a young girl, probably seven or eight, in front of the Eiffel Tower.

"I'm done with this, Janine," he announced as he opened the front door to leave.

"I doubt that," he heard back, and he glared at her. "You're too narcissistic to give up the good life of whisky and women. Besides, your clock may not be clicking but it is ticking and there's only so much life left in it, and in you. You'll be back."

Hitch ached to put Rousseau down, to let her know she was full of shit. Instead, he turned and marched out, leaving the door ajar.

Chapter Five

Over the following several months, Hitch spent as much time as possible trying to avoid his daughter while Edna spent most of her time consoling her, neither a surprise to either of them. Then one afternoon while he stood on his back porch overlooking the Potomac River, shirtless, and pumping out curls with forty-pound dumbbells in front of a full-length standing mirror, Edna stuck her head out the back door, clearly upset.

"Kitten called. She has an appointment tomorrow with Christopher's pediatrician and asked if we could be there. She wouldn't say why but I'm afraid…"

Hitch looked over questioningly.

"Oh, never mind." She disappeared without giving Hitch a chance to respond.

He knew what Edna was about to say, but then continued curling, successfully blocking the same thoughts from preoccupying his mind. "Seventy-three, seventy-four, seventy-five." After reaching one hundred curls, he carried the dumbbells to his exercise room and went to the bathroom to dry down and wash his face and hands. In the mirror he could see the V-Mark on his forearm; what looked like a multi-pointed starburst, the size of a quarter, uniformly Indian red in color. Without thinking, he touched it. He hadn't recalled doing that since…well since OJ. Not surprising, it was smooth, more like a tattoo than a birthmark, which is what he thought it was as a child. Most kids considered them birthmarks since they were vaccinated at birth. That was the law according to the Vaccine Assurance and Management Agency. All human inhabitants on Earth were to be vaccinated against the ERAM virus, and each human inhabitant carried the V-Mark on either the left arm or the right arm. VAMA was everywhere to make sure that happened. Their black hearse-looking vehicles floated over a roadway of air and displayed VAMA in bright yellow on both sides as well as down the back.

The following afternoon, Hitch, Edna, and Kathy squeezed together in a small examination room watching Dr. Ralph Delahunt inspect Christopher's V-Mark. Even from where he sat, Hitch could see how bumpy and dark red it was. Chills ran down his spine.

"Well, young man, you have been very cooperative," Dr. Delahunt said as he rolled down Christopher's sleeve and patted him on the back. Meanwhile, he looked at Hitch and Edna. "Maybe one of you can take him to the waiting room. The receptionist has several choice selections of candy waiting to be retrieved."

Before Hitch had a chance to do as the doctor asked, Edna volunteered, leaving her husband and daughter to face Dr. Delahunt, who already held Kathy's hand. "I've always been candid with you, sweetheart. The roughness and discoloration on his V-Mark along with the blood work… I'm so sorry."

Kathy went limp and began sobbing. Hitch tried to put his arm around her. She flinched, causing him to drop it. He moved to the door left open by Edna and stared into the waiting room where Christopher was unwrapping a piece of candy.

"I'm afraid I'll need some blood work from you, Oliver," Hitch heard Dr. Delahunt say.

He swung around. "Me?"

"You're a Beater. And, well you know, first OJ, now…"

Hitch held both hands up, as if to surrender, and shortly thereafter was in the lab area having his blood drawn. Two days later, in the afternoon, he and Edna were back in the doctor's office, without Kathy and Christopher this time. Ralph Delahunt sat across from them studying the lab report, nodding his head and shrugging.

"Well," he said as he handed them the report. "Two Preemies in one family does not appear to be coincidental."

"Are you saying it's because of…" Edna started to say without looking at the report.

Delahunt nodded at the report, as if the answers were there, and he didn't want to compound the pain by repeating the reasons aloud. All the time Hitch was studying the report and knew exactly what Ralph didn't want to verbalize. He was a carrier of the virus, of the plague. He was the fucking reason one grandson was dead and the other…

"Edna, Oliver, I'm so very sorry," Ralph said as Hitch tried to control himself, as he stared at the words in front of him, as he felt Edna's hand caress his shoulder. She meant well, he knew, but uncontrolled anger welled up.

"Don't be," Hitch said. "The Click is the will of God. Is it not? If you were the grandparent of two

Preemies would you continue to believe that shit?" He crushed the report in his fist and stormed out. Twenty minutes later he was at Hooligan's drinking all by himself.

Two hours later he found himself *knocking* at a door. The door opened slowly. "I'm surprised you waited this long," Janine Rousseau said.

****

Over the next several months, Edna saw little of her husband. Instead, she spent much of her time with her daughter, taking care of her and Christopher. She knew better than anyone how devastated Kathy was to lose OJ, and now even the thought that the only child she had left was in jeopardy made her… Edna couldn't finish the thought. She was there, close up, all those years Kathy tried to get pregnant but couldn't.

Her daughter was a lesbian, a lesbian in hiding, since being gay was a serious crime in the twenty-third century. This was made so by Smotec Innocent II, the Black Smotec, who Edna regarded with scorn ever since she left the Ecclesian Church as a young adult. Nevertheless, Kathy and her partner wanted children, so she secretly resorted to IVF, in vitro fertilization—secretly because IVF procedures were also seriously illegal. All those evangelists and the Black Smotec won that battle many years earlier after the Cūtocracy took political control of government after government. Edna knew her history.

Eight attempts at IVF all failed. As a last resort, Kathy went through the black market and hired a surrogate using her eggs and sperm from a black-market sperm bank. The combination produced OJ. A week after OJ's birth, Kathy's partner died in an automobile accident. After several years of grieving, she decided to have a second child, Christopher, the same way.

Edna and Kathy were in the kitchen one afternoon, spreading chocolate frosting on a cake they had baked earlier, when Christopher came bounding down the stairs from his bedroom. He rushed into the kitchen with a box of birthday candles. "Grandma, here. It's your birthday tomorrow. I remembered." He handed her the box. "How many candles should I put on it?"

Mother and daughter froze, but Edna quickly shook herself out of the anxiety that flooded her entire body, and hugged Christopher. "That's so sweet of you, my darling." He of course didn't know this was to be her seventy-fifth, a birthday no one celebrated. Nevertheless, she took seven candles from the box and had Christopher put them on the cake.

The following evening, after the family had dinner, Kathy brought out the cake, and Christopher helped his grandfather light the candles. Christopher sang Happy Birthday with total joy while his mother and grandfather followed along, trying to smile as best they could.

That day and for several months to follow, Edna neither heard nor felt the Click. Maybe it won't come, she thought on a number of occasions, but dared not voice those hopes believing they would jinx her. Maybe she, like her husband, was destined to beat the Click. She wasn't aware of two Beaters in the same family, but that didn't mean there weren't any. After all, they had two Preemies in the same... Even the beginning of that thought made her knees buckle and caused her to put the whole idea out of her mind.

Then one night, hours after she and Oliver retired, she screamed out, "Enough!" causing him to practically fall out of bed. "I've had it, Oliver. I can't take the waiting."

Less than a month later, they were meandering down a path in the park. Edna suddenly stopped. Her hands flew up to her temples. *Click, Click, Click.* Oliver led her to a bench nearby. They sat. Their eyes met and shared a deep gloom. Oliver grabbed his wife's hands and squeezed. The clicking, more like the intermittent winding of a grandfather clock, subsided. She had so hoped to beat it, not for her sake, but for Kathy's and Christopher's. They were all so close, and she wasn't entirely sure Oliver would always be there for them.

That night and for many to follow she went to bed terrified she would not wake up. Then one night several weeks after hearing the Click the first time, she knew the end was near. It was around midnight. She looked to her left. Oliver was fast asleep. Her eyes remained opened, wide, staring at him, then the ceiling. Just when she decided to roll over and try to sleep, she felt it coming. Seconds later, *Click, Click, Click, Click.* She reached over and shook her husband of almost fifty years. He knew. She could see it in his eyes. He held her tight. *Click, Click.* She felt her body dissolve into a heap of nothingness with each note in God's final song of silence. She trembled. She felt Oliver tremble. In her mind's eye she could see the hands approaching midnight! She peered beyond Death's final goodbye and saw nothing. No road to salvation as the Church of the Ecclesia had promised, no second chance in the greater world beyond, no singer of songs. Her final plea was to her husband.

"Oliver, make Christopher well. Promise me you'll make Christopher…"

She died in his arms hearing him promise he would do everything within his power. She also heard him cry. That made her happy and sad as she took her last breath on Earth.

Chapter Six

The only people Oliver Hitchcock had left were Kathy and Christopher. Nevertheless, Edna's memorial service at the cemetery, not long after her ashes were buried, overflowed with friends and neighbors—not surprising considering she and Oliver lived in the same city, in fact the same house, for over forty years. A number of Hitch's old colleagues were also in attendance.

Had the Hitchcocks been good Ecclesians and contributing members of the Church, the family and the others in attendance would have been invited there to celebrate Edna's life with the entire congregation. That was common Ecclesian practice whenever a believer died *naturally*—that is, according to God's clicking clock. Hitch and Edna were not good Ecclesians or even believers for that matter. As a result, once the crowd dispersed and Hitch sent his daughter and grandson home, he crouched down before Edna's headstone and placed fresh flowers into an adjacent vase he had partially buried earlier.

"I promise to do what I can," were the only words that seemed to be appropriate, as the tears ran down his cheeks. He then turned his attention to OJ's headstone, wiped his tears, and stared at the engraving—*He died too young*. He would do better for Christopher, he insisted as the tears returned.

He thought he was alone, but the feel of a hand on his shoulder caused him to recoil. He looked up and saw Rajiv Nadu, who had come all the way from Delhi to attend the service. He and Hitch were in India, in the covert service of their respective agencies, forever it seemed to Hitch, and they became inseparable friends.

"All those years together, the three of us. I will miss her deeply," Rajiv said in his thick Indian accent, standing tall, almost as tall as Hitch but twenty-five years younger. He pulled his old friend up and the two hugged. They spent several days together talking about the old times, about family, about friends, and about their many escapades hiding behind stereotypical trench coats and government supplied aliases. They talked about OJ and the fact he died a Preemie. Rajiv was traveling at the time and couldn't make it to the States to comfort his good buddy. He was surprised to hear how OJ died. Hitch hadn't told him, and now Hitch felt bad. Rajiv's reaction seemed, cautious, guarded, as if the Click and Preemies weren't topics he wanted to explore.

For many weeks to follow, just about every night, Oliver Hitchcock woke up at some point recalling Edna's plea, *please make Christopher well*. It was as if she were in bed next to him whispering in his ear— *please make Christopher well. Promise you'll make Christopher well, promise, promise, promise*. It was the echoing of those words, of his promise, and something Rajiv said that drove him to his study at three o'clock one morning along with a bottle of bourbon and a glass. Rajiv's voice rose within him. *In my country there's a...an old wives' tale, I believe you say here. Somewhere, someone knows how to combat God's death sentence. One just needs to know where to look for it. If only that were true.*

Those words stayed with him as he grabbed his scud and tapped it in a certain way, then set it down, causing a large holographic screen of scientifically focused light containing a holographic keyboard to project upward in front of him. With two hands he pulled the weightless keyboard to him and began typing. The letters E-R-A-M-V appeared on the screen after a series of taps and then, as if by magic, the full phrase he was looking for, ERAM Virus. He typed some more and a full page appeared. *Earth's Revenge Against Mankind—The Killer Virus.* Below the title—*The Coalition United for Theocratic Oversight races to develop a cure. Will the Cūtocracy succeed?* Hitch studied the title, then his finger flipped page after page in the same way he had moved the keyboard, studying each page carefully. Just when he thought he was getting nowhere, a link popped up—*Properties of the ERAM vaccine.* He touched the link wondering what the properties of the vaccine were and whether knowing that might give him a clue where to start. Start what? He couldn't imagine but he couldn't sleep either. Rajiv's words rang in his ears once again. Then suddenly—*This page has no content.* His fingers continued to flip the pages. *Research.* He touched the link. *Archives,* then *Mutations and Cell Divisions,* then… *Classified – Submit Authorized Code.*

Hitch continued, seeing the same roadblock, time after time, until finally he sat back in his chair and merely stared at the hologram in front of him. It gave off enough light for him to easily find the bottle of bourbon and empty glass. He looked at the clock on his desk. It was now approaching four o'clock. He poured himself a drink and quickly downed it, then began typing once again, and again. *Dissidents claim Click's a fraud* jumped out from the hologram, as if it had a mind of its own, and grabbed him by the eyeballs. *Higher Clearance required. Content removed.* Each time he returned to the dissidents—the same result—*Link Broken, Higher Clearance Required,* or *Content Removed, Content Removed, Content Removed.* "What the hell?" Frustrated, he grabbed the empty glass and flung it across the room, through the hologram. *Smack.* It shattered against the wall and caused the hologram to flutter, shaking away any feelings of hope.

By seven that morning, with at most a few hours of fitful sleep under his belt, he showered, shaved, ate, and was on the way to his old stomping grounds with *Dissidents claim Click's a fraud* flashing through his thoughts. He still had certain privileges at the CIA allowing him to easily access the building that housed the library. He hurried up the marble stairs, like a man who had a good night's sleep, two steps at a time, a man on a quest, a man who thought he was onto something. In no time at all, he reached the outside of a frosted glass door with *Julian Iscar, Chief CIA Librarian* silkscreened across its face.

He stepped quietly into a cozy space thick with carpet and soft amber lighting, a reading room not very large but furnished with several comfortable reading sofas, three rectangular tables surrounded by upright chairs, and a half-dozen stations. All the stations overflowed with computation shells lined up along one side of the room. Each station also defined a soundproof booth large enough for two plus a holographic screen twice the size produced by a scud. Behind the stations stood an equal number of government-issued metal gray steel floor-to-ceiling shelves filled with reading tablets and all types of reading material, both audio and visual, for use with portable discs. The shelves were separated by sound insulated listening booths and plug-in terminals. Authorized users had access to both the stations and booths and could listen to, watch, and search just about anything from the Earth's Spider Room Servers, and just about everything ever printed or in digital form anywhere. There were Spider Room Servers in just about every country on earth and each one was in communication with all the protolytes in space. In this way, data passed from one scud and computation shell to another.

Directly across from the entry door and reading room, Hitch eyed a raised counter and the back of a portly looking man bent over in front of it. He was short and bald and wore red suspenders over a long sleeve white shirt. Had Oliver Hitchcock not known that short, bald man, he could well have wondered what a seemingly harmless librarian with but a single arm could be doing in the most powerful library in the world. As he approached the counter, Hitch made a coughing sound, causing the librarian to turn around.

Julian Iscar's face lit up upon seeing his old friend of so many years. His deep blue-green eyes gave him away. He was anything but harmless. Hitch knew that well. They spent more than a day or two in trenches hidden from view, clandestine trenches only visible through classified glasses, and sometimes not even then. Before Hitch left "the Company," as it had always been called, the Special Operations Task Force had been formed and Julian was its leader. From time to time he would turn to Hitch for help in difficult matters. SOTF, or merely Special Ops, knew everything there was to know and how to deal with each and every contingency. With the exception of the CIA Director and the president of the United States, and those within its secret ranks, nobody knew it existed. All its operatives had other positions within the Company. Many were innocuous positions such as Chief Librarian, and Julian reported to the Director.

A few minutes later Julian and Hitch were sitting around a small rectangular table in a private reading room behind the counter. A pot of coffee and a bowl of chocolate covered almonds sat next to a number of *CIA LIBRARY* mugs, packets of sugar, and a jar of powered dairy creamer on a credenza along one wall.

"Please help yourself," Julian said, pointing to the credenza, "and tell me what brings you to my modest abode? Surely you have better things to do than continue associating with the likes of us?"

For the next few minutes Hitch explained why he was there, something personal that required some information he couldn't get elsewhere. He wasn't ready to divulge the real reason he was there. He needed to learn as much as he could about the Click, from a scientific standpoint. Why were some people Beaters and other Preemies, and was there a connection between Preemies and Beaters? But again, he wasn't ready to share all that with Julian, at least not yet.

After several cups of coffee, Julian led him through a triple locked door at the back of the reading room into a second reading room containing an ultra-high-speed computation shell. He entered several passwords into the shell, causing a floor to ceiling holographic screen to appear.

"It's all yours, my friend. I have things to do but let me know when you're done."

Forty-five minutes or so passed and Oliver terminated his search. He knew that his friend could easily check his whereabouts on the shell but probably wouldn't. In any case, he couldn't do anything about that and left the room looking for him.

"Well? Any luck?" Julian asked.

"Don't know yet. But somebody sure as hell doesn't want me to find it." The *it* Hitch was referring to had to do with a few links he discovered in his search relating to dissidents and outlandish opinions alluding to the idea that the Click might be a fraud. Outlandish, alluding! Not exactly hopeful links but it didn't matter. They were removed. Even one of the most powerful search engines in the world could not bring them back. So, who were these dissidents and why were their opinions expunged? Julian might know, Hitch thought, and he might have to ask him, but not yet. With that last thought, he found the librarian at his desk. "May need your help later, and if I do I'll fill you in on the details then."

Julian Iscar merely nodded and smiled. Both men knew about secrets, when to keep them and when to reveal them.

Chapter Seven

The Coalition United for Theocratic Oversight sat just outside the walls of Ecclesia opposite the Square on Via Dei Corridori. The large stone building was older than the Cūtocracy itself by at least a half century, and its location was no coincidence. Being within the shadows of Ecclesian power allowed the partnership between the Church and political arm of theocratic thought to both blossom and fester out of public view. In fact, early in their relationship, a tunnel was constructed between the Cūtocratic headquarters and the Casina of the earliest smotec, a building to the northwest of the majestic Basilica of Ecclesia, The Casina had been serving as the Academy of Sciences but became a private house for secret liaisons between the Church and the Cūtocrats after the tunnel was completed.

High Minister Robert McGivney knew the tunnel well. As the Chief Counsel for the Ecclesian Church and chief political adviser to the present Supreme Minister of the Ecclesia, Smotec Pius V, he spent much time traversing its ancient cracked walls and dank stone path. At that moment he hiked unnoticed through the dimly lit tunnel from Ecclesia to the Cūtocracy, wearing his usual black Cassock and matching skull cap. It took him approximately thirty-five minutes at his measured pace. There was no secrecy involved in his rendezvous. He could have easily driven or taken an Ecclesian shuttle but wanted to walk, to think. His sources told him Innocent's Smotecal Decretum had surfaced after more than a century. For what reason exactly? To harm the Church, the Cūtocracy? Did he even believe in Innocent's Decretum? Of course not. Nevertheless, there were cynics who would use the fairy tale to malign the Church. He could just imagine the PR disaster he would have to cope with until the lies were put to rest. That doesn't take into account the revenues lost every Sunday, he thought. "Mary, mother of God!" he heard slip from his lips and echo around him.

The tunnel ended in the basement of the Cūtocratic headquarters. The High Minister, a tall man with a slight limp, climbed one flight up to an elevator in what appeared to be a large janitorial closet. He took the elevator from there to a similar closet off the private quarters devoted to the Ecclesian Church for its use only and accessible only by the right set of keys. Those quarters included several comfortable chairs and a small conference table. General Edmond Rosewall, the Cūtocracy's highest military officer and director of VAMA's paramilitary, waited in uniform next to the table. He was alone and biting his nails.

"Your Eminence, I…" the general said standing erect upon seeing the minister enter. Rosewall was a short, ugly man with a scarred face and a mustache that extended well beyond his cheeks and below his upper lip.

"Don't give me that 'Your Eminence' crap, Rosewall. The smotec is on my ass and now I'm on yours. Do you have any more on that fucking Decretum that supposedly surfaced?" McGivney was in Rosewall's face.

"I have our best man on it, Your Eminence. Her name is Rousseau. She's a bulldog. If anybody can—"

"So the answer's no! Get on it now, God damn it, and remember who's paying to keep your Coalition solvent." The Minister stepped back having made his point, then sat down and lit up a cigar. "In the meantime, we have other business that needs attending." He blew out a puff of smoke and continued. "I want weekly updates on this Decretum matter, Rosewall. Weekly!"

Chapter Eight

For several weeks after visiting the CIA Library Oliver Hitchcock brow beat himself into believing he could find more on the Click, especially on those dissidents who seemed to have vanished into the blogosphere. At some point he gave up and called on his friend once again.

"Listen, Julian, I will explain everything, but not over the phone. Why don't we meet at the Pearly Gate… You've never been there… In that case we will definitely meet there. It's on E Street, North West, up from Seventh… Yes, tomorrow night at nine will work, and you're in for a treat."

Before he knew it, Hitch found himself meandering down Pennsylvania Avenue and up Seventh before turning right on E Street. There on his left stood the entrance to the Pearly Gate, big as life. *Ellen Dee Welcomes You to The Pearly Gate* read the marquee in alternating blue and white lights, chasing after themselves above the front entrance like greyhounds chasing a pound of flesh. Hitch felt comfortable seeing it. He spent many hours there before and after discovering he wasn't going to be done in by the Click. But then his feeling of well-being quickly dimmed dark, as if he were the pound of flesh caught in the grips of a man-eating puzzle he could not solve. This wasn't a social night out, nor was it a game.

"I'm sorry, sir, this is a private establishment. Entrance is by invitation only," a recently hired young man perched behind a standup desk and dressed in a tuxedo announced as Hitch was about to enter, as he tried to put behind him the frustration he felt.

Hitch pulled a membership card from his wallet and handed it to the young man. "I'm Oliver Hitchcock and I left a message to have Julian Iscar meet me in the lounge if he arrived ahead of me."

"One moment please, Mr. Hitchcock." The man behind the desk tapped on the screen of his ultrathin shell. Like other computation shells, it housed all types of transceivers, making it possible for the actual software processing to take place remotely, somewhere in the blogosphere, actually in Spider Rooms dotting the planet. From protolytes above, computations and data, in fact everything that makes the computation shell do its job, could be streamed into and out of the device. The shell could be designed as an ultrathin tablet—light weight, and extremely inexpensive to manufacture. Indeed, all computation shells and other such digital devices are built in the same way and they all fascinated Hitch. He loved the latest and greatest almost as much as a good bottle of whisky, a straight flush, a pretty woman, and a challenging covert operation.

After several more taps at his screen, the tuxedoed man made a call on his scud, and a minute later a beautiful brunette who couldn't have been more than eighteen appeared and introduced herself as Vanessa. "Follow me, Mr. Hitchcock." She led him across thick red carpet with bright gold edging down a wide hallway past a number of heavy double doors on both sides, each guarded by a tuxedoed sergeant-at-arms similar to the bouncer out front. One of the doors happened to open just as Hitch walked by. His eyes widened and he froze in place for a second, just long enough to take in a gigantic casino lit up like an indoor football stadium. He hadn't played on green felt for years, ever since graduating from Gamblers Anonymous. Fortunately, they continued on and stopped in front of a guard-free door labeled *Lounge C*.

"Here we are Mr. Hitchcock. Mr. Iscar is waiting for you at the bar."

Hitch stepped into what appeared to be a dark, empty room, but after a second or two his eyes adjusted. A man waved him over.

"Hitch, my friend, have a seat and buy me a drink. Apparently my money is no good here."

Hitched laughed. "That's right; but before we drink, let me take you on a tour."

Hitchcock led Julian from the bar into the wide hall, then they entered the first set of double doors on the right and found themselves in the back of a theater. In front of them were at least four hundred seats filled with an audience mesmerized as it watched a modern ballet up on stage—burlesque style, mostly naked women waiving semitransparent colored scarves four and five feet long. Reds and blues and yellows and greens swirled across the stage. A few minutes later they proceeded up the hall and edged into the casino that Hitch caught sight of when he first arrived. It was one of the largest he had ever seen, and he wished he were still playing. To his right, three steps up, a raised floor of poker tables popped into view, causing his heart to pound against his ribcage. Julian knew the look, no doubt, and quickly steered his old friend back out. After poking their heads into a fancy restaurant, a bowling alley/pool hall, and a large steam room, they wound their way back to the bar and ordered beers on tap from Rudy Havercamp. Rudy was originally from New Orleans, heavy set, white, and Cajun to the core. He wore a firearm, one of the classic low-level red lasers, on his hip. Hitch could never get over the idea of civilians carrying firearms, civilians who had no idea how to use them. But they did, and it scared the hell out of him.

"So, being the intuitive librarian you are, Julian, what is it you observed on our little tour?"

"That it takes big bucks to be a member in this palace of fine art."

"Yes, that's mostly true, but what else."

"I give up, what?"

"The people, the *members* as you call them. They are all men approaching seventy-five if not already there, well-to-do dirty old men waiting to die."

"Are you saying that all these people have heard the Click?"

"Many have heard it, felt it, whatever it is that happens letting you know the clock's ticking, or soon will. But in any case, they are waiting to die and, as you know, they only have around three months following the death knell until it happens. They take one day at a time. And if they can afford it, why not enjoy every last second."

"And their little women stay home darning casket liners?"

"Not at all. The women's version is just as elaborate, if not more so." Hitch once tried to get Edna to join. She would have nothing to do with it. "If I want to see naked men, I'll watch you take a shower," she said making her husband laugh out loud.

Julian picked up the napkin under his drink. *Ellen Dee's Pearly Gate.* "So, who is Ellen Dee?"

"Ha! Ellen Dee is a very profitable corporation. LND—your Last Ninety Days of life. We promise you'll enjoy them, at least that's what's mounted over the urinal in every Ellen Dee men's room, and all of the matchbooks and napkins include a reminder that the Click is your *key* to Ellen *Dee*. See for yourself." Hitch picked up his napkin and turned it over to prove it.

"Okay, I buy that, but what is it you're searching for?"

"Julian, do you know how this Click thing works?"

"Of course. Everybody does. It has to do with our genetic makeup that somehow got screwed up or accelerated during, during…"

"During the time of the great ERAM-V plague," Oliver Hitchcock was quick to add. "On the other hand, it could have been the Almighty or Mother Nature poking a nose in our business."

"Right. And when you hear the Click your biological clock begins winding down and you're gone within three months or so. But what does that have to do with you?"

"How old do you think I am?"

"I always assumed you were about my age, sixty-five." Julian looked around, then at his napkin. "God! I'm sorry, Hitch, I didn't realize you…"

"No, Julian, I'm not going to die in ninety days, not for a long while I hope. But I am well past the Click. I'm seventy-eight years old and while I thought I felt it once, nothing happened and here I am." Hitchcock drank the last of his beer and then let his glass drop to the table with a *bang* that got his friend's devoted attention. "I do however need your help because of the Click. You see, there are a fair number of people like me in the world, *Beaters* we're called, people who beat the Click, sort of like cheaters cheating death. The bad news is there are a fair number of people who experience the Click prematurely, as early as ten or eleven years old, and…" Hitchcock went silent. His mouth closed, his lips twitched, his jaws danced as if he were chewing on his own words in an attempt to swallow them without choking. He could see OJ being wheeled into the ambulance, but it wasn't OJ, it was Christopher.

"And," Julian said, breaking Hitchcock's momentary bout with guilt mixed with a trace of self-pity.

"And my eleven-year-old grandson happens to be one of those people who will die prematurely like my first grandson; he's what they call a *Preemie*."

"He felt the Click?"

"Not exactly, but he will soon enough, I'm afraid. I'll explain that later. For now, please take my word for it. And where you come in is this. I promised Edna on her deathbed that I would do whatever I could to save Christopher from that fate. I will need your help to keep that promise." Hitch gulped down the last of his beer and waved to Rudy.

"Another, Mr. Hitchcock?"

"Make it bourbon on the rocks, Rudy."

"And you, Mr. Iscar?"

Julian shook his head and looked at Hitch. "Still

drinking and gambling?"

"No green felt. As for the drinking, it gets me through the day. Ever since we lost Oliver Junior, then Edna. And now Christopher at risk."

"Are the doctors sure?"

"Yes. He's been subjected to just about every test. All positive. I need to know if there's anything out there that can save him."

"So, this is what you were looking for the other day?"

Just then Rudy started toward them with Hitch's bourbon. Hitch put his finger to his lips. He waited to answer Julian until Rudy came and went, then whispered. "Yes. I need access to those super search engine processing plants I know the Company has hidden somewhere in Virginia." He then described what he found in Julian's library search engine.

"Let me see what I can do."

Hitch said goodbye to his old friend at the door and walked to his car, trying to sort things out. As he retraced his steps, he couldn't help but notice all the VAMA hearses on the street, black with VAMA in gold across each side and down the back. They couldn't be missed, weren't supposed to be missed, Hitch guessed. But when did they start appearing so often, he wondered, as two passed by?

He never thought about the Vaccine Assurance and Management Agency until around his seventy-seventh birthday. During that entire seventy-fifth year, Edna woke up every morning thinking it was his last. Not Hitch. He was stubborn enough, and self-centered enough, to believe no such flaw would assault the perfection he knew his DNA to be. On his seventy-seventh birthday, long after they were both convinced of his infallibility, a late-night rap at the door caught him by surprise. Through the peephole he could see a young fellow in a pinstripe suit flashing his VAMA badge without saying a word at first. He didn't apologize for the surprise inspection or the late hour. Hitch had passed through the throes of the Click, was still breathing, and hadn't reported that fact to the authorities, something all citizens had to do no later than their seventy-sixth birthday if they were still living. The youngster wanted to know why he hadn't made a report and immediately demanded to see his papers and his V-Mark. Hitch would have shown him what to do with any fucking report or his papers if Edna hadn't intervened. After seeing Hitch's papers and V-mark, the pimple-faced moron instructed him to appear at the local VAMA office within the next thirty-six hours. He complied. What choice did he have? It was comply or face the wrath of Edna, the only person who really gave a shit about him.

He stomped into the local VAMA office at the end of Vama Way in upscale Alexandria, right at the river's edge. Upon stepping into the opened lobby under a two-story glass roof and sinking into heavy black carpet, he knew instinctively who he was dealing with, and it wasn't a bunch of bureaucratic shlebs. Only the Cūtocracy had the wherewithal to show off so lavishly. After extensive processing, they took blood, scraped some skin samples from his V-Mark. More than two hours later they let him go. Then nothing.

As Hitch relived his first encounter with VAMA, he reached his car. Hopefully Julian Iscar would be able to help him, although he wasn't sure what that meant or where that would lead.

Chapter Nine

Janine Rousseau, VAMA's youngest chief inspector at the age of forty-eight, sat at the desk next to her scud listening to General Rosewall's voice rattle out from its speaker and watching him on her new toy. It was a bright blue command center, a cube the size of a toaster with a keyboard, voice activation, and buttons. Rosewall appeared larger than life on a holographic surveillance screen seemingly draped over in a greenish-blue haze or fog so thick she felt like she could touch it. On several occasions, she stuck her hand in only to discover it turned greenish-blue and caused the optics to jitter and the images to look like they were in an earthquake.

"You heard me. Keep your damn toy under wraps. It's illegal as hell. If you're caught with it that's exactly where you'll be. You're only to use it to verify or squash the rumors about that stupid Smotecal Decretum thing and do it quickly or McGivney will be on my ass and I will be on yours. Do you understand?" Rousseau nodded as she glared at the short, fat man somewhat deformed by the greenish-blue haze that wrapped itself around his pulsating image. "Also, it's come to my attention that you should keep an eye on your friend Oliver Hitchcock. "Now shut down that damn thing."

Rosewall clicked off as she powered down her toy, causing the Hologram Surveillance Screen to vanish.

She wondered how Oliver Hitchcock figured into any of this but knew to keep her mouth shut. Minutes later she powered her toy back up and continued familiarizing herself with all its features, illegal as hell, as that may have been.

Later that evening, midmorning in Paris, France, she began tapping instructions on its keyboard. The holographic surveillance screen streamed up in front of her, going from dark to light, then displaying the words *Incoming Data* All of a sudden, an aerial view of a school appeared. Hopefully its schedule hadn't changed, a schedule she had memorized. After she held down one of many buttons, the school zoomed in, as if it were rising to the surface from the bottom of the sea. She saw a sandbox, swings, and other playground equipment, all within a greenish-blue haze of constantly changing density. She then zeroed in on a nine-year old child who glowed intermittently. That was the nature of the command center, or Blue Cube as she christened the new toy. It could find any subject based on their DNA and lock in on it so long as the subject was visible from the sky. Even without DNA, once an image appeared on the screen, it could be placed in memory and found no matter where it was. Once located, the image or target within the hologram glowed intermittently, as the child had, as Rosewall had. She watched the child's every move, smiling, until Oedipus Mertens walked in the room. His presence caused her to smack another button. The screen went white except for the words *No Data.*

Oedipus Mertens, a large-boned, gruff appearing lieutenant underling and loyal thug stood behind her watching the HS-Screen through one eye. The other eye was covered with a silver patch. "What ez dis?" he said with a slur he acquired as a child beaten to a pulp by a drunken mother, herself the product of abuse.

"Something that will be of great use to us. What would you like to see, my friend?" A sneer developed across her face.

"Mi ome. It ez so long since I bin der." He gave her a questioning look.

"Brussels, no?"

"Outside Brussels. Anderlecht, Belgium, on Rue Kinet, 77 Rue Kinet."

She began tapping instructions into the blue cube once again. The words *Incoming Data* appeared.

Then, suddenly, Oedipus's one eye went wide. He stepped closer to the screen as she zoomed in. "Dat's my ouse…and dat's…dat's Mr. Peeters, mi old neighbor." He poked his fingers into the greenish-blue haze causing Mr. Peeters and his house to dither, then quickly pulled his fingers out.

"Now watch this, Oedipus." She started tapping again. "Once I locate anyone, even without their DNA, I can lock on them." Suddenly, Mr. Peeters' image began glowing. Rousseau pushed away from her desk and the Blue Cube, holding up her hands to prove a point. Without doing more, as the subject walked down the street, the HS-Screen followed him as his image glowed intermittently.

"Is dees legal?" Oedipus wondered aloud.

"Ha!" Rousseau answered and was about to continue when her scud *rang*. She looked at it suspiciously, tapped the Blue Cube, and the screen vanished.

She clicked on her scud and looked at Oedipus

with a raised eyebrow. It was the bartender at the Pearly Gate.

"Havercamp! That was quick. What did you get?"

"What you asked for, a video conversation between Mr. Hitchcock and a Julian Iscar, clearly CIA. I tape everything."

Rousseau looked at the clock on the wall, then at Oedipus. "Good. We'll come by for you tomorrow evening. My man will call later to make arrangements."

"You'll make it worthwhile?"

Rousseau shook her head. "Worthwhile? Yes, of course."

The following evening a little before eleven o'clock, with Rousseau in the back seat, Oedipus drove his VAMA hearse down Pennsylvania Avenue and up Seventh Street where Rudy Havercamp waited. Oedipus pulled over and Rousseau waved him into the seat next to her.

"Well?" she said with an opened palm extended.

Rudy handed her a flash drive. "I got everything he and his one-armed CIA buddy said." He then opened his palm and began wiggling his fingers. "I believe what you got is mighty valuable as you'll see. A small cut of your laundry business and we'll call it even."

"Laundry business?" Rousseau was incredulous.

"I have contacts in the most amazing places. As I said, we'll call it even."

Rousseau shrugged then looked in the rearview mirror and caught the one eye staring back from the driver's seat. She nodded, then reached in her coat pocket. "I see."

Oedipus took off, maneuvered through the District, up and down one-way streets and angled thoroughfares teaming with open storefronts and a crowded populace seeking fun and frivolity. Eventually the hearse was lost in the formidable and downright scary Southwest quadrant where one wouldn't venture out at night without the armored protection of a VAMA tank. Suddenly the vehicle turned into an alley that refused to admit any form of light, as if to do so would have divulged the most hideous form of human poverty that the Cūtocracy claimed didn't exist. It also happened to be Rousseau's private dumping grounds. She pulled out her blue laser gun and shot Rudy in the heart. He quaked for several seconds before going silently dead. The car came to a *screeching* halt. Rousseau reached over, opened Rudy's door, and pushed him out. "Now we're even."

Chapter Ten

Once again Yennie Tawahada found himself in Dillon Burber's overly illuminated office long after sunset. A few minutes later, before Dillon could look up from the mess on his desk, President Wainwright walked in with her usual gracious smile and her old white tennis shoes she wore when no one was looking. She was matronly in looks when not provoked, tall but heavyset across the middle, and carried thick bushy gray hair balancing out the top—the grandmother type and she played it well. Indeed, she raised six children in the good Ecclesian tradition and doted over fifteen grandchildren who were constantly at the White House. Yennie had met most of them. She was a good president, he thought, but then she did have her difficulties, politically speaking, considering she had only been president for twenty months.

The fact that she was president at all was an anomaly. She had been President Roger Albritton's vice president before he died in a freakish boat accident. Albritton had been the typical ultraconservative fighting for a second term against an even more extreme and much better looking right-winger, one backed by the Cūtocracy. Albritton chose Andrea Wainwright as his running mate, replacing Robert Silber, who the Cūtocracy learned had Jewish grandparents on his mother's side. Although Andrea Wainwright was known to be somewhat moderate, the president needed the women's vote and despite her political leanings she was an extremely popular governor of a Southern state. As she became more comfortable in the White House, and more progressive, her political detractors intensified their efforts to bring her down.

"Good evening, Yennie," she said before taking a seat in the corner. "Sorry to drag you back but I'm afraid we need to call on you once again. It seems the little leak you orchestrated needs a bit stronger drip. There've been echoes of concern in faraway places or so I've been told, but they haven't made it across the ocean, at least not where they can do a whole lot of good." The president rose from her chair. "So, I will leave you here with Dillon while I take my leave. He will fill you in. Thank you for all your help."

Before Yennie had a chance to respond, the president disappeared, quietly in her tennis shoes, and Dillon Burber insisted they get down to business. "Do you remember that young man you mentioned a while back, Rajiv someone? He was here from India attending a memorial service for a retired CIA friend of his, Oliver Hitchcock. This Rajiv fellow said, or was it you who said the man, Mr. Hitchcock, would be a perfect partner to propel our Smotecal Decretum plan?"

"It was Rajiv who suggested Oliver Hitchcock. Rajiv Nadu."

"Good. Given everything you divulged about DanSheba and his connections there, I think we could use his help to make all this work. Besides, the president happens to know Oliver Hitchcock. For better or for worse were her words," Dillon added but had no idea what she meant, and it was clear she didn't invite him to ask.

In less than an hour Dillon explained their plan involving Hitchcock. Yennie excused himself and drove across Key Bridge to his condo in Rosslyn. On his way, he couldn't help but worry about exactly what he divulged to Dillon and the president of the United States. He cleared it with Meta, who was supposed to clear it with the elders in DanSheba, but he wasn't sure she had. It seemed too quick. The elders didn't work that fast.

After pouring a glass of milk and picking through a box of chocolate chip cookies, he carried his scud into the bedroom. A while later, he walked back out, talking on it. "Yes, I know you and Hitchcock are old friends, Rajiv. That's exactly why I called. I need you to do exactly as I asked… No, it won't. It will enhance your relationship, I promise, and it won't jeopardize anyone else… Yes, Meta knows what we are doing. She was the one who gave the Decretum to the president and she suggested involving Nagasi… I know you will do what you can, and we appreciate all your help."

Yennie clicked off and tried to organize his thoughts. He hadn't visited home in probably five years and his parents were not happy with him, nor were the elders who insisted that all DanShebans living abroad spend a month out of the year in DanSheba. They insisted, but he knew they hardly ever demanded it, especially when it came to individuals who did not rely on financial support from the village. Regardless, most DanShebans living elsewhere did make it home more often than Yennie. They brought with them the latest and greatest technology and gadgets from wherever it was they lived, a fact Yennie felt bad about, although he knew his parents felt even worse than him.

After glancing up at the clock over the kitchen counter, he turned on the TV and groaned. Dr. Roger Fielding, Director General of the World Health Organization, was being interviewed on Ecclesian Monitor TV. The WHO was the health and welfare arm of the United Nation which had control over VAMA, although most everyone knew it was the Cūtocracy that controlled VAMA, and some even believed it controlled WHO.

Yennie needed no introduction to Roger Fielding, who began pontificating. "Ladies, gentlemen, and children of the world, I am addressing you on this anniversary of the founding of the Vaccine Assurance and Management Agency, our beloved VAMA. Practically all of you—of us, have known nothing but prosperity in our lifetimes, good health, wonderful living conditions, no poverty, indeed a wonderful life. We don't know and can't envision hunger, disease, overpopulation, and we never want to see it firsthand, not as long as we live, nor do we want our children or grandchildren to witness these abominations. At the same time, because of our good fortune, we, most of us, have grown complacent. We have taken for granted what our governments have been able to achieve; what our beloved Cūtocracy and we at the United Nations, especially those able agents within VAMA, have fought so hard far. I wish to raise a glass to…"

"Enough!" Yennie barked out to the TV and turned it off by voice command. Maybe their little leak has had an effect, he thought.

Chapter Eleven

Oliver Hitchcock arrived at Washington Regis International Airport early. As soon as his passport was electronically logged in and he passed through an eye scan to establish his identity, he debated whether to call Kathy. The previous evening, she had called to tell him Christopher was running a low grade temperature. He decided not to call. It would only worry her more. Instead, he hopped on a high-speed people mover divided into fast and slow lanes, the former requiring overhead gripping bars given how fast it floated over its tracks. Even though he was in no particular rush, Hitch chose the fast lane. He always chose the fast lane regardless the circumstances and reached his gate area in enough time to have a leisurely breakfast.

After nabbing the only vacant table and punching in his order on a small device sitting next to the catsup and pepper sauce—a dumb waiter it was called—a glassy-eyed server in a stained brown *Feast & Fly* uniform eventually brought out his meal. A recent copy of *Washington Now* had been left on the seat. The cover story—*The Proud History of Washington Regis International Airport*. He thumbed through the article and had to laugh. The very airport he was sitting in exemplified state of the art use of federal tax dollars so that senators and congressmen could fly in style. *The rich and the powerful from inside the beltway are carried into the airport on high speed, solar powered air-rail in a matter of minutes. They fly out on jets made of light weight plastellic material, a unique combination of plastic and metal—jets faster than a speeding laser ray.* Well that was a bit of hyperbole. But the economy was surely thriving as the cover story claimed, wellness prevailed, and the population had been stable for decades. Peace and prosperity like never before, all thanks to God and the Cūtocracy. It was clear who wrote that article.

"The world may be at peace, but not me," Hitch shot back at the cover story.

After finishing breakfast and paying his tab on the dumb waiter by joining it to the app on his scud, he headed for the gate just as the agent there announced his flight to Mumbai was delayed. Something about a faulty warning light that required checking. Well some state of the art things never change. Just when he decided to call Kathy, his scud *rang*. She must have read his mind. Christopher's V-Mark seemed a little bluer than it had been. She wasn't one to check it as often as he had, that was too frightening, but her son's behavior bothered her too much to ignore it. "Keep an eye on him," was about all Oliver could say. "And have Ralph check his V-Mark if it continues to change."

On the flight to Mumbai, all of two hours and twenty minutes, Hitch reflected on the circumstances that brought him there. The immense Data Retrieval & Search Center that Julian made available did not impress him at first. He had expected a grand ballroom packed with endless bays of computer terminals and mammoth size holographic screens. Instead, he found himself sitting in what at one time appeared to be a large walk-in maintenance closet containing a single input/output shell and a small solid screen mounted over it. It was much like the relics in the National Technology Museum. However, he quickly learned how fast and thorough it was. Every thought he blurted into the handheld microphone produced on the screen an index of possible leads he might not have ever considered. Nevertheless, after several hours of chasing his own tail, it seemed, he learned no more than he already knew. Except! Except for the fact that he was not the only one who had been interested in the few links relating to dissidents alluding to the idea that the Click might be a fraud. Apparently, others had tried to retrieve those links from not only the very same computation shell he sat at in the Company's maintenance closet but from other computation shells around the world. There had been dozens of hits with no success. Who were those dissidents? How long ago was it? And who else was looking for them? Humm, Oliver Hitchcock wondered just as the flight attendant interrupted his thoughts and asked what he might like to drink. "Everything you have," he quickly responded but settled on bourbon over ice.

He would still be nowhere had he not received a call from his friend, Rajiv Nadu. Surprisingly coincidental and a bit strange, he thought, as he finished up his drink and looked for the flight attendant. Strange or not, he couldn't pass up the opportunity to see for himself. He doubted anything would come of it, but at least it was an excuse to visit Mumbai once again, and some of the gang he worked with way back when. Besides, he needed a break from Kathy and her… Damn it! That wasn't fair, he thought as the attendant approached again.

After he finished his second bourbon, the cabin lights turned off and the hypersonic plane cruised in the dark. Most of the passengers read by overhead light, some taking a catnap. Hitch, on the other hand, sat hard against the back of his seat studying the space between him and the seat in front of him. He was happy to be in first class where leg room was plentiful. He focused on such trivialities in an attempt to relax all the body parts. Not working so well. Too many things to think about. He unbuckled and strolled to the back of the plane for still another drink. A female attendant, Egyptian, in her forties, attractive, headed his way. He turned sideways to let her pass.

Just as she did, an elderly black woman rolled out of her seat and landed at Hitch's feet, trembling in fear, hands to her ears grasping.

"No! Please, I'm not ready. I can't…"

Hitch dropped to his knees, took her hand, looked into her eyes. The same desperation he saw in Edna's eyes the night she… As the woman shook, he imagined hearing the *click, click, click* that rang so loudly in Edna's last moments.

The flight attendant hovered over the two of them. Hitch looked up. "Do something, for Christ's sake."

"Sir, please get out from the aisle. One of my colleagues is getting a bag."

"Bag?"

"A body bag. Now, please step away." Without saying more, she walked back up the aisle leaving Hitch staring at her back.

"She's not even…" Hitch dropped closer to the woman and embraced her. He swore he heard a *click,* then a final sigh before she went limp in his arms.

Suddenly Hitch felt a hand grab at his shoulder, hard. He swung around, ready to strike. The flight attendant now standing over him, a man in his forties, stepped back, frightened at first, then agitated.

"Sir, please! International policy requires us to…" He stepped aside. Two other flight attendants swooped in and placed the deceased woman in a bright orange body bag, then zipped it up.

Hitch did little to prevent the disbelief and disgust permeating through his body from showing on his face. The Egyptian flight attendant looked on shaking her head. "You have no idea how many of these we see, all coming out of your country."

Hitch only half listened as he watched the bright orange bag being dragged down the aisle toward the back of the plane. What astonished him most were the other passengers. They seemed to take little notice. "Only you Americans seem to think it's okay to fly while in the throes of the Click."

Enough! Hitch had enough. He glared past her, went back to his seat and growled to himself.

After passing through customs, Rajiv greeted him with a hug, and they drove on a cushion of air from the airport to the Union Hospital in Chembur, a suburb of Mumbai on the east coast. Most of the way there, Rajiv made small talk, seemingly trying to avoid how it was he found Nagasi in the first place. At the same time, Hitch couldn't help but wonder why Rajiv thought there was a connection between Nagasi and Hitch's promise to Edna, a promise Rajiv recalled from their time at the cemetery.

Finally, after Hitch could no longer take the small

talk, he coaxed his good friend to open up. According to Rajiv, he happened to be visiting a relative at the hospital when he came upon Nagasi, a very old Ethiopian Jew, in the next room. Initially they thought Nagasi had Alzheimer's. Although rare, it was one of the diseases the past two hundred years of medicine had not been able to cure entirely. It seemed to raise its ugly head at the most inopportune times. While Nagasi claimed he was hit by a bicycle crossing the street, he got everyone's attention when he began babbling something about the ERAM-V vaccine being a death sentence. Rajiv was told he kept alternating between a state of delusion and total control of reality, mostly the former according to the doctors, as he continued to mumble about the vaccine and insisted on referring to it as a death sentence. The old Jew claimed he was one hundred and two years old, and again the doctors were convinced he was mixed up. But Rajiv wasn't so sure, especially after Nagasi kept jabbering about all his people living just as long, some even longer, deep in the jungle.

So, maybe coincidences happen, Hitch thought as they pulled into the hospital parking lot. A few minutes later he and Rajiv stood at an opened door looking in on Nagasi, who was either sound asleep or unconscious. He surely looked old, Hitch thought. He had shoulder length gray-white hair and a goatee, and his skin was black with blotches of chalky gray, proof he probably wasn't exaggerating too much about his age.

"This talk, people even older in the jungle. You believe that shit?"

"Storytelling and mythology are part of Indian culture, my friend. Like all cultures, sometimes we believe what we want to believe," Rajiv answered.

"Do we know where he lives?"

"I assume in the area. As I understand it, he was once the principal at the Jewish School of Learning not far from here."

"Jewish School of Learning?"

Rajiv put Oliver in touch with the head librarian at the city library, a Mrs. Ambika Patel. She spent most of her working life in Mumbai, in the Research and Analyst Wing of India's counterpart to the CIA, as an R&AW analyst, before switching professions. Hitch rented a convertible, punched the address into the auto pilot/navigation system which glided him to the city library with little effort on his part. He still wasn't convinced this trip would lead anywhere, but he had come this far and there was a certain strangeness in that fellow, Nagasi, that seemed authentic.

Considering how Hitchcock found Ambika Patel, she willingly shared some information with him. She confirmed Rajiv's understanding that Nagasi was the principal in a very private gated village, the Jewish School of Learning, just outside Chembur, a short distance from Mumbai's east coast. Everyone referred to it as the "Black Jews' Village" or merely the "School of Learning" because its inhabitants included only the black Jews, and because it was mostly made up of school houses for the village children from kindergarten through high school. Nagasi and the teachers lived in a separate home in the center of the village while the children and some parents lived in adjacent apartment buildings.

After visiting with Mrs. Patel, Hitch went to the village, but unfortunately it was closed and everyone gone. They just disappeared, or so he was told by several locals hanging around the chained front gate supporting a large red and white *No Trespassing* sign. They also told him the Village of Learning had its own grocery store, and bank, believe it or not, and that the villagers mostly kept to themselves. They did run a small fleet of fishing boats and sold some of their catch to the locals. No one was entirely sure where all those students and teachers went or where they came from. Apparently, most of the neighborhood imagined a hidden city deep in the jungle but that was because everyone seemed to romanticize these strange people and their ways.

Later that evening, well after dark, Hitch returned to the Jewish Village of Learning, this time with Rajiv. A brick wall almost as tall as Oliver surrounded the entire village. He estimated the village sat on at least a dozen acres. It was huge, he thought after walking the entire perimeter, huge and solid. The only entrance was through the main gate. It was constructed of thick steel posts that complemented the impervious wall. Between the steel posts they saw neglected landscape and debris held captive by the tallness of the walls and the absence of people. The apparent need for privacy and fortification begged the two onlookers to search the entire village, and scaling the wall was their best option. Before they did, however, they waited for the VAMA vehicles patrolling the streets to vanish. Christ! Even in this remote outpost across the world those bastards maintained a vigilance that could not be missed. Hitch never liked VAMA and now he even liked it less.

He happened to be a master at picking other

people's locks. As a result, they had little difficulty keying their way into the buildings and wound up spending nearly four hours searching the classrooms, offices, and personal residences. The village interior had been meticulously cleaned of any solid evidence that might have incriminated the fleeing occupants. The whiteboards were white, the wastebaskets empty, the drawers and closets devoid of even the leftover lint from clothing. And yet, all the tables, chairs, desks, beds, digital book readers, even computation shells devoid of incriminating data appeared as if they hadn't been moved during the cleansing process. Red dots were placed on all those items which were meant to stay, according to a poster on the wall. Anything with green dots was to be taken with them. It was as if the village citizens knew someone would be there in the middle of the night, begging for a hint of who they were. What better clues than the things they used on a daily basis, especially their book readers and the books they read?

The book that received most of Hitch's attention had fallen behind a heater. It had a green dot on its spine, which might as well have been a sign saying *read me*! And Hitch did, quickly, as Rajiv busied himself scavenging other areas. It was entitled *The First Coming*, and as best as he could gather it was about a community of Jews waiting for the Messiah to come.

"Hitch, we must hurry," Rajiv shout from another room. He closed the book and debated. Should he or should he not take it? He touched the green dot and looked at the heater. How did it get there? It was as if someone left it there on purpose. That thought, and curiosity, won the day. He stuck it behind his waistband under his shirt and went looking for his companion.

Chapter Twelve

Janine Rousseau hurried into her office, talking on her scud, making sure she doubled locked the outer office door. "Yes, yes. Thank you for the confidence, sir. I'm on it now." She rushed over to her Blue Cube and punched the power-up button. Seconds later its holographic surveillance screen appeared larger than life with *No Data* flashing across its face. She quickly typed in some key coordinates and the name given to her by Rosewall. *No Data* changed to *Incoming Data*, the HS-Screen went greenish-blue, then all of a sudden the Ecclesian Basilica in Rome appeared. She zoomed in, hit the target button, tapped on the listening mode, and turned the volume up.

High Minister McGivney in his black Cassock and skull cap, his image intermittently glowing within the greenish-blue haze, paced in front of the Basilica talking to someone on his scud. Rousseau knew him by reputation. A onetime vicious prosecutor in Rome with alleged ties to the Italian mafia before being drafted by Supreme Minister Pius early in the smotec's term, he was thought to be a closet Opus Dei by some. Others even believed he was a Tarsusian, the more extreme wing of Opus Dei that was made up of the followers of St. Paul, who was born Saul of Tarsus. In any case, she had to keep tabs on him for her own good if not because Rosewall insisted. She watched with interest and listened after adjusting the sophisticated sound filter that took her some time to master.

"I don't give a damn how remote it is. If the Smotecal Decretum surfaced you must find it or else the church will have hell to pay," he said sharply to someone on the other end. "Of course it's bogus but since when does that matter. I need you to stay on this." Rosewall wanted Rousseau to find out who McGivney was talking to.

Just then, a priest approached from behind him. "Minister McGivney."

McGivney whirled around. "What?"

"Excuse me sir, but His Sacredness, the smotec, wishes to see you right away."

"We'll talk later, and I expect results," McGivney said into his scud and clicked off.

"Damn it," Rousseau yelled to no one in particular and powered down the Blue Cube. "Who in the hell was he talking to?"

"Who wez who talken to?" Oedipus asked as he walked into her office after unlocking the outer office door.

"None of your fucking business. At least not yet," she said, still steaming. "However, I do want to show you what I recorded earlier, and that will be your business."

She powered up the Blue Cube once again and typed in some instructions. Oliver Hitchcock appeared through the same greenish-blue haze, leaving the airport in Mumbai with another man, an Indian. Hitchcock glowed intermittently. They were then seen going into and out of a hospital. Rousseau paused the holographic content and laughed.

"Had it not been for Rosewall and my dead bartender friend Rudy, I would never have keyed in on my even better friend, Oliver Hitchcock," she said looking at Oedipus and laughing once again. "Imagine him involved in this mess I have been asked to clean up. If this isn't a juicy coincidence I don't know what is?"

"Ya, and your dead friend wouldn't be so dead if he wadn't so greedy." Oedipus laughed.

"Now this is what I really want you to see." She unpaused the holographic content, and they both watched Hitchcock go into and out of the Mumbai City Library. Again, his image intermittently glowed. He was then followed into and out of a taxi where he stood in front of what looked like a school.

"Now comes the best part," Rousseau announced.

The HS-Screen went fairly dark since what had been recorded had taken place at night, but the images were clear thanks to long-range infrared technology that projected from the protolytes above. Hitchcock continued to glow intermittently, this time in shades of gray, as he stood at the front gate of the Jewish School of Learning with his Indian friend. They saw the two jumping the wall. They managed to get into the buildings. What they found, Rousseau's magic Blue Cube could not tell, since the Cūtocratic Protolytes it relied on could not pierce through opaque objects, unfortunately Rousseau thought. Nevertheless, she would find out.

"Wat es the CIA doin in Mumbai?"

"Clearly Hitchcock is not on CIA business or they would have scrambled our signal. This is personal."

"Why botter wit heem. He's a Beater trying to save

heez kid, dats all. Ezn't dat wat we learned from da dead bartender?"

"Oedipus, this isn't just any Beater. He's up to something."

"Like wat?"

"Not your problem. Orders are to scare the hell out of him."

"Dat's all?"

"Dat's all. I mean that's all, for now." Rousseau sneered at Oedipus. "You better watch your Belgian butt. The man's a living legend. Mess up and he'll cut your throat. You leave for Mumbai tonight."

The following morning Rousseau sat at her desk eating banana slices and blackberries while talking with Oedipus on her scud. She had him on holographic mode which meant his face and all of its warts were close enough to touch.

"Where are you now?"

"Sittin een my ATV een front of heez friend's ouse. Once ee leaves, I will follow eem and, as you say, scare dee ell out of eem."

"All right. You don't have to call back when he comes out. I'll have both of you on my little Blue Cube." She clicked off and Oedipus's holographic image vanished. After leaving her bananas and berries, she moved to where the Blue Cube was hidden, pulled it out from under a stack of files, powered it up, and typed in the necessary instructions. Less than a minute later Oedipus appeared on the HS-Screen sitting in his opened all-terrain vehicle, his image glowing intermittently. Hitch's friend's house appeared within the greenish-blue haze.

Rousseau beamed. She could not get over her toy.

It was so much more powerful than even the best scud. At the same time, she knew having it was utterly illegal and if discovered could get her thrown in jail. The General assured her that would not happen. Nevertheless, she kept it under a blanket of files when she was not there, and she kept the outer office door locked even when she was there. The only other person with the combination to that door was Oedipus and he could be trusted with her life. That was because he owed his to her. When she was CIA spying in her native Paris for the Americans, God that was years ago, she was the field officer in a major sting operation that involved Oedipus as a minor player. Something about him played well within her gut and she cut him loose. Otherwise, he would still be in someone's dungeon deep underground, if not already dead.

She engrossed herself in another project when a short squeal came from the Blue Cube as Oliver Hitchcock stepped out of his friend's home. She quickly tapped in some additional instructions calling for a split screen, and the HS-Screen showed Oedipus on one side and Hitchcock, now intermittently glowing, on the other side. She sat back in her chair and smiled. "Okay my love, this little venture should let you know we are keeping tabs on you."

Hitchcock drove along the streets of Mumbai with Oedipus close behind, although it didn't appear to Rousseau that Hitch knew he was being followed. Just as she was thinking that, his convertible rose higher above the pavement and accelerated. Even she could hear the whine of his electrotomic isothermal engine responsible for both the air cushion below and the propulsion pushing him forward. He made a quick right turn and then a left into an alley. Rousseau could only imagine Oedipus's grin as he kept up. She didn't know a driver as good as him.

Once Hitchcock exited the alley, he made for the highway and the two raced neck and neck as the ATV, also whining as it chewed up hydrogenated acetylene fuel, careened into the convertible's side several times. Hitch reversed thrust and slammed on his brakes, allowing Oedipus to take the lead, then rammed into his back end. They seemed to be playing with one another. This time Oedipus slammed on his brakes and maneuvered behind Hitchcock. Again, the convertible accelerated, dipped slightly, and veered off at the next exit. It merged onto a narrow road paralleling a mildly steep ravine on his right. The ATV stayed close behind. Within seconds, it easily caught up, crashing its heavily reinforced front end into the convertible with sufficient force to cause the convertible's blanket of air to quake under the chassis and its tires to slam to the ground. For a moment Rousseau thought Hitchcock was going to vault into the ravine. "God damn it, Oedipus, we need him alive!" she yelled at the HS-Screen.

Just then the convertible's cushion of air regained its footing and moved Hitchcock into the left lane where she saw him reverse thrust and slow down, allowing Oedipus to catch up. Now neck and neck, each swerved into the other, *bam, bam.* Hitchcock sped up and moved into his right lane where he slowed down once again. Oedipus moved to his left and overtook the convertible. Just as he turned into Hitch's front end, the convertible engine's reverse thrust slowed him down as he turned hard to the left. It caught the ATV's unprotected backside, *bang.* Oedipus lost control and spun into the ravine below. Hitchcock dropped to the ground and slammed on his thrusters. He stopped at the top of the ravine as a ball of fire shot up into Janine Rousseau's office. She sprang from her desk and practically fell into the greenish-blue haze being engulfed by the flames. Oh my! She was witnessing the demise of her lieutenant. She could feel the tic pulsating in her eye and her lower lip quivered.

Hitchcock raced from his car down the ravine, searching to his left and right. The ATV smoldered, but Oedipus was not in it. Seconds later, she saw him glowing, intermittently, within the bushes a hundred feet down. Hopefully he was still breathing. She quickly turned the volume up on the control center and to her relief heard her stooge groan. Apparently, Hitchcock heard it also as he rushed farther down the ravine toward him. By then, the Belgian seemed at best semiconscious. Hitchcock pulled out Oedipus's scud and his wallet then tapped on the scud. Even Rousseau could see VAMA flash onto the scud screen. "Jesus!" And it only got worse. She watched Hitchcock undress Oedipus until he was entirely naked. She then watched him tap once again on Oedipus's scud. Suddenly, she heard a *ring*, and she flinched. Resolved not to show weakness, she picked up her scud from the desk and took the call. He switched the scud into view mode and placed Oedipus's naked body within its crosshairs.

"Hey, Janine. Next time don't send a boy to do a man's job." He disconnected and headed up the hill toward his convertible with Oedipus's clothes in one hand.

Rousseau swiped her bowl of half eaten bananas and berries onto the floor, *crash*, and shut down her toy.

Swish, the HS-Screen vanished. The tic in her eye began ticking once again.

Chapter Thirteen

All the way back to his hotel, Hitch couldn't have been more delighted. Now more than ever he knew he was on to something. Janine would not have sent her thug all the way across the world just to play games, and clearly she didn't want him to use deadly force. He couldn't help but smile as he threw pieces of clothing from the convertible, one at a time. Once he scattered Mr. Oedipus Mertens across the road, he had to think carefully. Why was she taking him so seriously? Did it really have to do with Christopher? But what else? Hell! Nothing else! But what had he learned? He learned that some unknown bloggers, probably before he was born, took issue with the Click and were expunged. And then there was Nagasi, an old man, quite probably delusional, who claimed to be a hundred and two. And he claimed not to have been vaccinated. Hitchcock swore he saw a V-Mark on Nagasi, but maybe he was mistaken. And what about Rajiv? Could all of that have been a coincidence? Hitchcock didn't believe in coincidences. Nevertheless, he was willing to put common sense aside when it came to his grandson.

As he approached his hotel, Hitch was no closer to solving the mystery he called Janine Rousseau. Early in his career he met her in Paris, where she was a translator by day and an operative at night, using seduction and charm where necessary. She had been recruited by an operative friend of his. It didn't take her long to seduce Hitch, and thereafter their relationship became tumultuous to say the least. That lasted for almost a year. But then Rousseau blew her cover in one too many ventures and pissed off some higher ups, landing her on the streets of France, where she disappeared. At the time, Hitch was relieved considering the extra-marital relationship had begun boiling in a pot too hot to keep the lid on—a pot he was afraid might spill over into his private life. The next time he saw her she was wearing a black leather jacket with VAMA in yellow down one sleeve.

It was well after midnight when he reached his hotel and brought out the booze. After packing up for the morning flight and pumping out a hundred pushups on his knuckles, he found himself wandering in and out of the hall while listening on his scud to the other end of a conversation. A half-empty bottle of whisky sat on the coffee table along with an empty glass.

"No, not to kill me. I believe the shit was out to scare me… Yes, damn it, I know this is Janine's work and she knows I know it. The question is for whom and why?"

Hitch walked out on the balcony and thought he got a glimpse of a VAMA shit, one of those ubiquitous black hearses. "Julian, I'm going to need your help on this. I'll be home tomorrow morning."

The following day, after arriving at Washington Regis and passing through customs, he was once again on the phone with Julian Iscar. He raced through the airport, dodging the crowd of travelers. "What? You'll see what you can do?" Hitch became more incredulous as he listened. "Rousseau and VAMA! I already told you that. So what… Yes I know what I'm getting into, damn it… No! Just find out what it is they're getting into, and what an old fart who claims to be from some mysterious fucking village in the jungles of India has to do with anything."

Hitch clicked off, still steaming. He decided to skip the people mover, but practically trotted alongside, hoping to calm himself down.

Upon arriving home, he passed a VAMA hearse across the street and then from the driveway saw his front door ajar. He reached for his laser gun and opened the garage door at the same time. After pulling in and closing the garage door behind him, he jumped from his car and crept through the door in the back. Hitch dashed down the brick steps and under the overhanging deck. He peeked through a basement window and saw nothing but his own reflection. The rushing river below carried away with it suspicious sounds, if any, including possible footsteps overhead. Taking advantage of the river's roar, he unlocked the basement door and tiptoed through the dark to the head of the stairs. Inching his way up, step by step, with one hand gripping the handle of his laser gun, he no longer heard the river. The only sounds he could detect were the squeals under his shoes. Then a *crash* when he reached the top of the stairs. He raced through the door into the kitchen, ready to fire, then into the living room where the front door was wide open. Gusts of wind blew sheets of paper everywhere. A glass vase had fallen from an entry hall table to the tile floor below and shattered.

Hitch looked around dismayed, at first thinking the chaos was merely the work of nature. Then he noticed all the open drawers in his den and possessions thrown everywhere. "What the hell?" He raced for the door and looked out briefly. The VAMA hearse had vanished. He locked up and spent a good deal of time looking for video cameras and hidden mics. If they were there he'd find them. The place was clean. He took a deep breath, then turned and surveyed the mess that surrounded him.

It took several hours to put the house in order. When Hitch finally finished, he faced piles of printouts covering most of the counter space in the kitchen, the kitchen table, and much of his study. He checked the clock, 3:55 p.m. He sat at his desk and tapped on his computation shell. *Ring, ring, ring.* A hologram of Rajiv appeared. He was in his bed making love. "Oliver?"

"Rajiv, are you free?" The hologram disappeared.

"Oops! Oliver. What did you ask?"

"I asked if you were free, but now I'm not seeing you."

"Better that way. Am I free? Not exactly, but I am available, but just for a moment."

"You were supposed to check in on Nagasi."

"I did. I'm afraid he disappeared."

"What?"

"Discharged in the middle of the night. I checked all the hospitals. No record of a newly admitted patient named Nagasi."

"Shit!" Hitch swiped his hand across the desk causing papers to fly once again.

"Do not worry my friend. When the school opens, I will let you know. Early appointment in the morning. Must go."

"In that case, I hope she doesn't keep you up all night."

"She is twenty-two and gorgeous. I'm afraid she might just do that."

Hitch watched the signal disappear on the screen of his computation shell only to be replaced by silence. He jumped up from his desk chair and kicked the papers on the floor, then remembered *The First Coming*, still in his suitcase. Five minutes later, he sat on the living room couch with a bottle of beer in one hand and the book in the other hand, the green dot still on its spine. An hour in and he was convinced it was a book of fiction. Something about the Queen of Sheba in the Old Testament visiting King Solomon. The king supposedly seduced her, and that seduction resulted in the Tribe of Dan, one of the lost tribes of Israel defeated by the Assyrians and exiled from the land of Canaan. They eventually settled in Ethiopia, but generations later found their way to an idyllic meadow in the underbelly of India where, according to the True and Rightful Prophesy, they were to settle. Settle and wait for the Messiah. Jesus! This is lunacy, Hitch thought. Who were these people who read this stuff? By the time Hitch finished the book, he wasn't sure whether or not the Messiah ever came or who those people really were.

Chapter Fourteen

Yennie Tawahada stood at the open door to the oval office talking while President Wainwright sat on the edge of her desk listening. Dillon Burber sat in a chair in the corner watching.

"It's only a matter of time until they discover DanSheba. Oliver Hitchcock found our man Nagasi thanks to our mutual connection," Yennie attempted to say matter-of-factly. He was conflicted. DanSheba was his home, the home of his family and ancestors for so many generations he couldn't count that far back. He also agreed with Meta. The time was right to do what had to be done.

The president chuckled. "Knowing Oliver Hitchcock, it will be sooner rather than later. We can't have him discovering DanSheba without the public on our side. No, we'll need to speed things up."

"What do you suggest?" Dillon piped in.

"Something to shake up the public. Make them think for themselves. Something that will make headlines."

"Like?" Yennie asked. Each additional day he worked for Andrea Wainwright was a day he realized more fully how cunning she could be.

"Let's just say that Dillon here, our beloved Press Secretary, will have something juicy to feed to the press corps, yes, juicy enough to make the faithful want to burn me at the stake." She smiled a very wicked smile.

****

Janine Rousseau stood in the living room in front of her opened wall safe, filling it with bundles of hundred-dollar debit notes she took from a briefcase on the credenza below the safe. She listened to General Rosewall on her scud while admiring the photo of the child on the wall.

"Rousseau, are you there?"

"Yes. Yes. You were saying?"

"I was saying that I had someone check out the hospital in Mumbai and that's as much as I know. Nagasi somebody or somebody Nagasi. So just stay close to Hitchcock. We need to know more."

****

Minister McGivney sat against the arm and back of a red and blue sofa elegantly beaded in pink pearls, listening on his scud. He became so agitated he began picking at the pearls. "I see. Very interesting, and bothersome. Nagasi you say and the Indian jungle." He hesitated, deciding whether or not to verbalize his thoughts. "For years we've heard rumors about a tribe of wild black people in the jungles of India who could never be found and were never vaccinated. We always put that down as active imaginations running amuck."

McGivney started to end the conversation when another matter occurred to him. "Do you remember me mentioning a professor last week… Yes, Bloom, he's the one. He is part of a group of deniers; actually, he's the leader. We've been keeping an eye on him ever since his father won the Nobel Prize. I'm thinking that he might be interested in Mr. Nagasi and his so-called connection with India if your friend Hitchcock is…

Yes, right away. I think that could be to our advantage. And one more thing, find out if that bitch Rousseau knows about Nagasi."

The Minister clicked off and looked across the room at the smotec, who appeared angry.

"You didn't mention the Smotecal Decretum, Robert. That must be our priority."

Chapter Fifteen

The morning after learning about Nagasi's disappearance, the papers from Hitch's desk remained on the floor, reminding him of the setback. As he passed his office before exercising, he noticed the mail icon on his computation shell blinking. He trampled across all those papers to reach it. A note from Julian appeared across the screen along with three attachments. The note merely told him the attachments might be of interest and wished him luck.

He opened the first one, which contained the CV of Dr. Elana Wu, Professor of Immunology at American University. She had been a Senior Associate under Professor Emeritus Barnaby Bloom before he retired. Elana Wu came from mainland China to attend George Washington University at the age of fifteen and was considered one of the rising stars in the biotech world. Her CV briefly described her as the chair of a program in which recombinant DNA techniques, cell fusion, and bioprocessing techniques were used to alter organisms for specific purposes. A footnote to her CV boasted that she and other researchers successfully increased crop yields, developed more efficient biofuels, and improved medical diagnoses through genetic testing. It also mentioned her expertise on the interplay between DNA and vaccinated cells in the human body, which Hitchcock highlighted in yellow.

That attachment also included a photo of Dr. Wu. "Humm," Hitch said to no one in particular, "this should be interesting." *Hopefully she still looks like that,* he thought to himself, assuming the photo was probably taken in college.

He opened the second attachment, an article on Professor Barnaby Bloom. According to the article, Professor Bloom was the leading expert in the world on vaccine chemistry and came from a rather famous family. Both his father and grandfather were Nobel Laureates in the field of Bio-Science.

The third attachment started with a note. *For your eyes only—Julian.* It was more like a dossier on Dr. Wu, clearly not something easily available to the public. *After leaving China to attend George Washington University, she remained a citizen of China and became a converted Ecclesian since arriving to America. Like most religious converts, any and all criticism directed to "her church" she considered blasphemous, even though she had taught human evolution to graduate students. She was even more insistent in her conviction that questioning the government was something one didn't do, certainly not in mainland China where she grew up and knew better, and not in her foster country either. Doing something wrong and being deported always danced at the edge of her thoughts, and she made that clear to anyone who would listen. She also claimed that one day she would return to China to teach and take care of her parents, but then they died in an automobile accident.*

Hitch finished reading this last attachment, then looked back at the first one including the photo of Dr. Wu. He shook his head and wondered how Julian was able to get all that information on her, but then remembered who Julian Iscar was. He reached for his scud to call Dr. Elana Wu.

Dr. Wu agreed to meet with Hitch, but the only time she had free was lunch on Thursday, her secretary informed him. If that worked, Dr. Wu would meet him at *The Imperial Garden* in Georgetown at one o'clock. He agreed. To even get that far, Hitch had to explain that his grandson was a Preemie and that he hoped Dr. Wu's expertise would shed some light on the situation. Even that didn't seem to work. Then Hitch mentioned that Edna had worked as a research assistant in the Biotech department at American University some years earlier. Bingo!

Hitch was early, as usual, but more so on that particular occasion considering the importance of the meeting, or so he hoped, and possibly because he was looking forward to matching the real with the photo. Upon arriving, he discovered a reservation had already been made in Dr. Wu's name, clearly a regular in the very upscale Chinese restaurant. The hostess, an older Chinese woman, led him to a table in the back, away from most of the lunch crowd. Dr. Wu had not arrived yet, but it was only 12:50. Just when he began checking his scud for messages, an approaching figure caught his eye. Her looks jolted him out of any other thoughts he might have had at that moment. She was stunning. Thin, but well built, taller than he had imagined. Absolutely beautiful. Combining that with her obvious intelligence caused Hitch to remain spellbound as he heard her voice, soft but self-assured.

"Mr. Hitchcock?" She offered both hands, feminine but firm, her nails polished high gloss magenta, her lips a somewhat lighter shade.

"Everyone calls me Hitch or Oliver." He stood to greet her.

"All right, Oliver. I am Elana, so please, let us both sit, eat, and talk."

"It was very nice of you to meet, especially considering you don't know me." Hitch loved looking at her smile. It seemed so pure and cunning at the same time.

"But I do know you, or at least of you, and I have always wanted to meet a real CIA spy. I'm afraid many of your exploits are public knowledge, Mr. Hitchcock, I mean, Oliver."

"Retired CIA."

"Really? You look too young to be retired."

Was she flirting? Hitch sat up tall and smiled. "And you look too young to be a full professor and expert on the interplay between DNA and vaccinated cells in the human body."

"Touché," she countered.

Just as they seemed to be trading flirts, the server, a young girl who looked very much like the hostess's daughter, approached with two menus.

"I don't think we'll need those, SuLynn. Just a double order of the regular. Oh and bring us each a Naale."

"A Naale?" Hitch asked as SuLynn left them alone.

Elana laughed. "A very strong Chinese beer from my home, Shanghai, and by the way this is my treat."

By the time they finished lunch, six emptied Naale bottles sat on the table. Earlier formalities gone, there were periods of comfortable silence, as Hitch evaluated Elana, as Elana evaluated Hitch, or so he thought.

"As I said earlier, I am awfully sorry for your situation. I mean, about Christopher, but I'm not sure how I can be of much help other than to let you know what to expect."

"Well, considering your expertise, what can you tell me about the ERAM-V vaccine, not just its makeup but like how it came about, into existence that is, and why there were people way back who believed…"

In midsentence, Hitch watched Elana stiffen as her eyes turned to the entrance of the restaurant. He followed her gaze and saw Oedipus and another thug even larger than him. Both wore VAMA leather jackets. Oedipus pointed to the back where they were, and the two of them followed the hostess to a table between them and the front door. Elana looked back at Hitch.

"I'm sorry, Oliver. What were you saying?"

"The virus. How it…"

Elana began to quiver and the pitch in her voice increased, as if she wanted to be heard from a distance. "I'm sorry Mr. Hitchcock. I'm afraid I can't help you."

"But…"

"No. I can't." She quickly stood, stared at Oedipus and his friend, started for the front door, then quickly did a hundred and eighty and rushed out through the *Exit Only* behind them. Oedipus's companion jumped up from his table and started to follow her out. As he passed Hitch's table, Hitch stuck out his foot and the bruiser tripped and fell. He rose quickly and started for Hitchcock when Oedipus, through a hand gesture, signaled him to follow Elana, at least that's what Hitch guessed. In the meantime, their server left him the check. He picked it up and walked over to Oedipus, who still sat, watching, and dropped the check on his table.

"Give this to Janine. It's the least she can do." He started to leave but turned back after only a few steps. "The next time you want to run someone off the road, you might try autopilot. And given what I observed between your legs forget about ever putting the move on your boss."

Oedipus started to rise. Hitchcock broke an empty glass on the table, pushed Oedipus back down, and put the broken glass to his throat. Their eyes met, anger in Oedipus's, amusement in Hitch's, which he hoped showed. After a few seconds, he dropped the broken glass in Oedipus's lap and walked out as nonchalantly as someone fully satisfied with a great meal.

Chapter Sixteen

For several days Hitch paced through the house in a funk. He was infatuated with Elana Wu, pissed she couldn't, or wouldn't help him. The only joy he got out of their meeting, besides her surprising beauty, was shoving a broken glass against the throat of Janine's thug. He looked at his watch. Almost noon. Kathy and Christopher were coming for lunch and would be there any moment. He rushed to the deck and turned on the grill.

They ate burgers and chips in the fresh air and watched the hikers parallel the Potomac with wires dangling from their ears. Christopher talked about school and his history project. He was studying how early Christian theology evolved into a religious Ecclesian monopoly, which in turn evolved into a political and social imperative for the betterment of humankind. Hitch listened with interest. His grandson was only eleven and already being indoctrinated. As a nonbeliever, Hitchcock made his views known, even to Christopher, and that aggravated his only daughter, who attended the Liberal Church of Spirituality at least twice a month. At one point, she tried to get her parents to attend, but neither of them would budge, Edna in particular. She had studied Christianity, especially Catholicism, in college and wasn't sure which was worse, the Catholic Church or the Church of the

Ecclesia.

Later, while Christopher played on his grandfather's computation shell, Kathy and Hitch cleared off the dishes. Kathy spread out on the kitchen table at least a dozen photos she had taken from her purse. Hitch stared at them in disbelief, as if they were the last thing in the world he expected to see.

"It was Dr. Delahunt's idea," she explained. "He said if I take pictures every day we will be able to monitor the progress."

"I know, sweetheart, but isn't that a bit over the…"

Just then Christopher showed up announcing he was ready to go home. Kathy pulled her father close and whispered. "Does it look to you like it's getting worse?"

"No, absolutely not. Now go home. Get some sleep and don't take a picture but once a week. I'm sure that will be fine."

Hitch kissed Kathy and hugged Christopher before guiding them through the front door and onto the porch. As he did, a VAMA hearse drove past the house. After watching Kathy drive away, he rushed inside, then to the living room window where he caught another VAMA hearse pass by. He stepped into the kitchen, looked at the dozen pictures of Christopher's V-Mark, and grimaced. It clearly grew darker and rougher by the day. He pulled out a magnifying glass from a drawer and could even see the blistering and general roughness reflected off the flash of the camera. Filled with anger, he picked them all up and threw them in the trash compressor. *Hummmmmm.*

He grabbed hold of his scud, tapped in a number, and paced. A hologram swelled up from his scud showing Rajiv Nadu making love with a different woman. Suddenly the hologram disappeared once again.

"Bad timing again, old man. The answer's the same. Talk to you soon."

Before Hitch could respond, he heard the other end disconnect. "Son of a bitch!" He stomped into his bedroom, removed his shirt, and headed for the mirror, where he preened and flexed his muscles in anger. He picked up a pair of dumbbells and began curling until it hurt. He returned to the mirror, preened once again, then stared at his V-Mark, feeling its smoothness with his fingertips, observing its uniform Indian-redness. Distressed, his eyes shifted back to his reflection, which returned a thousand-mile stare, as if haunted by what it saw. Only his reflection could know his deepest insecurities. He tried shaking it off and quickly opened a cabinet. Every shelf was covered with bottles of vitamins and supplements. He took one labeled "Primo—*Get Raw Hard Rock Muscles in Minutes.*" He opened the bottle and swallowed a handful. That made him think about Elana Wu.

After flopping into an easy chair in the study, he pulled out his scud, did a quick search, and tapped on the results. Seconds later he could hear *ringing* at the other end. An answering machine clicked on. "You have reached Barnaby Bloom. Please leave a message."

Hitch decided not to. What he had to say was far too complicated. Instead, he clicked off and jumped from the chair. From the corner of his eye he could see through the window a vehicle lingering on the street. He poked his head out and the black VAMA hearse moved on.

He stepped out from the study onto his deck where the falls could be heard. The afternoon sun had just crept behind a thick cloud, and a cool breeze seemed to lift his spirits just a little. He wasn't planning on running—too much to do—but the crashing cry of Potomac whitewater and the sweet smell in the air made for an invitation he couldn't refuse. After changing into shorts and running shoes, he drove off with *Rigoletto* plugged into his ears. It took him only a few minutes by car to reach the beginning of his favorite trail, and off he went; first to the left, then the right along the river's edge, and then up a steep hill overlooking the Potomac river. It reminded him of the ocean waves assaulting the beachheads in Cape Town and Rio de Janeiro, and the sun baked boulders along the river's edge in so many cities in Neuropa. He loved running along water, but not today it seemed. Today *Rigoletto* scratched across his temples like new chalk across a whiteboard. Today his memories pulled him back only as far as his last visit with Dr. Delahunt, with Edna.

In the far reaches of his peripheral vision he saw the doctor chasing alongside him pointing to the report, huffing to keep up, yelling above the roar of the river, "carrier of the ERAM-V virus, carrier of the ERAM-V virus, carrier…" Delahunt's words, repeated over and over again, drowned out *Rigoletto*, crushed his innermost ego, assaulted the high opinion he had of himself. He was the reason OJ died; he was the reason Christopher… Fury ignited the muscles in his thighs, in his calves, his feet pumping and pumping, faster, faster in hopes that the body could escape the suffering soul. He had to outrun the guilt that would only paralyze him, that would only reduce to a silent prayer his ability to keep his promise to Edna.

The trail itself passed under foot as if it were invisible, while his favorite opera underscored his profound shame and provided the beat for each painful step he took. The pounding in his chest would not chip away at his disquietude. He was no less responsible for the death of OJ than Rigoletto was responsible for the death of his daughter, Gilda.

The sweat bled through most of his t-shirt by the time he reached the front door. He was hungry but couldn't think of food, too much on his mind. He had grown even thinner since Edna's death and the promise he made to her, a promise he doubted he would be able to keep. Before OJ and Christopher, he stood up straight, all six and a half feet of him. Lately, he found himself stooping over, as if his thinness refused to support the weightiness carried within his every thought.

Since he seldom carried his scud during a run, before the front door had a chance to close, habit drove Oliver into his study to see if anyone left a message. The red light on his computation shell was blinking, almost in synchrony with the yellow light on his phone tablet. He quickly called out. "Messages please."

"Mr. Hitchcock, this is Barnaby Bloom. I see you called. I was wondering how long it would be before I heard from you. Please give me a call at your convenience."

Chapter Seventeen

Hitch tidied up the house, pulled out of his driveway for Charlottesville shortly after ten o'clock, and charged toward the speedway where the minimum speed limit was 100 kilometers per hour and the maximum depended on how many horses rode under one's electroatomic isothermal pedal, and how heavy a foot stomped on it. He was in a hurry and he knew his sorry state would relish the freedom to fly, quite literally.

Throughout most of the trip, as the speedometer hovered at 275 kilometers per hour and his wheels flew almost six inches above the road at times, he played out in his head where all this was leading and whether it made any sense. Assume the best, assume the worst, and assume all the possible ways of reaching either end result—standard operating procedures in the field. The worst seemed obvious. He wasn't going to save his grandson. But could his best save him? That question ate into Hitch's bones and percolated through the pores of his skin as he raced past the other vehicles seemingly parked in the slow lane. He kept lining up the possibilities, like foot soldiers on a chessboard trying to protect their own king. They were all pawns fighting bishops—he, Julian, even Rousseau and her idiot minion, all of them.

Let's say this Professor Emeritus really does wish

to become involved, and suppose we magically discover the Click is a big hoax on unsuspecting seniors, and terrible fallout for innocent children. How is that going to help Christopher in time?

Just for a second, Oliver Hitchcock thought about initiating reverse thrust and turning back toward home. Was he doing all this merely to anesthetize his own anxieties while his daughter's only child died in front of his eyes? A repetitive thought; an unwelcomed visitor constantly reminding him of reality and his own ineptitude. Wouldn't he be better off spending more time with Christopher while he has the chance, or must he get beyond a single child and the unthinkable idea of surviving a grandson, two grandsons? He knew there would be hundreds of other kids following in Christopher's shoes, and what about all those youthful seventy-five-year-olds who have so much to live for, like Edna before she died? Whatever the reason, selfish or selfless, he had no choice; the rubber had to rise above the road. He had to zoom on.

His navigator easily found Barnaby Bloom's house, a sprawling red brick ranch, sitting a good forty yards in from the country road that carried him up and down the Virginia countryside without his wheels ever touching the ground. It was the only house within two acres of anyone else. The narrow road caused him to pull behind a black Trident Racer on a gray asphalt driveway blistered by age and the Virginia sun. As he did, Oliver noticed a table under a bright red umbrella behind the garage and thought he saw a young woman standing next to it, probably the professor's daughter.

A voice, low but clear, greeted him as he opened his car door. "Hello there." The man called out, ambling onto the driveway from the long, narrow front porch that stretched across the entire front of the house. The owner of that voice was short and stocky with long white hair, somewhat bedraggled, clinging to his shoulders, and an equally white mustache painted thickly across his face.

Barnaby Bloom held out his right hand from the sleeve of a jacket at least a size too large. "Dr. Livingston, I presume?"

As Oliver stepped out of the car, he looked up somewhat puzzled.

"Obviously you are not Dr. Livingston. But you recognize the name? No?" Barnaby was smiling.

"No, I'm afraid not. I'm Oliver Hitchcock."

"Quite so, quite so."

"And you are Professor Bloom, I gather?"

"Barnaby, just plain Barnaby."

****

Janine Rousseau sat in an unmarked beige SUV with tinted windows a half mile down the road from the Bloom house. She was aggravated; pissed was the word that rang through her mind, as she played snoop for General Roseshit. With the aid of binoculars, she watched through a crack in the front passenger window as Hitchcock shook hands with the white-haired old man while she took note of the black Trident in the drive way. Just as she jotted down its license plate her scud *rang*. She looked at it and groaned.

"Yes, General?"

"Are you on him?

"Yes, but I'm no fucking Patrol Boy, damn it!" She continued to watch Barnaby Bloom as he walked his guest into the house.

"You are what I say you are, and right now you are my eyes and ears. The Cūtocratic council is concerned. They've decided they want the son-of-a-bitch out of their hair."

"I thought they needed him to find the Shmuckie Decretum, or whatever the hell it's called?"

"That's the smotec's concern, and McGivney's. The Council doesn't believe the damn thing exists. So do what I say. And while you're at it, they want that Wu woman to disappear also."

Rousseau couldn't keep up with the schizophrenic changes in strategies. "But…"

"No buts, Rousseau. Just remember I'm the one who pulled you from the gutter when the CIA abandoned you. I'm the one who allows you to run a money laundering business for that kid of yours. Do exactly as I say or you're fucked."

****

Barnaby Bloom led his visitor onto the back patio. The woman standing there, with her back turned, was feeding a doe that froze then scampered away when the patio door slid open.

"I believe you've already met my colleague," the professor said to Oliver Hitchcock.

Elana Wu hesitated for a second, to add drama to the moment she had to admit to herself, then turned around, smiled, and extended her hand. Hitch grinned, accepting it in both of his. For the next two hours, the three of them talked through lunch and a large platter of chocolate chip cookies.

"So that's the story. I was ready to give up. Then this black Jew, Nagasi, Ethiopian from what I understand, popped into the picture."

"Quite so," Barnaby said, then turned to Elana, who shrugged. She wasn't sure how all this was going to play out but was concerned they all might be treading in deep water.

"I think Elana and I will be of help. We will consider joining your team to save Christopher, if that's possible. But let us give thought to how that will happen."

Barnaby then rose, and Elana followed suit thinking she could no longer feel the bottom of the pool. Hitch took their hint, following close behind the two of them as they crossed through the house and onto the porch out front. Before reaching Hitchcock's car, Barnaby said his goodbyes to his visitor and let Elana walk him the rest of the way.

"Oliver, you will forgive me?"

"Pretty sure that was the first time a beautiful woman offered to pick up the tab then stiffed me."

"Oh. Do I owe you…"

"Definitely, but not the tab. That's been taken care of."

"Then you knew why I had to…"

"I'm not that retired and certainly not feeble-minded."

She chuckled. He opened the car door.

"Do you like pizza?" Hitch asked as he maneuvered behind the wheel.

She flashed a curious but playful look, she hoped, and nodded. He smiled back and drove off under ominous clouds gathering overhead. As Elana watched him turn the corner, Barnaby joined her on the driveway.

"He doesn't realize you've just accepted him into

the Cause," she said, holding on to his arm with both of her hands as they walked back to the house. "He thinks you have agreed to become a member of his team of one."

"Quite so. Well, whether the drink flows into the pitcher or the pitcher falls into the drink, the pitcher will fill up. Besides, we need new blood, especially someone with a cause close to home, and a deadline."

"What if he compromises my work? I surely won't be much help in the dungeons of China."

"From what I've learned, Oliver Hitchcock lives to survive. It's an obsession. And now he's obsessed with saving his grandson."

"Sounds like a dangerous man."

"Our people, the people I trust with my life, and yours, welcome him. That said, we need him for one very important reason."

"Which is?"

"His connections. India and the old Jew, Nagasi, may be our last hope."

Elana wasn't entirely sure where Barnaby's scheme would lead but she trusted him with her life. He stood by her when everyone else said she was too young to make tenure, when everyone else said her Chinese roots, and belief in God, would sabotage their goal. He was there when her parents died and she had no one else to turn to. Besides, she wanted what they wanted, and for the same reason, for the sake of humanity. The church hadn't totally brainwashed her.

Chapter Eighteen

Oliver Hitchcock left Charlottesville on a high. When he first saw Elana Wu standing under the red umbrella everything fell into place. He was invited there to talk about the Click. Why hadn't he figured that out earlier? Everything he learned about Barnaby Bloom from Julian begged him to reach that conclusion as soon as he received the invitation. Elana had been a student of Bloom's, and an associate before the professor was forced to retire. But even had he made those connections, in his wildest imagination he could not have predicted he would be flying home with such allies on his team. What started out as a fight by one, a single grandfather, against the gods, had increased to three. The professor and his student were critical, most critical indeed, the three Musketeers and Julian, their d'Artagnan.

He hadn't driven more than twenty minutes when the sky began dumping waves of precipitation against his windshield. Nevertheless, he felt good, relaxed, as he hummed over the news on the radio. Suddenly what he heard got his attention.

"...the Virginia senator is planning to ram the bill through with the full backing of the Cūtocracy. It requires all tax returns to include religious affiliation and actual church membership."

Hitch glanced in his rearview mirror and spotted a

VAMA hearse coming up fast.

"Senator Boudreau and like-minded followers believe the bill will withstand a constitutional challenge considering that eight of the nine justices on the court owe their allegiance to the Cūtocracy."

He quickly jumped onto the next exit ramp and accelerated, hoping to put more space between himself and his tail.

"Everyone knows that the pagans are multiplying, particularly American Muslims and atheists, a scary thought for the Cūtocrats who rule the spiritual world. Obviously, they want to know who their enemies are and where they live..."

Once again VAMA jumped into his rearview mirror, this time approaching much faster, soon filling up the entire mirror. Hitch slammed down the thrust controls on his brakes and watched the black hearse zip past him as he veered over.

"...especially their enemies in the United States, the ones who could do the most harm."

He shut off the radio and was about to pull back onto the road when he saw through his windshield two tail lights race toward him. The VAMA hearse *screeched* to a stop and slid sideways. Seeing he was blocked in front, he dropped into reverse thrust, but then a quick glance in the mirror let him know he was going nowhere. A beige SUV came barreling up to his rear bumper. *Bam*! Clearly, there was no way out.

As hard as the rain pounded against the windshield, his wipers were of little help. He could hardly make out someone with a weapon drawn coming toward him. It was Oedipus. At the same time, through his rearview mirror, he could barely see another VAMA thug jump out from a second hearse behind the SUV.

Then came the amplified voice from within the SUV. "Looks like you've got nowhere to go, Oliver," Rousseau chided. "Get out with your hands in the air."

With his right hand, Hitch grabbed his laser gun and a flare from the console next to him. With his left hand, he opened the driver-side door, partially. "Okay. I'm coming out. Please don't shoot. I'm too old for this shit."

Using his left leg, he pushed the door open, ignited the flare, and tossed it onto the ground. It exploded into a *flash*, temporarily blinding both Oedipus and the other thug. They shot wildly into their blind spots, *zing, zing*. Red laser tracers ripped through the air. In the meantime, Hitch rolled over the console, pushed open the passenger door, and *fired* at the thug, who went down.

He rolled back over the console as Oedipus raced around the other side and fell out of the driver's door, spotting Rousseau hovering over the downed man. Seeing Hitch, she reached for the gun on the ground, but before she could get to it, he pounced on her. Oedipus fired, *zing*. Hitch took it in the upper left arm but held on to his own weapon in his right hand. From behind, he wrapped his wounded arm around Rousseau's chest with his hand inside her jacket, pressing against her bare breast.

He put his gun to her head. Blood from his arm trickled into her cleavage. Oedipus approached and demanded Hitchcock let her go.

"There are two things that can happen here, dipshit," Hitch said as the barrel of his gun pressed against Rousseau's temple, as his left hand pressed tighter against her breast. "Either you pick up your buddy and take off, and don't look back, or I put a large hole in the head of this very sexy lady."

"You don't hav da ball," Oedipus snarled back.

"I say he does. Now do what he says," Rousseau snapped.

Hitchcock laughed. "See. Smart lady."

Oedipus hesitated, then dragged his wounded, semiconscious partner to his hearse. Hitch held Rousseau tight until Oedipus disappeared. Only then did he let her go. She spun around to face him and was greeted with a famous Oliver Hitchcock grin.

"The last time I saw that smile, we were in bed together. Better days."

She stepped closer, pushed his gun aside, kissed him with passion, then stepped back and strolled to her SUV. Once there, she turned back around and with one finger stroked the bare part of her breast, wet with rain and Hitch's blood. She then circled her mouth with the same finger, licked her lips with her tongue, and gestured for him to come close. He approached as excitement built within his loins. She kissed him passionately once again, then pushed him away.

"Be careful." With that, she climbed into her SUV and drove away as Hitch laughed.

Chapter Nineteen

It was well past the dinner hour when Elana Wu finally left Charlottesville for home in the outskirts of Georgetown. She gave Barnaby a hug good-bye and zipped away in her black Trident Racer. After swerving around the corner, she discovered a VAMA hearse tailing her. All the way through Virginia it followed close behind as she switched from one lane to another. At one point she swerved to the right and climbed up an exit ramp, successfully losing her tail, she thought. After travelling along several side streets paralleling the speedway she jumped back on and VAMA was waiting. "How in the…"

Finally, somewhere just before her speedster reached the Potomac River, it disappeared. She took a deep breath and crossed the bridge into the District wondering what she was getting into. It seemed forever ago that she received her student visa, a challenging but straightforward feat with no complications. Her work visa after graduating number one in her class with a PhD was another matter, more like navigating the top edge of the of Great Wall from end to end on one foot. The Chinese government paid for her entire education and wanted their investment back—wanted her back— the deal she agreed upon and was comfortable with before her parents were killed, before she and Barnaby became so close. She kept requesting extensions on the grounds that what she was learning in her position at the university was invaluable. They would do anything to get her back, she thought, while periodically glancing in her rearview mirror and not seeing any signs of a tail. How long would she be able to stay, especially if she wound up doing battle with the Cūtocracy and VAMA?

Less than fifteen minutes later, she dropped to the ground, rolled into her designated slot, 27A, and stepped out of the speedster. A VAMA hearse, maybe the same one, came to a *screeching* halt less than three feet away. Startled, she recoiled as Oedipus and a new partner jumped out and grabbed her. With one very large hand that smelled like a mixture of bacon lard and shrimp peels cupped around her mouth, she could do nothing but struggle in the arms of both men, who dragged her into the hearse and sped away.

By the time she found herself sitting on a backless stool in a small room filled with all types of contraptions, her legs ached and her head sagged from exhaustion. A hot light shined down, like that in a dental office, practically blinding her to the strange face just inches away. The words kept echoing around her. *What were you doing there, there, there? What did you talk about, about, about, about? How do you know Oliver Hitchcock, Cock, Cock, Cock? Why were the three of you meeting, eeting, eeting?* She could hear herself respond. *We're all friends, friends, ends, ends. That's all, all, all, all.*

Rousseau turned off the hot light and stepped back. "You're lying!"

Oedipus jumped in between them and gave Elana a backhand across the face with such force she fell to the floor, causing her glasses to fly.

"Get up, bitch," Rousseau demanded as she picked up Elana Wu's glasses and threw them at her.

Elana did as she was told, tasting the blood oozing from the edge of her mouth. When the room finally stopped spinning, she saw Oedipus hand Rousseau a transparent plastic bag filled with white powder. Rousseau dangled it in front of her, back and forth, back and forth, much like a hypnotist looking for answers. "Interesting. How did this high grade China White find its way under the carpet in your trunk?"

"It's not mine and you know it."

"Ah, but it is, and this little bag may just be your one-way ticket back to Shanghai."

"No one who knows me would believe that."

Rousseau laughed. "I'm sure you will be long gone before anyone who knows you is told. So tell me the truth! And wipe that hellish blood from your mouth."

Oedipus threw Elana a box of tissues.

"I told you the truth," Elana insisted as she pressed a tissue to her lips.

"Hitchcock, Bloom, friends? You told me nothing. The three of you were conspiring to…"

"Yes. We were conspiring to have a lovely day and evening. They played chess most of the day and I read."

Rousseau jumped back into Elana's face. "Chess, my ass. Now, if you want to stay out of a Chink dungeon, tell me about your work and how Hitchcock is involved."

Elana tried her best to explain what it meant to be professor of immunology and her focus on recombinant DNA techniques, cell fusion, and bioprocessing techniques in hopes of boring Rousseau to death. She clearly avoided vaccination science and anything else that could be tied to the Click. She lost count of the number of times she had to repeat herself and continuously insisted her work had nothing to do with the ERAM-V vaccine.

Finally Rousseau sat back, as if she were terminating the inquisition. The clock read 2:55 in the morning. Elana, weary and exhausted, yet defiant, fidgeted on the stool and glared at her. She may wind up back in Beijing but she was going to go with dignity.

After that brief respite, Rousseau jumped from her chair. "One last time. What do you know about the ERAM-V vaccine?"

"Again, about as much as I know about chess. Nothing."

Clearly frustrated, Rousseau grabbed Elana by the collar, yanked her across the room, slammed her against the wall, and looked over to Oedipus. "Drag the bitch downstairs."

Oedipus gripped Elana by the shoulder and led her to another room. He pushed a keypad on the wall, and a sliding door opened up to a downwardly spiraling staircase. He pushed her down the staircase to a series of empty dungeon cells and locked her in one of them.

Clink! The small steel door, more like a child's playhouse door or large doggie door, seemed to seal Elana's fate. The only light snuck through the door's small window, exposing a mattress sitting atop a wooden frame. She could barely see the cruddy toilet and sink in one corner. As she approached the mattress and saw how terribly soiled it was, she quickly turned to the toilet and vomited.

Chapter Twenty

All the time Oliver Hitchcock showered and shaved, Rousseau remained the focus of his attention—her bare breasts, thick lips, and his groin. He wiped the steam from the mirror and stared at his body, recalling her warning the last time they slept together. He wasn't getting any younger, and he would return to her bed, or so she predicted. At the time, he believed her regardless of his declaration otherwise. But no longer, considering his promise to Edna, and his hookup with Barnaby. Rousseau was now an enemy he had to stay clear of. Nevertheless, that didn't stop him from thinking about her in bed.

After dressing and strolling into the kitchen prepared to boil some eggs, he realized there was little counter space left for such menial tasks. Stacks of printouts, news stories, and the like were everywhere except on the stove top and in the oven. He had to clean up. Besides, he was concerned that VAMA, which seemed to have set up an office out front, might decide to expand into his living space once again.

It was that latter thought that prompted him to pull up the carpet across the fifth step on the stairway to the second level. He lifted the hardwood underneath exposing an elongated safe extending the width of the step. He pulled it out and pried open the board underneath, divulging a larger space spanning several steps, then placed there his more recent work product that might incriminate him.

Once he finished that task and tidied the rest of the kitchen and his study, he was about to boil his eggs and brew some coffee when he heard his scud *vibrating* on the desk in the study.

It was Barnaby. Elana Wu was missing. He was clearly upset and Hitch tried his best to calm him down.

"Yes, it's true. Sometimes, she does go off for days without calling but I'm worried nonetheless. I mean with all these VAMA cars that now…"

"Barnaby, please, give it a couple of days. If she's not in touch by then I'll see what I can do." While Hitch acted nonchalant, he was worried also, and for the same reason—those VAMA shits. He immediately thought of Julian. Surely, he would be able to find her if she was in their grasp.

"All right, I guess," Barnaby acquiesced. "But in the meantime, I think we need to talk. I have an appointment at American University tomorrow morning. Can I come by after that, say around eleven?"

"No. I mean yes, eleven will work," Hitch said. "But I have a better place to meet than my house," he continued while poking his nose out a window and watching a VAMA hearse drive by.

****

Among Oliver Hitchcock's talents was his uncanny ability to shoot fast and accurately. That didn't come naturally. He worked at it constantly, even after he retired from the Company. Just about every Thursday morning, he would spend at least an hour at the shooting range not terribly far from his house. However, in the last several months he only managed to make it there a couple of times and welcomed the chance to kill two birds with several zings of the trigger, so to speak.

It took ten minutes to calm Barnaby down, after which Hitch showed off his skill firing at human shaped targets with his laser rifle. *Zing-zing-zing*. And with each zing, Barnaby flinched.

"Enough!" Barnaby hollered out over the noise. "You can continue after I leave. For now, please tell me what you're going to do about Elana?"

He took off his earmuffs and so did Hitch.

"I will have someone extremely reliable on it if she doesn't call by tomorrow. I promise. Now, this Cause you said you wanted to talk about. What the hell is it?"

Barnaby approached Hitch and took his rifle from him. Held it close, as if he were inspecting it then set it down on the bench close by. Hitch stared at Barnaby, then at his rifle. "Jesus, Barnaby, are you afraid I'm going to shoot you?"

Barnaby laughed. "No, but I am afraid we haven't been entirely candid with you."

"Not what I want to hear, my friend. My new friend. There's too much at stake."

Barnaby shook his head. "We had to be careful. I apologize."

Hitch picked up his rifle and without earmuffs approached the target line. *Zing-zing-zing-zing*. "I don't have time for any bullshit, Barnaby. My grandson doesn't have time."

Barnaby sat down on the bench and motioned for Oliver to join him. "The Cause goes back three generations to my mother and father and his father, my grandfather, all enemies of the Cūtocracy. Today, we are over 100,000 strong worldwide."

"What? Who?" Oliver Hitchcock started to sit next to Barnaby but changed his mind. He thought better on his feet.

Barnaby stared at Hitch for a moment, as if he were not sure he wanted to confide in him, and that was seriously aggravating.

"Barnaby, this is no time for gamesmanship, not with my grandson's life at stake and Elana Wu who knows where.

Barnaby nodded. "The *who* are anonymous men and women, and the *what* is their conviction that the Click is the Cūtocracy's fraud on humanity."

Hitch stared at his new friend and was about to respond. *Zing-zing* exploded from a stranger who had just begun shooting two lanes over. This time he flinched. "Wait! You're saying you believe the Cūtocracy is responsible for the Click?" Hitch whispered even though the stranger had earmuffs on.

"Believe? I'm saying it's a fact. They hid it within the ERAM-V vaccine in order to control population growth ever since the Ecclesian Church insisted on outlawing abortions and birth control way back when. That was their quid pro quo."

Hitchcock turned his back on Barnaby and froze as he observed the stranger zero in on the enemy. *Zing-zing-zing*. The sign flashed 'Enemy Eliminated' in bright yellow. It's one thing to believe the worst, another to know it's true, he thought, and tried to shake it off. Finally, his attention turned back to Barnaby. "So, where does Elana fit into all of this?"

"Coming up with the antidote and a Clickless vaccine. She's our only hope. She's the only one with the knowledge and intellect to put it all together."

Hitch shook his head in disbelief. "Really? And what do you want from me?"

"Blood, unvaccinated blood. Elana will need lots of it."

"Unvaccinated blood?"

"For the antidote. We need lots of unvaccinated blood. We've been scouring the Earth with no real luck. For every person we have in the field searching, VAMA has dozens vaccinating the masses."

"So this is all about…"

"Mr. Nagasi, and India. Elana's bit of blue sky. And yours too, Oliver."

Hitch shook his head. "You really believe he's for real? Nagasi?"

"You're the expert. That's for you to determine."

Without much hesitation on his part, Hitch agreed to return to Mumbai, but first wanted to know everything about the Cause, not merely what amounted to an elevator speech.

"Well, that calls for sustenance," Barnaby suggested, and the oldest and newest living members of the Cause walked across the street to a café at the corner and dined on duck salad and discussion. After giving Oliver even more than he had asked for about the Cause, he reminded his new charge that Elana must be found.

Several hours later, Hitch stood on his back deck taking in the rising mist over the Potomac, punching in numbers on his scud. "Julian…"

Once satisfied that Julian was now in the loop and up to speed, Hitch disconnected but remained within the shroud of mist that now surrounded him. He had decided not to mention Elana Wu or that she was missing, at least not then. She's probably off on her own, he thought. No point complicating a situation already fraught with complications.

Chapter Twenty-One

Oliver Hitchcock was once again at Regis on his way to Mumbai. With Kathy and a cranky Christopher on either side, the three stepped off the people mover just ahead of Security. Christopher offered one hand to his grandfather but stared off to the side. Hitch stooped down to hug him, and with a turn of the head, he brought Christopher into eye contact, then smiled and kissed his grandson's tightened brow. Disappointed, he looked up at Kathy hoping to evoke some kind of sympathy. He received none.

They hugged without words, then he headed toward Security. As a second thought, he turned back and watched them disappear in the crowd, the only family he had left. Hitch turned back and seconds later reached an agent who stamped his papers and inspected his carryon luggage. After receiving a nod from the agent, he stepped up to one of many eye/hand scanners where all five fingers and both eyes were analyzed. His picture and name appeared on a monitor above the apparatus. A gate automatically opened.

The area around Gate C27 to Mumbai buzzed with excitement as passengers began boarding. Hitch stood under the TV watching Dillon Burber's press conference when his scud *rang*. After edging away from the TV and the crowd, he picked up the call. It was Kathy. He clicked her onto screen-view mode and immediately saw the fear in her eyes.

"On the way out he heard it, Dad. What am I supposed to tell him?" she whispered. "And his V-Mark, it's much bluer and blacker. Dad, my God. Ninety days! That's how much time Mother had."

"This is the final call for Flight 67 to Mumbai. All remaining passengers should board at this time."

"Kathy, maybe he didn't hear it. Call Delahunt if it doesn't get better in a day or two and let me know what he says. I have to go."

"But, Dad…"

Hitch clicked Kathy off in midsentence and hustled into the jetport. Within minutes he found his seat in First Class.

"We will be departing for Mumbai momentarily. Please make sure…"

Ring, ring. It was Hitch's scud again; this time he could see "Barnaby Bloom" across the screen. He put it on voice only mode. "Barnaby, what's…"

"Elana hasn't returned. I have to call the police."

Hitchcock cringed, then sighed. "No! Not yet. I will have someone look for her first. He's a safer bet. She'll be fine. I promise.

Barnaby was not happy but agreed to give Oliver one more day before he would involve the police, which also meant involving VAMA. Hitch was sure of that. He had to reach Julian before they took off and complete the picture he had not quite finished painting earlier. He did, and Julian assured him he would find Elana if VAMA had her, and even if they didn't he would find her.

Now he could relax, at least until he reached Mumbai. Rajiv had made all the arrangements. He would be meeting in late afternoon with Ambika Patel, the librarian he had met during his previous trip. That was his mental segue way back to the Cause and Elana Wu. Barnaby had been more forthcoming than he expected.

Shortly after graduating from George Washington University, American University hired Elana to work under Barnaby, who recruited her into his secret organization. Back then, she was an unwilling participant but had a gift for the science they needed like no one else he knew. Eventually, she came to trust her mentor even though he was a nonbeliever, a Jew no less, and she a practicing Ecclesian. That was in part because he had already stepped in to help her on a number of occasions, Barnaby confided in Hitchcock, but also because the mentor and student were truly fond of one another. As a result, he minced no words when the time seemed right. The Cause needed her; God needed her so He or She wouldn't be made a mockery of; and mostly the human race needed her.

As Barnaby explained it to Hitch at the café, he had become a chieftain in the war against the world practically at birth. They were all underground of course—Jews, American Muslims, and atheists. The secret mission of the Cause was to rid humanity of the Click and find an antidote for that dreadful vaccine, that geriatric euthanasia that plagued the world, a mission Barnaby's grandfather and father began. Both mysteriously disappeared, never to be heard from again. Yes, Barnaby Bloom and the others already knew what Oliver Hitchcock had hoped for with no more evidence than linkless references to imagined dissidents, wishful thinking, and several bottles of scotch.

But how do a handful of activists, relatively speaking, fight a sophisticated bureaucracy controlled by the major countries of the world under the watchful eye of an all-powerful Cūtocracy and VAMA, its ubiquitous enforcer? For the longest time Barnaby wasn't sure, and wasn't confident their knowledge and their fight would amount to anything. Then, Oliver Hitchcock and his connections with India and this man Nagasi fell into Barnaby Bloom's lap as if it were meant to be, as if the dissidents could only be quieted for so long.

"What we need with absolute certainty," Barnaby explained to Oliver at the café, "are large numbers of adults who have never been vaccinated. Only then will Elana and the Cause be able to learn how to make the antidote and begin making it in order to un-Click large populations. It has to do with infusing clean blood with Click-containing blood in a very sophisticated way and then subjecting the combination to a complex process of DNA swapping."

For years the Cause scoured the planet for such people, but with no success. According to the intelligence developed over the years by the Cause, there were hints that such a group, and only one, existed somewhere in the unknown and impenetrable wastelands of India. That's where Oliver and his newly found discovery, Mr. Nagasi, came in—hopefully.

"It's just a matter of finding a large group of unvaccinated souls and the ballgame is over?" Hitch remembered asking.

Barnaby wished it was that easy, but unfortunately it wasn't. He explained that they had to not only discover large groups of unvaccinated people but first they needed to prove to the world that the vaccine contained the Click; that it wasn't part of God's design.

But even if the Cause could prove to the world that the Click was man-made, goodness would not necessarily be drawn to their side. Government after government and their handpicked population experts paid homage to the Click. Without its presence, divine or not, they argued humanity would swell its way through all its critical resources, eventually into war, and ultimately extinction in the not so distant future. The Click was God's way of protecting a most valuable creation, the Earth and its inhabitants, and if not God's way then Mother Nature's. Either way, the Click still served to keep in check humanity's inability to temper its need to procreate to reasonable levels. That's what the Cause was up against. Barnaby was not going to paint a prettier picture than that for its newest member.

But first things first, Hitch recalled him saying. Hopefully, if they were able to prove the present vaccine contained the Click and could produce an antidote in large quantities, they would then worry about doing battle with goodness and the issue of future overpopulation, especially if the antidote worked on people in the throes of the Click, and that included Christopher.

By the time Hitch finished that happy thought, he was jolted back to the present by turbulence and a shaking scotch and water on his tray. *Ding*, the "fasten seatbelt" light went on. He thought about Kathy and how abrupt he had been during their last conversation. He would call her as soon as he met with the librarian, Ambika Patel.

It was early evening when a taxi stopped at the

dead end of a cul-de-sac cramped with parked cars. Hitch asked the driver to wait, then got out and took a deep breath. He heard Indian music before reaching the sidewalk. As he weaved around several vehicles double parked, his scud *rang*. Barnaby's face appeared on the screen. He clicked on and was immediately bombarded with concern.

"Oliver, they seized all her work including her research on ERAM-V. Now they know everything, even that we're looking for an unvaccinated population."

Hitch tried to sift through his own thoughts about that revelation while the Indian music continued to blast through the house he was approaching as if its sole purpose was to annoy him. "Well fuck 'em. We'll let the whole world know what it is she, you all, already know. I must run now but I will shoot you over some contacts at the *Washington Herald*, one in particular. Her name is Amy Winkler. Send her everything that VAMA seized."

"But…"

"Gotta go, Barnaby. Do as I say, and I'll get back to you later." Hitch clicked off and *knocked* hard on the door to compete with the voices and music on the other side.

Ambika Patel opened the door and standing behind her was Rajiv, which didn't surprise Hitch. He followed the two of them into the house ringing with laughter and song, through bellowing pungent clouds of smoke from the sweet aroma of hashish. Several people stood around a piano in one corner singing in their native tongue, Marathi, a language he once could understand if spoken slowly. All the people celebrating were Indian except for two black men.

Mrs. Patel led Hitch into a combination guest bedroom and study at the far end of the house, and the two of them sat down between guest wraps thrown across the bed. A few minutes later Rajiv brought in two glasses of red wine and quickly left.

"Welcome to my home, Mr. Hitchcock," Ambika Patel said with a thick but enchanting accent he recalled from their last meeting as she raised her glass to his. "It is true that my dear husband, Kailash, left us less than three weeks ago, and it is equally true that this is how we mourn his passing. He was a school teacher living an honest, happy, and productive life and died a timely and peaceful death. What more could one ask for? We are happy for him and this is how we show it."

What more could one ask for? Quite possibly ten or fifteen more years of happiness and productivity, Oliver Hitchcock thought. He then explained what brought him to her home, originally planning to talk for at most twenty minutes. It took far longer than that at his host's insistence. He described Christopher, his daughter Kathy, and both Barnaby and the Cause. Most important, he explained what they knew about the Click and how desperate they were to find large numbers of men and women who had never been vaccinated. All the time, Mrs. Patel listened intently without giving away her own thoughts. That made Hitch uneasy. She hadn't flinched at the idea that the Click was manmade, and yet she hadn't argued with him. It was as if…

"I don't know if I can help you, Mr. Hitchcock. I have people I must talk to. In the meantime, please come into the living room and have some refreshments. I am sure Rajiv will join you."

Hitch followed her into the living room and his old friend was there standing by platters of Indian delicacies he hadn't enjoyed since leaving his post there a decade ago. *Rajima-Chawal*, a curried red kidney dish beyond description. *Pork Vindaloo, Rogan Josh,* and *Chungdi Jhola,* a spicy gravy-based prawn curry, his favorite. Twenty minutes or so later the two black men he had seen earlier, owners of the East Bombay Fishing Company, were introduced to him. They were relatives of Mrs. Patel by marriage, she explained. After the introductions, Mrs. Patel led him back into the guest bedroom and left him alone. He waited patiently but was anxious to learn whether this trip would bear fruit. Who were those men really, and what did they have to do with his quest? Before he had a chance to ponder those questions, they appeared and began asking their own questions. They listened to the entire tale that Mrs. Patel heard an hour earlier. The older of the two men asked if he could see a picture of Christopher, and Oliver quickly pulled one from his wallet. After smiling at the photo, he asked if Oliver had a picture of Christopher's V-Mark. Oliver found several on his scud. Both men studied them then the older one stepped into the hall and looked over at his host, nodding. The relatives by marriage then excused themselves and were gone before Oliver could even digest their presence. Once they left, Mrs. Patel led Oliver to the door and handed him a sealed envelope. Rajiv was nowhere in sight.

"Take this, Mr. Hitchcock, and go with God."

It wasn't until he climbed into the awaiting taxi that he opened the envelope and read the message.

Seek out Meta DeCarlo in Greve, Italy. Tell her the fishermen of Bombay sent you.

After he read the note and before they pulled away, he looked back at the Patel house. In the opened living room window, he saw Nagasi standing, smiling, giving him the two-finger peace gesture. He quickly opened his window, extended his arm out and returned the gesture. There was hope after all, he thought as they drove away. He would meet this Meta DeCarlo and Julian would retrieve Elana. Thank God for Julian!

Chapter Twenty-Two

Janine Rousseau stretched her calves and her spine in an attempt to relax as she stood next to General Rosewall in Rome. They waited for Minister McGivney, who would be travelling the tunnel from Ecclesia to the Cūtocratic headquarters, or so she was told by the general. Rousseau was aware of the tunnel but had never been in it or the room she was now standing in. She was nervous. McGivney's reputation was not one of piety or good cheer. He would just as soon slit your wrist as shake your hand if he thought you showed any sign of resistance to his agenda.

The Minister was tardy but finally arrived and now stood comfortably in the quarters devoted solely to the needs of the Ecclesia. He wore a black robe trimmed in hot pink and a thick hot pink belt-scarf wrapped twice around his waist. He towered over the general, and his face seemed to exude an ogre type charm—a deadly charm, Rousseau thought. At the same time, the pockmarks under both eyes and rounding out his cheeks on opposite sides of a larger than usual puffed-up nose looked like a throwback to an earlier plague.

General Rosewall stepped forward to greet him and then introduced Rousseau.

"Ah! Ms. Rousseau. You are a beautiful woman, not the bulldog Rosewall speaks so highly of."

Rosewall cringed slightly and Rousseau laughed.

"Cannot a bulldog be beautiful also, Your Eminence," she suggested as the Minister took her hand and kissed it.

"You are quite right, my dear, but keep in mind we need your bite to be more brutal than your bark. There is important work to do, as I informed your General earlier in the day." With that tit for tat behind them, Minister McGivney, seemingly satisfied, turned back to General Rosewall and gave him a stern look. Without saying it, he conveyed his displeasure with Rosewall's choice. Not that she was a woman, although there was that, thought Rousseau who seemed to read his mind, but mostly because she was sure he saw vulnerability in her eyes. It was a weakness she knew showed when nerves got the better of her, a weakness that would bubble to the surface at the most inappropriate times. Meanwhile, a figure stepped into the room quietly and stood in the shadows. Only Rousseau seemed to notice him or her enter.

"We're doing what we can, Your Eminence," Rosewall countered, clearly trying to ignore the Minister's flirtatious ways with Rousseau and his stern look.

"Not enough! I tell you this Dr. Wu is a problem, more so than that pesky CIA agent or ex-agent, or whatever the hell he is."

"We can take care of her," Rosewall insisted, then turned to Rousseau who puffed out her chest.

"For sure. After all, she's vacationing in one of my luxury suites."

"And if the Supreme Minister's not worried about the Smotecal Decretum, we should eliminate all of them, the Chink in the dungeon, Oliver Hitchcock, and this Professor Bloom. Cut the legs off the so-called Cause," the General continued.

A burst of laughter rose from the shadows. A man stepped into the light, causing McGivney to snap at him. "You're late."

"Who might you be?" General Rosewall asked, clearly agitated by the intruder's presence and the surprise.

"I'm sorry, my dear General. Let me introduce my secret weapon. Julian Iscar, please shake hands with General Rosewall, chief Mountie for the Cūtocracy. I believe you know his bulldog, Ms. Rousseau."

Rousseau glared and Julian winked back after shaking hands with the General.

"Your Eminence, if it pleases, may I have a quick word with you in private?" Julian asked.

The Minister stepped into a far corner, waving for Julian to follow. Rousseau eyed the two whispering for several minutes before they returned to the center of the room.

"General, I've had second thoughts. For now, I do not want you to eliminate anyone. If there's anything to the old black Jew, who no doubt you are aware of, and an unvaccinated village in India, we must find out exactly what it is." The Minister gave an order, not a request. He then turned to Julian and purposely ignored Rousseau. "The General and I have other business to discuss. If you don't mind we can carry on a bit later, possibly at dinner this evening."

Julian nodded then took his leave prompting Rousseau to catch up. She was pissed but hid her anger well as she raced past him, then sauntered into the hall with Julian shuffling behind her.

"The Church can handle this," Julian said.

"No! VAMA will take charge." Rousseau turned back to Julian hoping her confidence was enough to put him down.

Instead, he snickered. "You had your chance with Hitchcock and blew it, you and that Belgian buffoon of yours."

Rousseau marched into Julian's face. "Don't fuck with me, Julian, or I'll let Hitchcock know who you really work for."

Without looking for a reaction to her threat, she pivoted away and once again sauntered through the lobby and onto the street like the sexy siren she was. She drew second looks from the Italian men as they passed by and relished every ogling glance.

Rousseau exited Regis International Airport the following morning just as Oedipus pulled up to the curb in their VAMA hearse. She started to get in the back but instead rode up front. After buckling in, she sighed.

Oedipus looked over. "Not happy?"

"Rome is a bitch. Let's go."

"Maybe dis will cheer you up," her driver said as he handed her a satchel. "Your share of da laundry."

She unzipped the satchel and peeked inside. Wads of paper cash. She grinned as Oedipus peeled away over the whine of his electroatomic isothermal engine and rose to a cruising level inches above the ground.

He dropped Rousseau off at her house. Once inside, she immediately proceeded to the wall safe and hid away the cash. After closing the safe, she stood there staring at the photo of her and her daughter in front of the Eiffel Tower. She kissed her fingertips then touched her daughter's lips. At the same time, she spoke softly in French, "*Pour toi mon amour*. For you, my little darling."

Chapter Twenty-Three

The White House press room was nervous with noise waiting for Dillon Burber, the Press Secretary, to make his grand entrance. Reporters sat at desks in semicircular rows around a podium standing on an oval platform. All the desks were outfitted with computer shells and the names of the organizations assigned to those desks. More than a dozen cameras and their operators stood on another platform behind the reporters. Dillon was only five minutes late when Yennie, sitting to one side in the corner, began shaking his right foot in nervous anticipation. He and Dillon had gone over a number of times what they had hoped to accomplish. At the same time, he—they—didn't want it to seem staged, nor did the president. Nevertheless, he knew how unpredictable a press conference could be and the whole world was watching. Yennie hadn't seen that many TV cameras at any of the previous sessions.

Just when he thought he should go back and check on Dillon, the Press Secretary stepped into the room.

"Sorry I'm late, guys, and I apologize for the short notice," Dillon Burber said as he walked up to the podium. "Before I take questions, let me address an explosion in the recent news cycle."

The room went silent, and everyone focused on the White House press secretary whose hair was slicked back as if he were attempting to cover up a number of sleepless nights. Clearly he was tired, which only reinforced the monotone in his presentation. That was saying a lot considering the entire press corps had dubbed him the king of drone. Nevertheless, every journalist in the press room seemed to be sitting on edge waiting to hear why he called an unscheduled session and how he planned to address the explosion in the recent news cycle, at least Yennie hoped so.

"As all of you know, serious allegations have been made that the Click is not a God-given or natural occurrence of aging but rather a result of the ERAM-V vaccination process. If you haven't read about the work that Professor Elana Wu from American University has been conducting, I suggest that you go online to the *Washington Herald's* site. It's all there thanks to Amy Winkler."

It was as if he were speaking in an echo chamber. The entire room reverberated with the words—*the Click is not a God-given or natural occurrence of aging*. Of course they had all read it by then, either on the *Herald* site or on at least a hundred other sites around the world. Nevertheless, hearing it uttered by the president of the United States' official spokesman had to be electrifying.

Before the room quieted down, Dillon glanced down at Amy Winkler and nodded, as if thanking her for having the courage to publish Dr. Wu's work. She nodded back. He then briefly discussed the details of that work and explained the reason for him being there. The president wanted her fellow citizens and the world to know that she was not dismissing the allegations, outrageous as most everyone thought. Of course, that wasn't the real reason for Dillon Burber being there.

The real reason was coming, and Yennie smiled as he continued to shake his foot.

"Now let's begin this press conference with Gabriela Link of the World Network News Service," Dillon suggested.

She wanted to know why the president wasn't doing more to push back on the Chinese who continued to flood the US market with low cost vehicles manufactured outside the Universal Trade Agreement. Everyone knew that Chinese workers were being paid below the minimum set by UTA, and in many cases they were underage. Dillon fielded that question and its follow up quite easily—in the minor key of E flat. At the same time, Yennie wondered why even she would lead off with such an inane question immediately following Dillon's preamble to the session. Surely his comments trumped the press's need to protect the American worker, at least for the moment.

The next several questions were equally tedious, but at least related to Elana Wu and the Click. Then just as Yennie had hoped, Agatha Guthrie of the Ecclesian Monitor woke up the press corps. She wanted to know why President Wainwright had not been attending church regularly, for the past fourteen Sundays in fact, especially given that for eleven of those Sundays she'd been in town.

Had she not asked that particular question, Dillon was prepared to ask it himself and then answer it. Yennie knew she would, given how he managed to leak a teaser to her editor, someone he played poker with regularly. Dillon's retort was clearly unanticipated by the press corps and caused an uproar the likes of which even Yennie had not been prepared for just as President

Wainwright had predicted.

"Well, Agatha," Dillon said in more of an E sharp tone, "President Wainwright has decided to leave the Church and take a break from religion itself. She chooses to be unaffiliated, if you will, and please don't bother with a follow-up question. Now let's see who's next?"

Agatha Guthrie jumped up from her chair. "Wait Dillon! Just one follow-up. Given that nonsense Amy Winkler is spewing in the *Washington Herald*, does the president's decision to leave the church have anything to do with the Click and the ERAM-V vaccine?"

Dillon looked over at Amy who seemed to shrug off the insult, then back to Agatha. "I cannot comment on the president's decisions regarding her spiritual commitments. Thank you all for coming. I believe that is enough for today."

As the decibel level in the room cranked up, Dillon quickly disappeared and Yennie follow close behind.

****

General Rosewall and Minister McGivney took their time finishing other business after Rousseau and Julian Iscar left them. Finances for one. The Cūtocracy needed additional funding to combat the barrage of bad press resulting from the publication of Elana Wu's work and to beef up both VAMA and their private army that Rosewall was in charge of. They also had to establish a line of command. Rosewall thought he could win that one, but again money spoke louder than brass medals.

"Just keep in mind, General, I hold the purse strings, and should you get out of line I will cut those strings as quick as a razorblade can cut through the veins in your wrists."

Twenty minutes later, General Rosewall stomped down the street thinking about razorblades and the Minister's balls. At the same time, he talked to Rousseau. "They're both assholes, McGivney and Iscar, but that's beside the point. Just kill Wu, but find out what she knows first, God damn it. Take care of your friend Hitchcock also. And fuck McGivney. I can handle him."

****

After Rosewall left, McGivney remained by the window and watched him leave the building. He didn't trust the sniveling snot but for now he needed him, or at least he might need him depending on how things evolved. If it's true that a large population of unvaccinated old people... He couldn't complete that thought. It was too... He shook his head and started back for the Vatican. The tunnel seemed more confining, the humidity more oppressive, the sound of his sandals pounding the pavement more disconcerting. It was as if he were walking a tightrope unravelling under his feet with the entire church and his beloved smotec on his back. There couldn't possibly be a large tribe of people living well beyond seventy-five. God wouldn't allow it. Neither he nor the smotec himself had that luxury. After all, they were God's disciples and God's disciples lived and died under God's grace.

Ten minutes later, alone in the tunnel, he was on his scud with Julian. "Yes, that's what I said, keep working with Hitchcock. Do what you have to but get Wu. If there really is a hellhole in the jungles of India, I have a feeling she will come in handy."

Chapter Twenty-Four

Oliver Hitchcock sat in his tiny hotel room listening to the traffic in downtown Mumbai through the open balcony door. He sipped on a scotch while he tried to reconcile uncomfortable thoughts flowing through his mind. Does he fly directly to Italy or go home first? Christopher's V-Mark remained bluish-black, even more so, and the blistering seemed to be spreading. Kathy begged him to come home. She even intimated that Christopher might not live long enough for him to arrive in time. That was enough to make him decide to fly back to DC before meeting with Meta DeCarlo. He was about to make arrangements when he once again unfolded Ambika Patel's note.

Seek out Meta DeCarlo in Greve, Italy. Tell her the fishermen of Bombay sent you.

Once again, he wasn't sure what to do. Not like him. In the past he would have… "Damn it! This is not the past." He decided to call Delahunt, hoping the doctor would be more optimistic than his daughter. Dr. Delahunt was out of the office. Could one of the other doctors help him? Christ no! Jesus, he had to make the decision himself. He inched around his hotel room with the note in hand hoping for an epiphany, then walked down to the bar and ordered a martini. Two martinis. Doubles. The TV over the bar was on the travel channel but muted. As he sipped his third martini, he watched a pretty young American girl with blonde hair walking across the Ponte Vecchio in Florence, Italy. The bright red Duomo rose in the background. The bartender looked over at him. "Have you been there?" he asked.

"A long time ago." Hitch hesitated, then nodded to himself. "But I'm heading there from here." Good! He'd made a decision.

In less than twenty-four hours, he sat on his balcony in Florence. A cool breeze crossed the Arno River and brushed over his face as he watched the tourists marching across the bridges. They took photos, carried bags, and held hands. For three days, he sat on that balcony, off and on, and Meta DeCarlo, whoever the hell she was, had already canceled twice on him. Even if she were to lead them to an unvaccinated tribe of Ethiopian Jews, Elana Wu remained missing and without her nothing could be done. He was losing hope. He tried to shake the feeling by focusing on his immediate surroundings. By then, he had become a familiar guest at the Lungamo Hotel on the south bank of the Arno River.

The cool breeze, now chilly, seemed to beach itself on the balcony. He shivered as his thoughts left his surroundings and came back to the problems at present, especially to Christopher's condition. A few minutes later, his scud *vibrated* and he picked up the call after enabling its holographic mode. He could practically touch Barnaby's furrowed brow.

"Oliver, where are you?"

"If you activate your holographic mode, Barnaby, you will see I haven't left my hotel in Florence," Hitch said sarcastically. "It appears this mysterious Ms. DeCarlo does not want to meet with me after all. And if she does…" He paused and finished up the scotch. "Like I've got all the fuckin' time in the world."

"What about Elana?"

"My friend is taking care of it, and I trust him with my life."

"Well, as long as he gets her back."

"He said he will, which means he will," Hitch barked into the holographic image in front of him as he refilled his glass.

"Quite so."

A few minutes later Hitch clicked off and moseyed down to the hotel bar close to the TV. After a few minutes, a news bulletin flashed across the screen. He and everyone else at the bar stared up at a demonstration in Washington, DC, taped earlier.

Crowds of people, Ecclesian Crusaders according to their signs, marched down 15th Street heading toward Pennsylvania Avenue and the White House demanding that the president resign. They were practically rolling over the reporter trying his best to remain standing as they rushed by. Before he had a chance to speak, one of the signs smacked him hard on the shoulder and knocked the poor fellow down.

No *I'm sorry* or *excuse me*, Hitch thought. Apparently, true believers didn't have to apologize. Besides, they were all in a hurry to crucify Queen Wainwright. In fact, two of the spirited many racing past the reporter carried a banner in bright red letters as if written in blood urging those who could read to *Burn Witch Wainwright just like they did the witches in Salem!* The reporter stopped them and asked if they really meant that.

"I not only mean it, but I would happily strike the

first match," Father Winterhaven exclaimed after he introduced himself and moved closer to the camera. He bore a toothless smirk across his face ruddy red from drink.

"I guess that says it all," the reporter declared. "I'm Gary Smith in the Nation's Capital."

The anchor quickly appeared on screen. "That was late morning, Washington, DC time and was just one of hundreds of anti-Wainwright demonstrations around the world," he announced from behind his desk. "And besides railing against the President of the United States, Cūtocrats everywhere are asking, who is Elana Wu? According to a recent *Washington Herald* poll, as many as thirty-two percent of those polled believe the Click could be a fraud. At the same time, rumors continue that Dr. Wu is really a heroin dealer who…"

The anchor paused in midsentence as he cupped one hand to his ear piece. "More news from Washington, DC I'm afraid."

The TV screen switched to a reporter standing on Pennsylvania Avenue with the White House behind him. The anchor's voice could be heard off screen. "We go immediately to Robert Mabry on the scene. What's happening Bob?"

"Well, Judd, we are told an assassination attempt on President Wainwright less than an hour ago has been foiled. According to my sources one of the conspirators involved was a secret service agent assigned to guard the president. According to one particular source the agent is believed to be a member of the secret society known as the Tarsusians…"

"Tarsusians?" the anchor interrupted.

"An extremist arm of the Ecclesian Church that has

been around since the early nineteen hundreds. They're a more violent spinoff of Opus Dei I'm told, but they have stayed deep in the shadows doing God's work according to the strictest principles of Catholicism before its meltdown and the rise of Ecclesian religiosity."

"And how exactly was the plot foiled, I mean…"

Just then Hitch felt a tap on his shoulder. "Mr. Hitchcock, please follow me," a server said.

He jumped from his stool and followed the young man through the bar's small kitchen and out the back door to an opened, stripped down, high-tech Speedster painted deep maroon with stainless steel strips running across the center of its hood and trunk. An attractive black woman with coal black hair, around fifty years old Hitch guessed, sat behind the wheel.

"Please get in, Mr. Hitchcock. We must hurry," Meta DeCarlo said.

****

Rousseau pulled out the Blue Cube, fired it up, and began pouncing back and forth along the edge of its HS-Screen as *No Data* blinked within the greenish-blue haze. She was on her scud talking to one of Rosewall's lieutenants in charge of the mission. "He has to come out sometime, George. He's been cooped up in that fucking hotel for three days now which means I've been cooped up here, and I don't like it."

"How do you think we feel out here waiting?"

Just then the HS-Screen went live capturing Hitch as he stepped into the open and began glowing intermittently. "Hold on, there he is, behind the bar, getting into… Now stay with him, George, and take him out or Rosewall will have your ass, God damn it!"

Rousseau clicked off her scud and stepped up to the greenish-blue haze close enough to breathe in its magical ability to transport visions across the world. "As much as I hate to do this, Oliver, it's beyond my control." It surprised her how unemotional she was, considering the order she just gave. She and Hitch had history, good and bad, serious and indifferent. He was the… She stopped herself; had to live in the present. This was the mission. If she was to survive, there was no room for sentiment or even ambivalence. After turning her back on him, she crossed the room and faced the wall mirror close enough to examine the blood vessels in the whites of her eyes. "I mustn't be vulnerable," she said to herself, aloud, to make sure it sank in.

From there, through the mirror, she saw the Speedster wind through the countryside. George's black SUV carrying him and two other lieutenants followed at a distance, laser guns fixed to its hood. Overhead, an armed VAMA drone tracked their path. She swirled around and *clapped* her hands.

****

The power of whatever sat under the hood of the maroon and silver striped Speedster kept Hitch glued to the back of his seat as Meta DeCarlo, seemingly relaxed and casual, cut corners at high speed and accelerated on every straightaway, sometimes lifting them as much as a foot off the ground. All types of alarms on the dashboard screamed with fright while the souped-up engine's high pitched *wail* killed any conversation. He was mesmerized by the beautiful woman sitting next to him; her long hair blowing back, her steady hands on the wheel, the picture of something out of the movies.

As she exceeded 275 kilometers per hour, he tried to stay cool and stare ahead, but his eyes had trouble leaving her.

Finally he yelled out. "You always drive like this?"

"Only when we're being followed," she yelled back, first pointing skyward, then behind her.

Hitch pivoted to the rear. No car, then glance upward. No plane that he could see. He looked for the side mirror but it wasn't there, then to the rearview mirror. It wasn't there either. "How the hell do you know?"

"Please, Mr. Hitchcock, just hang on."

The Speedster dropped to the unpaved road below with a *thump*. It broke hard and slid sideways creating a rising trail of dust between them and the black SUV that had just come into view. It then raced toward what appeared to be a dead end as a steel shield rose from its rear. *Zing, zing, zing.* Hitch heard laser shots ricochet directly behind him while the *roar* of the SUV closed the gap. The VAMA drone dipped downward through the clouds and seemed to magically appear. Still glued to the back of his seat, Hitch couldn't believe what he was witnessing, didn't expect such excitement, as the speedometer registered 185 kilometers per hour He looked over at Meta DeCarlo who calmly steered the Speedster toward high brush without a discernable roadway.

"This may get a bit choppy, so once again hang on," she suggested.

****

Rousseau became entranced with the chase, so much so that she pierced the holographic images in front of her. She even clapped her hands in anticipation of the catch and the demise of her dear friend. The optics caused the images to momentarily quake and Rousseau to jump. He and that woman were heading into a raised thicket of green that clearly would provide little support for the pneumatic blanket of air that normally maintained proper altitude. Surprisingly, it glided over at least two hundred yards of entangled weeds as if they formed a landing strip before dropping downward and bouncing onto a rock bed of sorts. Then up again it went. From Rousseau's line of sight, the speedster seemed to fly over a narrow crevice and fishtailed onto a slightly tamer raised gravel road. After straightening out and rising, it flew down that road leaving the black SUV to suddenly reverse thrust its engine in braking mode. Clearly George did not know how to cope with the crevice and the higher ground on the other side.

She watched in frustration but was still hopeful as the VAMA drone circled wide in order to swoop down, then followed the Speedster paralleling railroad tracks. From her vantage point, she saw the road veer away through an open field, making it a perfect target. Rousseau held her breath. Finally, she could check Hitchcock off her list. All of a sudden, instead of veering into the open field, the Speedster dropped down and slammed on its brakes, creating more dust.

"What the fuck?" Rousseau stared into the HS-Screen wondering what the hell they were doing. In the meantime, she saw the drone coming back around behind the stalled Speedster. Closer, closer, dropping, dropping. Rousseau was so close she could practically pee into the greenish-blue mist that would witness Oliver's final demise.

****

With the Speedster dead still, Meta looked back at the drone, then at her companion. "This could be dicey," she declared just as rockets rained down on them. Not only could they hear the *explosions* to their left and right, but they were so close they could feel the ground vibrate their cushion of air. All of a sudden Hitch felt the back of his seat give him a huge kick between the shoulder blades as Meta floored the Speedster. Within seconds they were straddling the railroad tracks doing 225km/h as the explosions behind them caught up.

Less than a mile up the tracks a tunnel popped into view. "What the fu—" *Whoosh.* Everything went black. The Speedster raced out of the tunnel and into a thick forest, invisible from both protolytes and drones.

****

As soon as Hitchcock disappeared in the tunnel, *No Data* began blinking on Rousseau's HS-Screen. "Damn it! Damn it!"

She hurled an empty tin coffee cup across the room just as Oedipus entered. He ducked. *Smack.* It bounced off the wall and onto the floor. "Why can't anybody make a decent product?"

"Wat?"

"This damn Blue Cube. You'd think it could see through a fucking forest. What the hell good is it if anyone can hide from it by standing under a shittin' tree?"

"So wat do we do now?"

"We find out who in the hell that woman is, that's what!"

Oedipus nodded and left Rousseau searching the

area for Oliver Hitchcock, without success. In frustration, she turned the Blue Cube off just as Oedipus reappeared.

"Some olt German guy eer. Calls eemself, Herr Volkmar."

"Never heard of him."

"I'll get reet of eem."

"Do that."

Oedipus turned to leave. "Sometin 'bout a proposal…ant Elana Wu."

Rousseau did an about-face. "Elana Wu?"

"Yeah."

"Bring him in." Rousseau quickly wheeled the Blue Cube in a corner and covered it with a blanket.

Oedipus led an elderly gentleman in. Without being asked, he sat himself down in Rousseau's favorite chair, put one leg over another, and pushed back as if he were making himself comfortable in his own study. Right away that pissed her off just enough to bite her tongue. She would teach this old fart whose office he was in but first needed to know his connection with Elana Wu.

****

Meta DeCarlo's Speedster pulled under an overhang adjacent to a two-story stone home surrounded by a vineyard and trees sufficiently dense to guarantee privacy. Two levels of outdoor stone steps led up to a porch along both the side and back of the house. Meta led her guest up the stairs and onto the porch where he could just see the piazza in Greve over the vineyard and trees.

"Welcome to my home, Mr. Hitchcock."

"Oliver… You are certainly wicked behind the

wheel."

Meta grinned. "Necessity is the mother of reckless driving, I'm afraid."

"Reckless? I'd say reckless would have been letting those rockets explode in our back seat, Meta. May I call you…"

"Yes, please, just Meta."

****

Oedipus stood by the door as Rousseau sat across from Herr Volkmar, still sitting comfortably in her favorite chair. She seethed but managed to laugh nevertheless as a bag of white powder hung down from one hand.

"You may be a friend of Dr. Wu, Herr Volkmar, but you see we have no choice. We have to make sure she is no longer a menace to the good citizens of this country. And since she is a Chinese citizen…"

"Are you done?" the old man said in a drawn-out German accent before Rousseau could finish her thought.

"Done? I'm just getting started." This time she didn't laugh.

"I think not. You see, as we speak, Dr. Wu is now in my custody."

The old man's penetrating glare convinced Rousseau he was serious.

"Check it out," he continued and sat up as if he were about to depart. Rousseau wanted to shove her fist between his eyes and rip off his large German nose but once again bit her tongue. She nodded to Oedipus who stepped out while Herr Volkmar smirked in her direction. She glared back with the intention of killing the bastard any moment.

Oedipus returned and merely shrugged. Rousseau went weak in the knees and flush in the face. She didn't need a mirror to feel it. Nevertheless, she managed to gain her composure.

"Now for my proposal. You will call off any attempts by VAMA to harm Oliver Hitchcock, Dr. Wu, Barnaby Bloom, and anyone else assisting them."

She began laughing uncontrollably. She couldn't help herself. "And why in the hell would I do that?"

The old man stood and stepped toward Rousseau, close enough that she could feel his breath. "Because if anything happens to them, I'll give the order to tear out that black heart of yours and have it rot in the vacant cell below." He smiled and started to walk out. "Oh, one other thing. Don't bother following Hitchcock or the others with the blue toy you're hiding. I've had the signal scrambled."

Herr Volkmar scooted past Rousseau, picked up the tin cup she had thrown at Oedipus earlier, and handed it to him.

****

Yennie Tawahada sat comfortably on the couch in his office, having just clicked off his scud.

"Well?" Dillon Burber asked standing in the doorway.

"You can tell President Wainwright that Oliver Hitchcock is with Meta now. They are just about to have lunch together."

"And Elana Wu?"

"I'm afraid she's still missing, at least that's what Meta was told by Mr. Hitchcock."

"All right, but keep me posted." Before Yennie could respond, Dillon was gone.

Chapter Twenty-Five

Meta DeCarlo led Oliver Hitchcock into the den from the dining room after a lengthy lunch, each carrying a glass of wine. Meta took a seat on the sofa and motioned Oliver to sit next to her. A computation shell sat on the table across from both of them.

"I'm afraid it's true. The rapidly changing discolorations on his V-Mark confirm it, and he's heard the Click more than once and…" Oliver's scud *rang*. He pulled it out from a pocket. "Speaking of that, this is my daughter. Excuse me please." He jumped from the couch, walked onto the porch, and answered in visual mode. Hitch saw immediately how distressed and weepy she was. She leaned against the opened door of Christopher's hospital room. Christopher lay in a bed behind her.

"It's Christopher. I'm here at the hospital, he's been admitted. I'm…"

"What? Already?"

"I need you here. Now, Dad, I…"

"You know I can't do that, Kitten."

"Yes you can."

"You expect me to just stop and…"

"Of course not. Off playing spy games. You were never there for me when I…"

"That's not fair, Kathy. You know what I'm doing here. It's for…"

"You want me to believe this crap about black Jews in India? Some mysterious woman in Italy. What's this have to do with Christopher?"

"Everything."

"No! It's about you. It's always about you."

"Kathy, you don't understand."

"Oh, don't I?"

She clicked off. "Kathy? Kitten."

Hitch took a deep breath and held it until he could gain his composure. He walked back to the den carrying a smile and an overall demeanor incongruous with the hurt that rumbled within. He returned to the couch next to Meta. "As I was saying, Christopher and the others need the antidote, and for reasons I don't understand Dr. Wu needs a large group of people who haven't been vaccinated."

Meta shook her head. "What your Christopher needs, Oliver, is DanSheba. I've waited all these years to avenge the death of my great, great granduncle Jonathan, all because of Innocent's Smotecal Decretum. And now it appears I will be getting a lot more."

"Decretum?"

Meta laughed. "The ever so secret Smotecal Decretum issued by Supreme Minister Innocent II, but there's more. For now, take this. It shows Jonathan's involvement." She handed him a memory stick. He looked at it, wondering what he was going to discover.

"Dr. Wu is right, of course. It's all there. We need her and the Cause in DanSheba. And please bring your daughter and Christopher. It truly is his only chance."

As soon as Hitch returned to his hotel in Florence well after dark, by bus so as not be noticed, he plugged the memory stick into a port in his scud. During the next forty-five minutes he came to know Jonathan DeCarlo and how he accidentally learned about the Smotecal Decretum. He learned how it caused Jonathan to lose his life, presumably. From what Hitch now knew, the Church of the Ecclesia voted against the rest of the Cūtocracy, although he couldn't guess what the vote was about. Only later would he understand why the so-called Smotecal Decretum was so important.

Just as he began to think more about that, his scud *rang*. It was Julian. "Well, my friend, give me good news. Without Elana, I've got nothing."

"Like the old days, Oliver. Dr. Wu won't be going to China after all. Your old flame, Rousseau, on the other hand probably wishes she were."

"Ha! Would love to have been there. Where did they have her, and how did you pull it off?"

Julian laughed. "Rousseau had her in a VAMA cell below her office. How I pulled it off is my trade secret. However, I will tell you that my disguise was a masterpiece. Hopefully, the good frau will have many nightmares about German spies interrupting her sleep." He laughed again. "So, tell me where and when I need to deliver her. What about your plans?"

"No details yet, but I know I'll need her before we leave for DanSheba, wherever in the hell that is. I'll explain later." Hitch clicked off and resumed the saga of Jonathan DeCarlo. The last thing on the memory stick was Jonathan's voice, quite possibly the last words he ever spoke.

"And so, Juliette, my dearest sister, it will be up to you to make sure the world knows what's going on here. I did not intend to participate in mass genocide. You must believe…"

Jonathan ended his plea abruptly, as if he were interrupted, never to be heard from again.

Time to go home, Hitch thought as he looked around his hotel room. It was an event filled week. He wasn't sure what to make of Meta DeCarlo or her invitation to DanSheba, and what could she have possibly meant when she said Christopher's only chance was to go there. Wherever there was. As he started pulling his things together, he received another call. He stared at the screen as a questioning frown spread across his face, than clicked it on.

"Dr. Delahunt? Ralph?" Hitch dropped onto the edge of the bed and put him on screen view.

"Oliver, I'm truly sorry for bothering you but…" Dr. Delahunt hesitated. Hitch saw him look around as if he were worried someone might be listening.

"Ralph, what is it?"

"Oh! I'm sorry. I just wanted to make sure your daughter had not returned. She went to the cafeteria for a bite to eat. We need to talk. Is this a good time?"

"Of course. Any time's a good time when it comes to Christopher. I assume that is what this is about."

"Yes, yes it is. You see, Oliver, it's only a matter of weeks, two or three at most. I'm afraid I don't know how to break that to Kathy. I'm afraid she's under an illusion that it's just not going to happen. I thought…"

"Ralph, now listen to me. I will need those three weeks. There is a plan. We are getting close. I can't explain to you right now what it is but you must do everything you can now, I mean today, to make sure Christopher will be able to travel and will last out those three weeks. Do you understand?"

"Yes, but where…"

Hitch jumped up and began to march across the room. He took large, nervous strides. "Again, no time to explain, but I will be having a Professor Barnaby Bloom come to the hospital. He will explain our plan to you and Kathy. Now listen to me, Ralph. This is critical if we are going to save my grandson. When you hear the plan you are going to think it's insane, as will Kathy, especially Kathy. No matter what, I need you to stay calm and support the plan. Do you understand?"

Hitch saw how confusing this was to Delahunt. "Please, Ralph, can you do that for me?"

"Unfortunately, I see no other plans in the horizon. But..."

"No buts. I have to go. Now please make sure Kathy listens to Professor Bloom."

Hitch clicked off realizing he wasn't going anywhere for now. He planned to wait until he got home to discuss everything he had learned from Meta along with her "invitation" with both Kathy and Barnaby. That couldn't wait. Unfortunately, the clocks were ticking, Christopher's and theirs. He picked up his scud and called the professor. They talked for more than an hour, first Hitch filling him in, and second making plans to go to DanSheba. Barnaby indicated he would meet with Kathy right away.

Hitch then called Meta and told her about his discussion with Dr. Delahunt. Her response was immediate and decisive.

"In that case, we all must leave for DanSheba right away and, Oliver, just remember it is critical that Dr. Wu be there."

"There is where?" Hitch asked. He needed details and she provided them, as if they had been made and memorized long before he called. He was dumbfounded. This DanSheba couldn't be for real, not the way she described it. What had he expected, a luxury health clinic in the heart of Minnesota. For the life of him, he couldn't wrap his arms around the idea. India? The jungle? A village? A state-of-the-art hospital and research center? How in the hell was he going to wrap himself around all that? How was he going to wrap Kathy around it?

Jesus, Elana! He had to reach Julian. He tried several times and only succeeded the following morning after a sleepless night. He relayed the plan to his CIA buddy and let him know exactly when and where he was to bring Elana.

"And Julian, keep in mind that VAMA is everywhere. We can't afford to lose her."

"We will arrive incognito but we will arrive, my friend," Julian promised.

After clicking off, Hitch began packing up. In doing so, he discovered the book he took from the Jewish School of Learning, *The First Coming*. He stopped and stared at it. Who were these people who waited centuries for the Messiah? How did a whole village manage to avoid the long arm of VAMA? A state-of-the-art hospital?

"Jesus! I need a drink!"

Chapter Twenty-Six

There was much to do. It had been a while since Meta visited DanSheba. She wasn't sure how long it would be before she returned to Greve. Her essentials were out and ready to go. Everything else was packed away. Now she had to sit down and contemplate the future.

DanSheba! She thought about the tiny village with deep satisfaction; its history over thousands of years rich with tradition and mythological hyperbole. From the beginning, it was first and foremost the place that would receive the legitimate Coming, the Messiah, with all his humanity intact. No one who understood the Old Testament believed the Messiah would be any more than a mortal being blessed with the gift of spiritual and battle-ready leadership, and the ear of the Almighty. It was sometime in the twenty-first century when the village supposedly received him, at least that was the story told by the villagers around the tall pole in the square. Whether the Messiah really did come, Meta could not say.

What she could say with a smile wider than the Arno River was that her Messiah was coming. Elana Wu would bring sufficient expertise to destroy the Click as surely as the earlier Messiah would have addressed, or did address, the myth of a divine Jesus described in the New Testament and the hope for life eternal in some celestial Garden of Eden.

She tried to think back to the first time she visited DanSheba. She couldn't have been more than twelve. In early afternoon on a gloriously sunny day, she sat with her mother in a small corporate jet secretly owned by a DanSheban corporation. It flew south from Delhi toward Bangalore, the high-tech capital of India. Because the small jet could fly at a relatively low altitude, she had exceptional aerial views of the country's jungled midsection. Somewhere between Nagpur and Hyderabad, Meta recalled being glued to her window and the terrain below. The sun appeared to fall to the earth and bounce back into her vision. A powerful glare disappeared before she could look away, as if it had been swallowed up by the jungle floor.

"Did you see that?" her mother asked.

She remembered nodding but didn't know what it was she saw.

Her mother kissed her on the head. "That my darling is DanSheba. That is where you will be spending a good deal of your life and that is where you will learn both Hebrew and Amharic."

The homes were modest, mostly stone and wood, and yet the technology that connected that tiny hidden village to the rest of humanity was the most sophisticated in the world. And yet there were no motorized vehicles. If the people wanted to get from one end of the village to the other, they either walked or rode a bicycle, or hailed a bicycle-powered taxi. Both extremes amazed Meta as she acclimated to her new surroundings that summer when she was twelve.

In addition to computation shells of all sizes and varieties and other digital gadgetry, there were books of every type—fiction and nonfiction, not necessarily the most current editions, but eventually they came. DanSheba could be described best as an intellectual community hidden within the long forgotten and mostly irrelevant underbelly of India, she thought years later. After all, its people had nothing else to do but read, argue, and spend money the village made on the Ethiopian diamond mines it owned. And much of that money was spent on travel the world over, education, and more recently a state of the art hospital and medical research facility. The facility was right there, within a tin can kicking distance from the main square and the tall pole that stood watch, the very same pole that the Messiah supposedly climbed up to reach the ear of God. DanShebans thrived everywhere in the world and it was from those places its people would bring back home the most recent technology, books, and ideas.

Because DanSheba occupied a small amount of land, its young people were encouraged to live in other parts of the world. The village sat within a grand meadow pressed up against steep, barren sides of a mountain. The cliffs encircled all the meadow except for a small opening around a hundred yards wide. A river providing the only way in and out flowed alongside the opening and served as DanSheba's umbilical cord to the outside world. It was the means of obtaining reading material, medicine, and other necessities from those outside, as well as much of its food. Looking up from the wharf at the river, the mountainside appeared to be formed of polished granite that glistened in the sun. That glare and the mountain shadows were enough to hide the meadow and its inhabitants from the daylight sky.

Meta shook herself back to the present. Time was running out. She jumped from her chair and gathered her belongings. After making several trips down to the Speedster, she started back up the stone stairs to lock up. Pounding footsteps echoed behind her. Before she had a chance to turn around, two masked thugs grabbed her and dragged her back into the house. She fell to the floor and hit her head. Blood oozed from above one eye. When she finally looked up to see what was happening, the barrel of a laser gun pressed against her temple. One of the thugs, short and thin, holding the gun in one hand, reached down with a handkerchief in the other hand. Before she could take it, the second thug, much taller and heavy around the middle, pushed him aside and got into her face.

All of a sudden, she felt a knife against her throat. The panic seemed to cause her eyeballs to jump from their sockets. Her scud *rang*. She tried to reach for it. The thug grabbed her wrist.

****

Yennie was on his cell leaning against the outer gate of the White House, listening to continuous *rings*.

"Darn it, Meta. Pick up."

Where was she? They had talked earlier. She should have been on her way to the airport in Florence. There was no reason for her not to pick up.

****

Meta was now in the basement standing before a large safe hidden within what looked to be a second furnace. Blood still dripped from the gash above one eye. Her scud *rang* again.

The overweight thug flashed his knife in front of her eyes. "Leave it."

The smaller thug came down the steps with a wet cloth. He placed it above her eye. She took it from him, held it firm, and nodded a thank you.

"What the hell are you doing?" the other thug growled out.

"Shut up," the smaller thug barked back. He then leaned closer to Meta and whispered, "Open it before he cuts your throat, and he will."

Meta jerked back, trying to appear defiant. "No."

"Lady, I can put this safe in your lap and blow it up," the fat thug said then began poking the tip of his knife into her chest. Her scud *rang* again. "But I won't. I'll cut your throat instead, then I'll blow up the safe right where it is. Now, I'll count to five. One, two…"

Meta nodded and bent down to reach the safe. She worked the combination until it popped open. She reached in and pulled out a brown leather valise, the only thing in the safe. The thug with the knife grabbed the valise and looked in the safe to make sure nothing else was there, then opened the valise and pulled out the Smotecal Decretum. The smaller thug took it in his hands. He ran over its entire surface with his fingertips. He bent the edges, and bit into the gold colored trim. He stared at the signature.

"Is it the original?" the fat thug asked.

"Yes."

"Are you sure?"

"I know real gold when I see it. Let's get the hell out of here."

He and the other thug raced upstairs and were gone by the time Meta reached the top of the stairs. Once she heard the roar of their high-powered pickup truck speed away, she plopped on the couch in the den and called

Yennie.

"Are you okay?" he asked.

"Yes, of course. I had visitors. It seems they knew I had the Decretum, and think they have the original."

"Not surprising. My sources tell me there's a VAMA spy close to Hitchcock."

"What! Any ideas?"

"I'd look for anyone with a connection to Opus Dei or quite possibly the Tarsusians."

Meta looked at her watch. "I have to go. I will be meeting Oliver at the Mumbai airport and want to make sure I'm there before he arrives."

"And the others?"

Meta thought about that. "Barnaby Bloom will be bringing Oliver's daughter and grandson directly to the school. I've arranged for that with the transportation people in DanSheba."

"And Elana Wu?"

That was a more difficult question to answer. Meta shrugged. "Oliver said she will be there but wouldn't tell me how or by whom. Let's hope he's right."

Chapter Twenty-Seven

Barnaby stood in his living room peeking out the window through the closed drapes. He saw two VAMA hearses parked on each end of the street. They were in plain sight and obviously didn't care. The few things he was taking with him were waiting at the café in town. He ate breakfast, lunch, and dinner there for the last two days, and with each meal he brought some of his belongings from home. He was sure neither of his VAMA tails suspected.

This is it, he thought, then locked up the house and left for the café. By the time he reached his destination and pulled into a space, both hearses drove into the shopping center. He left his car and entered the café where a young woman, a member of the Cause, quickly led him out the back and into the alley. He climbed into an awaiting white van with dark brown print on both sides: *Pinochet Bakery Products*. He and his belongings sat in the back under a sheet surrounded by loaves of bread.

"Hold your breath, Barnaby," the young woman called out from the driver's seat. "One of your friends just pulled into the alley and will be passing us any second."

"Don't forget to throw him that magical smile of yours," Barnaby said under cover and laughed. Once they were out of the alley and sure they weren't being followed, Barnaby pulled off the cover, sat up, took a deep breath, looked at all that bread, and tapped on his scud.

****

Ring, ring, ring. Kathy stood in Christopher's hospital room watching several nurses connecting and disconnecting tubes and wires in preparation for them to leave. She quickly looked for her scud. It had fallen from her pocket onto the chair next to his bed. She picked it up to see who was calling and frowned. She really didn't want to go. She really didn't believe all of this was happening. And she wouldn't be going if it hadn't been for Ralph Delahunt.

"Yes, Barnaby?"

"How's Christopher?"

"Raring to travel halfway around the world, I would guess, but how would I know. I'm only his mother." She dropped her shoulders and sighed as Ralph came into the room with another doctor. "I'm sorry, Barnaby. He seems okay. They're about to sedate him and, yes, we are ready to go."

"I'm sorry too, Kathy, but…"

"I know. We will see you in a little bit." She clicked off and looked at Ralph.

"Kathy, sweetheart, this is Dr. Ringthaller. He will be attending Christopher during your journey."

Twenty minutes later, Kathy found herself keeping pace with Christopher's gurney and all the connected devices as they sped through the hospital toward the kitchen in the back. Before long they were in the kitchen's receiving area preparing to step into a large empty supply truck—Kathy, Dr. Ringthaller, Christopher, and two paramedics. She had hoped that

Ralph Delahunt would come along. After all, he talked her into going on this insane wild goose chase. "We are all out of options," he said. "Who knows? Maybe this is God's plan." That wasn't terribly comforting considering that Ralph was as much an atheist as her father. Ralph couldn't come along. He had other seriously ill patients to look after. That wasn't comforting either since her only child was well beyond seriously ill. It could be worse, she thought. At least there will be a doctor making the trip with them.

****

Barnaby waited on the tarmac next to a corporate jet. Whose it was and how it was paid for, he didn't know but apparently this mysterious Meta DeCarlo made all the arrangements. He looked at his watch. They should be here any moment, he thought. How he managed to convince Kathy to come at all wasn't entirely clear to him.

When he first approached the subject not long after introducing himself, she stared at him as if he had just escaped from an institution for the mentally challenged asking her to run away with him.

"And how many times have you been to this…this DanSheba?" she finally asked.

"I…well I… I've not been there, but…"

"But you have no choice if you want any chance to save Christopher's life," came the words from behind both of them. It was Ralph Delahunt. He was a tall, thin man with gray hair above both temples, bald on top, and a thin white mustache. Barnaby liked his no-nonsense manner immediately, maybe because he saw kindness in the man's eyes at the same time.

"Ralph," Kathy barked out.

The doctor approached and took both of Kathy's hands in his. "Kathy, there are no answers here. Christopher will die for sure if you stay and…"

"And if we go to that Godforsaken place in…in…" Kathy stopped herself and began to cry. Dr. Delahunt pulled her to him and held her tight. Barnaby saw him tear up.

"I have no answers, sweetheart. Only an engine of hope and a large number of people who are greasing its gears and programming its computers to ensure it reaches its destination."

As Barnaby relived those moments, his only regret was that Ralph was not able to go with them. He shook his head and looked up just as the supply truck came into view. The paramedics on board carried Christopher into the jet on a stretcher. He was fast asleep by then.

Kathy approached and Barnaby stiffened, trying to prepare for another battle. All of a sudden, he felt her hands grip his shoulders and watched in disbelief and relief when she kissed him on the cheek.

"I'm sorry for being such a naysayer, Barnaby. I will try my best, but I can't make any promises." She tried to smile, or seemed to, but couldn't.

Under the circumstances, who could, Barnaby Bloom thought as they followed Dr. Ringthaller onto the jet.

Chapter Twenty-Eight

Hitch packed up all his belongings and now had to get back to Mumbai without VAMA on his ass. If they discovered he chartered a helicopter in Siena for Rome, they would stop him for sure on some pretext or just kill him on the spot like that damn drone tried to do earlier. He opened the balcony drapes wide enough to see a VAMA hearse standing guard. "Jesus!"

How was he going to deal with this? He was sure they had someone behind the hotel. They probably had someone in the lobby, by the elevators. Hell, the place would have to go up in flames for him to get out unseen.

"That's it!" He sat and thought out his brilliant idea. After a few minutes, he rushed into the hall. First he went left all the way down to the end, then to the right. Halfway down, there it was, a bright red fire extinguisher and alarm in a recessed glass case. He rushed back to his room, picked up his things, and ran back to the glass case. He broke the case with the heel of his shoe and set off the *alarm*. He raced to the stairwell and hobbled down to the next level with only one shoe on and did the same thing just as guests began streaming into the hall. More noise, more people.

He followed several of the guests into the stairwell and waited at the lobby level for a larger crowd. At least twenty of them rushed into the lobby where they merged with more guests, and everyone headed for the street. Hitch maneuvered his way through the crowd and traffic until he was several blocks from the hotel on the other side of the Ponte Vecchio. He flagged down a taxi heading away from the hotel and jumped in.

An hour or so later he exited the taxi, paid the driver, and rushed to the helicopter he had chartered. From there he travelled to Rome, and in Rome he boarded a commercial jet to Mumbai. He had suggested to Meta that maybe they should travel under fictitious passports since no doubt VAMA would be tracking them. "Not to worry," she told him. "They will only be able to track us to the School of Learning. We will easily lose them there." Hitch didn't know how but Meta seemed so confident he didn't press her on the issue.

Travelers around the world hurried into and out of Chhatrapati Shivaji International airport in Mumbai. Hitch, being one of those travelers, exited Customs with little difficulty and saw Meta waiting. She greeted him with kisses on both cheeks then rushed him through the closest exit to a line of taxis. Hitch started to approach the first one in line when Meta grabbed his arm and shook her head. She led him around the corner where a lone taxi waited. The driver, a young black man, sat behind the wheel as Meta opened the back door and motioned for her companion to get in.

The streets were snarled with traffic in downtown Mumbai, a necessary route to where they were heading, as the driver dodged and weaved under a canopy of colossal glass skyscrapers in the shadowed heat of morning. All the glass, all those people standing behind it, staring down at him, he thought. It was as if the entire Mumbai population was keeping track of his every move.

Early in the ride, Hitch updated Meta on Christopher's situation according to his last conversation with Barnaby Bloom. At the time, Barnaby and his entourage were just leaving the States. Hitch conveniently left out the fact that his daughter was anything but thrilled with their travel plans.

"And Elana Wu? Where does that stand?" Meta asked.

"That's taken care of. They will meet us at the Jewish School of Leaning per your instructions."

"They?"

"Yes, they." Hitch did not elaborate. He wasn't about to compromise Julian, who certainly didn't have to involve himself in saving Christopher—and he did so at great risk to himself. The less anyone knew of his participation, the better.

Meta did not respond. She remained almost stoic, Hitch thought, but breathed easier once he realized she was not going to force the issue.

For several minutes neither of them spoke, making the sound of heavy traffic that much more invasive. Suddenly Meta turned his way. "We have a problem. A very reliable source told me we have a mole."

Hitch glared, then jerked his head toward the driver.

"He's one of us."

"Who's the source?"

"Never mind that. Someone knew we were meeting at my place and why. And it wasn't a DanSheban. I assure you of that."

Hitch pushed back against his door and twisted

around to confront Meta. "My people? Not possible."

"You know it's possible. Now think. Who?"

"Your source first. You tell me…" Hitch was not going to be bullied into accepting such an outrageous accusation.

"No names, but this comes from deep in the White House." Meta pulled out her scud and began tapping on it. "Maybe this will help."

A hologram rose from her scud. *Subject: Opus Dei/Tarsusian Sect.* Underneath, Hitch saw a symbol, an oval surrounding a human figure standing with arms outstretched and feet together like a Christian cross.

"Have you ever seen one of these?" she asked.

"What is it?"

"Opus Dei. No, actually it's the Tarsusian spinoff. A fanatical sect that was instrumental in transforming the Catholic Church into the present-day Church of the Ecclesia."

Hitch started to say *never* but then turned away from the hologram and Meta. He stared out the window and began racing through his mind's eye as it shuttled him back through the years. Every few seconds that symbol flashed in and out with greater resolution. Then nothing, no not nothing. Sand, endless sand. Then *explosions* all around him, endless sand and *explosions*. A man down. He couldn't see. Desert sand continued to blow through his mind's eye. Blood oozing up through the sand began coloring his vision. An arm? A man's face. His body twisted away from his arm. He's breathing, alive. Hitch digs his way under the sand, around the torso. He lifts him. Blood everywhere. Hitch looks down. The arm remains. He spots the oval with the figure inside, all covered with sand, with blood, on the arm. He carries the man across the battlefield. He wants to go back for the arm, but can't.

Hitch turned back to Meta and sighed. "Yeah. I've seen it." He tried to make sense of what he saw. He rewound and hit play several times. Nothing changed. The same sand, the same arm, the same Tarsusian symbol. Impossible! No, nothing's impossible. He shook his head and kept his thoughts to himself.

****

Minister McGivney sat across the table from the Supreme Minister having tea and reporting where matters stood regarding the so called Smotecal Decretum. The smotec was less than happy with the report.

"You were supposed to take care of this…this abomination," he screamed turning his back on McGivney who tried his best to hold himself together. Smotec Pius then turned back. "You still haven't the slightest idea where the Decretum is, the original?"

That took McGivney by surprise. *The original*, for real, he thought. "The Smotecal Decretum, Your Sacredness? But I thought that was all made up."

"Made up! Made up! It's as fucking real as the poxes on your face, and it could destroy us. Do you hear me, McGivney? It could destroy the Church. And that's not all. If there really is a shithole in the jungles of India harboring hundreds of octogenarians happily living into old age, they must be destroyed. It must be destroyed before the world learns of its existence. Do you hear me McGivney? For Christ's sake, we don't even get to live into our eighties."

The smotec's tirade thundered down the High Minister's spine as he traveled the streets from the

Vatican to the Cūtocracy. He needed to breathe fresh air. The tunnel was not an option this time. It reeked of pious hypocrisy. As he approached the Cūtocratic headquarters, he looked at his watch. Upon entering the lobby, he heard Rosewall's irritating voice around the corner. He slowed down and peeked over a large vase with artificial flowers observing Rosewall's tirade. He was tired of tirades.

The General had Rousseau by the collar. "Fool! Idiot! I should have let you rot in Paris. How could you let her go?"

The Minister stepped into view. "You're the fool, Rosewall." He approached the two of them and pushed them apart. "She didn't let Wu go. We took her, and for good reason. We need to find that fucking village in the jungles of India."

****

After the taxi carrying Meta and Hitch put Mumbai's downtown behind them, they approached the Jewish School of Learning on the east coast of the city not far from Chembur. The atmosphere became carnival-like, astonishing Hitch, although from where he sat Meta seemed unruffled. Cars, trucks, the media, people everywhere, and holograms emanating from every possible device filled the streets with a rainbow haze of overlapping images. They were no more discernable than a jigsaw puzzle under several pounds of sludge. He saw children eating cotton candy and sucking on lollipops as the taxi pushed and shoved its way through the hordes of onlookers. And signs everywhere. Some extolled the Click, others rejected it. One group held up a banner—*UnClick Us Now*. Another group of priests and clergy brandish their own battle-cry—*The Click Is Divine*. VAMA hearses dotted the landscape like a heavy dose of pepper on the white of an egg.

As they pushed through, slowly, a crowd gathered around an eccentric-looking preacher who stood on the hood of a car with a megaphone. Nearby, a woman and six children of all ages sang *Amazing Grace*. Hitch opened his window in order to better hear the preacher.

"Rally around the Cūtocracy and our beloved smotec. The Click is God's way of protecting the Earth and its children from overpopulation." Hitch counted all the children and had to laugh.

The taxi maneuvered its way through the crowd and moved closer to the preacher. Hitch turned back and noticed a shuttle bus on their tail as the carnival atmosphere thickened.

"What the hell? How did all these people and the media know where…"

Meta smiled. "I'm afraid it was me. Let the world know the truth and it will act. That's my motto, Oliver."

Hitch started to respond but was cut off by the preacher, who continued on. "We have known nothing but prosperity. No cancer. No heart attacks. No war since the Great Plague."

As the taxi pulled closer to the curb with the shuttle right behind, the preacher droned on. "And it was the Almighty who saw fit to provide us with a means for attaining the prosperity we have come to take for granted. God has given us a gift, the Click. Now, a war is being waged against the peace we cherish. Now, the Almighty's enemies are hell-bent on taking it away from us! The devil is among us, dear people."

****

McGivney vanished as fast as he came, just long enough to harass them, Rousseau thought. He took Wu? The shit-ass German worked for McGivney? She looked over at Rosewall after watching the High Minister close the door behind him. "What now?"

"I don't trust the son-of-a-bitch. I'm going to need you in Mumbai, near that so called Jewish School of Learning. The powers here at the Cūtocracy are a thread's thickness away from convincing the UN to pull back and…"

"Pull back?" Rousseau wasn't following.

"The entire UN fleet under VAMA's authority, under my authority, are convening in Mumbai as we speak. It has the ability to destroy everyone at that so called School of Learning if it has to and I don't want McGivney or the UN to fuck it up." The General nodded as if satisfied with his pronouncement then turned to the window and looked out. Rousseau followed his stare. She saw McGivney walking toward the Vatican.

"What about the village in the jungles of…"

"There is no God damn village. McGivney is delusional. And if the UN doesn't have the balls to pull out the plugs, then, Rousseau, you and I and those loyal to me, and only me, will do what needs to be done. Do you understand?" He looked over at her.

She smiled. "Anything you say, boss." Christ! Am I on the right side of battle? I have Rosewall on one side, McGivney on the other side, and Hitchcock in front of me, Rousseau said to herself as she continued to wonder. For sure I'm not going to get in bed with that one-armed asshole, Julian Iscar. Maybe it's time to retire and look after my kid.

Chapter Twenty-Nine

With the help of a group of black men, the taxi and shuttle wedged through a storm of journalists who caught them stopping near the gate of the School of Learning. Hitch jumped out from the taxi and pulled Meta with him. Most of the black men, DanShebans Hitch guessed, held back the crowd, allowing them to reach the gate.

He watched two of the DanShebans enter the shuttle and lead Barnaby off, followed by Kathy, and then someone Hitch didn't recognize, Dr. Ringthaller he presumed. Kathy waited by the shuttle door as the two DanShebans went back on and brought Christopher off in a gurney along with an IV bottle and tubes.

Before Hitch realized it, Barnaby was standing next to him. "He's sedated and no changes for the worst," Barnaby whispered.

"And Kathy?"

"Up and down, I'm afraid. I have a feeling actually being here, not in the abstract, is going to throw her for a loop."

Hitch nodded, then approached the gurney and looked at Kathy. She glanced away. He inspected Christopher's V-Mark and bit his tongue, trying not to grimace. It seemed larger and blacker. The roughness around the edges was blistering and migrating to the center. He couldn't help but wonder whether he had the three weeks he told Delahunt he needed to…to what? He looked around. Jesus! What have I done? With that question rumbling through his brain he turned back to his daughter.

"Kathy."

She stepped toward him as a soldier ready to do battle with the enemy might and confronted him with venom in her eyes. "What are we doing in this hellhole? Christopher's death will be on your soul, just as…" She stopped herself.

As he was about to say something, not sure what considering he was asking himself the same question, he felt the immediate presence of an older man and younger woman, both Indians. He felt the man tug at his sleeve.

"As promised. Here she is." Julian announced in a whisper.

Barnaby, obviously overhearing that, rushed over and put his arms around Elana just as the gate to the Jewish School of Learning opened. Julian turned to leave when Hitch stepped in his path.

"I think not," Hitch barked.

"I delivered," Julian shot back, now close enough for Hitch to smell the Indian makeup that transformed his friend into his enemy.

"I can see that but what's the rush?"

Julian tried to step around Hitch. "I wasn't planning on…"

Hitch laughed. "Consider this Plan B." He took Julian by his real arm and coerced his friend through the gate which closed behind all of them.

Meta, who now stood next to Hitch, picked up her scud and made a call. "We're here as planned… Yes, all of us including Dr. Wu. It's like a circus outside the gates, as I had hoped… I will. And let the president know."

Meta led them past the one-room school houses that Hitch recognized and a long one-story building that contained all the administrative offices. Near the far end of the campus grounds, she directed them into the Teacher's House, a three-story home large enough to house many people comfortably. A late evening buffet of cold cuts, fruit, salad, and brownies for dessert monopolized the large dining room table. Coffee, tea, and juices sat on the sidebar under the dining room window. In the meantime, three of the DanShebans gathered up every one's luggage and personal belongings and took them away.

"I suggest we all take a deep breath, relax, and eat up," Meta announced as she took a clean plate and stepped to the table.

"Shouldn't we get settled and unpack?" Kathy asked.

"I think we can wait for that, my dear," Meta said as she continued to fill her plate.

For the next forty-five minutes, the group—including a number of the DanShebans—sat in front of a fire blazing within a beautiful used brick fireplace. It served as the focal point in a very large living room. Barnaby, Kathy, and Hitch ate in one corner around a game table with Christopher in his gurney next to her. Kathy only nibbled, refusing to look at her father. Dr. Ringthaller sat on the other side of the gurney close to his charge. The doctor looked to be about forty, Hitch thought. He was a quiet man, thin, with thick red hair and wore dark rimmed glasses. Hitch was glad he came along.

Just as everyone was finishing, Elana stepped into the living room carrying a full plate, with new clothes and looking like herself. Hitch couldn't help but stare.

Kathy looked at her watch and then glanced over at her son. "I think it's time we retire. She jumped from her chair and walked around the gurney to talk to Dr. Ringthaller. Hitch bit his tongue and followed his daughter's every move.

Elana sat in the now empty chair next to Hitch. He took her hands in his, below the table's edge so no one would see. Their eyes met. "I was beginning to think we might never have that pizza together," he said with a smile that was meant to be more than a smile.

She squeezed his hand and, ignoring any onlookers, reached over and kissed him on the cheek. "Thank you for getting me out of that place."

He wanted to kiss her back but stopped short after glancing over at Kathy, who glared at him.

Elana shifted her attention to the three figures across the room, Julian sitting on the steps with a DanSheban on either side. She looked back at Hitch, questioningly.

"It's a long story. Later." He rose from his chair and approached Kathy and the doctor. She turned her back on him and marched toward the bathroom.

Just as Kathy returned, Meta stepped into the living room. "If everyone has had enough, please leave your plates where they are and follow me."

Rather than lead them up a beautiful light oak winding staircase to the bedrooms on the second and third floors, as everyone had expected, she directed them along a narrow hallway, down a dozen steps, and into a large dorm room. Meta asked everyone to step away from the center of the room when a large rectangle in the tile floor began pivoting downwards, as if by magic, exposing an opening into what appeared to be a cellar. Shortly thereafter, a set of portable stairs leading downwards mysteriously appeared from below.

Just as all the confusion rang loudly across everyone's face, a DanSheban in a black T-shirt and blue denim overalls came up the steps from below, nodded to Meta without saying a word, and dropped back into the shadows below.

"I believe we are ready," Meta said and began leading the entire party into the cellar. "There are twelve steps down so please be careful and hold on to the railing."

It took three DanShebans and Hitch to bring Christopher down on his gurney. Once they were all below ground, Meta motioned them to move up against one wall forming part of a large dimly lit basement. A set of what looked to be railroad tracks ran across the floor from a tunnel less than fifty yards away. No one spoke. They were too astonished and as they took in the scene, two DanShebans rolled the stairs out from under the opening and into one corner of the basement. The floor automatically moved back up to close off the subterranean ceiling. As it did, Hitch felt the ground rumble under his feet. A miniature train with engines on the front and back appeared out from the tunnel as if by magic. It rounded the corner before stopping in front of them.

"Would someone pinch me," Barnaby finally said and everyone burst out laughing.

The engineer, another DanSheban, jumped from

the front engine and hurried to the back engine while the passengers were helped on by the DanShebans that had brought Christopher down. Two of those DanShebans stayed with Julian while Hitch sat with Elana, and Barnaby sat with Meta. There was a flatbed car behind Hitch for Christopher's gurney. Dr. Ringthaller sat behind the gurney and Kathy sat in front of it. Hitch turned back to Kathy who again looked away. He took a deep breath and sighed.

Elana squeezed his arm and whispered in his ear. "She'll be fine. You'll see."

The train hummed through miles of underground passages that made Hitch wonder. How long ago were they dug? How did the DanShebans managed to dig them without anyone knowing? One thing was for sure. These were people to reckon with.

Each turn to the left and right, and there were many, bolstered his confidence that they were on the right track. He laughed aloud at the unintended pun. Elana turned and smiled. She surely was beautiful, he thought. Hopefully she was just as smart when it came to the vaccine. That thought caused him to look back at his grandson and his daughter. She leaned over Christopher and combed her fingers through his hair. Hopefully Elana was right; Kathy would be fine, but only if her remaining son lived. He clinched his teeth and closed his eyes trying his best to sidestep his role in this genetic debacle.

Before long, they pulled into another large cellar similar to the previous one. Several DanShebans escorted them up the same type of portable stairs and into the back of a warehouse. From there two black men wearing black jackets with *East Bombay Fish Co* printed across their backs led them out of the warehouse and onto a dilapidated wharf. In the distance a flotilla of large VAMA warships could be seen at the East Bombay Wharf, and that image quickly deflated Hitch's confidence.

Chapter Thirty

The party boarded a large wooden barge with thickly varnished oak-paneled sides. It was built high off the water requiring everyone to navigate a half dozen ladder steps before reaching the deck, surrounded entirely by a three-foot-high wall. Here again Christopher had to be lifted up with the help of Hitch and several DanShebans. Once aboard, they were all directed to tables and chairs under a roof covered lounge with openings all around.

Within no time at all, they left Mumbai and headed east through the various inlets, creeks they were called. Before long the barge glided across the water under a moonlit sky into the underbelly of India, into the shadows of its jungle thicket, into a new chapter in the fight of Oliver Hitchcock's life. For several hours they meandered to the left and the right and the left again, taking different forks in the river as it snaked its way deeper into the heart of darkness.

Hitch stood at the bow, alone, gazing at the moon's reflection on the water and the constantly narrowing and widening shorelines on opposite sides. Beyond the frontage walls of moonlit green, he saw only snippets of the jungle's ever-present eyes peeking out of utter blackness.

"Our magic carpet to DanSheba," Meta declared as she stepped up to the railing beside him.

Hitch wondered about that. "What I don't get is how you've managed to keep DanSheba a secret. VAMA technology has…"

"Geography, my friend. You'll see. And thousands of years of practice. Secrecy is part of the DanSheban's DNA."

"At your house we talked about educated DanShebans throughout the world constantly in touch with your not so little village of high technology."

"Too crazy for you to believe?"

"So crazy I couldn't tell Barnaby."

Meta shrugged, as if she understood. "So Julian is a Tarsusian?"

"Is? Was, that's for sure."

"But he is our spy? Yes?"

Hitch hesitated. He knew the answer to that question but was having trouble making sense of it, and more trouble spitting it off his tongue. "Yeah, but why deliver Elana?"

Meta stared back without an answer, then turned away from Hitch and headed for the stern. "You're the expert."

Much later, as the group sat in the covered lounge watching the partially clouded sky, now moonless but sparkling with other heavenly bodies, one of the DanShebans began dropping down thick transparent plastic sheets from the roof. "In a few minutes you will see why we have done this," he explained with a smile that said he could not wait for his guests to see what was about to happen. "Please, hold tight to your seats. We will be making a very sharp turn to the right momentarily."

Sure enough, a few minutes later, as they

experienced serious turbulence, the barge started into a sharp right turn. To everyone's surprise they headed directly into a gigantic waterfall at least six stories high. By then, Christopher was sitting up on his gurney and *hooting* loud enough to be heard over the thunder of crashing whitewater. They continued straight ahead through one edge of its majestic curtain. The mist was so thick, the sound so deafening, Hitch could hardly see the others or hear his own thoughts of amazement. Once they passed through the backside of the waterfall, the churning river turned to glass, the roar to silence, and the mist to seemingly crisp dry air. They moved smoothly into a cavern void of light other than what came from the barge. For the next hour or so, they talked quietly across an immense seemingly shoreless lake before exiting into a narrow river imprisoned on both sides by walls of jungle thicket a hundred shades of green made visible by the rising sun.

****

Rousseau couldn't get to Mumbai fast enough. At Rosewall's insistence, she brought the Blue Cube, ever fearful that it would be discovered by authorities more powerful than the general. She reached her hotel near the East Bombay Wharf in Mumbai, hid the Blue Cube as best she could, and then took a taxi to the wharf. The entire area had turned into a multi-ring circus, actually more like a citywide festival of competing interests. Hordes of people assaulted the streets, restaurants, and shops—onlookers, the media running around with cameras and microphones, and angry demonstrators from both sides. Many of the signs read *Down with the Cūtocracy*; others, *Atheist America—Burn in Hell*; and still others *Only a Clock should Click.*

She had never seen so many VAMA agents blanketing the area. They patrolled the streets, poked in and out of the shops, and monopolized the water. A dozen battle-ready riverboats serving as battleships and carriers for helicopters overwhelmed the wharf with their flags waving in the breeze; VAMA India, VAMA Neuropa, VAMA China, and others. Why were they there? Where were they going? She knew the answers but still could not wrap her arms around DanSheba. Certainly they weren't all needed to flatten a schoolyard filled with dissidents.

As she wrestled with all that, her scud *rang*. It was Rosewall.

"Are you there?"

"See for yourself." She clicked her scud into view mode and scanned the area with it.

"Good. Just stay alert. I have a meeting with McGivney in a little while and will learn more. He's been somewhat secretive. Not sure what's up but just be ready. And one other thing. I want you to get into that Jewish School of Learning before we blow it to hell. One of my sources at the Vatican told me they didn't believe Hitchcock and his people were still there."

"Impossible! Half of VAMA has to be here and they must have the entire school surrounded. It would have taken a resurrection for Hitchcock to get out."

"Well I doubt that God's on their side so let's assume they're still there."

"And this Spanish Armada that I'm looking at, do we know where in the hell they're going?" Rousseau asked.

"I can only guess. McGivney is pulling the strings at the UN. Hopefully I'll know more soon."

****

Two DanShebans guarded Julian Iscar in a cabin below deck the entire time they were afloat, and Hitchcock hadn't talked to him since they entered the gate at the School of Learning. At the moment, he sat with Meta in a cabin across the hall but could see Julian's back.

"Oliver?" Meta said as she nodded toward Julian, but Hitch ignored her.

"These Ethiopian Diamond Mines that DanSheba owns, they fund everything?"

"More than enough and have forever. What about Julian?"

"And there are DanShebans secretly living everywhere in the world shipping in new technology."

"Yes, and books. But we've already discussed much of that. Don't change the subject."

"Yeah. It's time I talk with my good friend." He put it off long enough, he knew, but had difficulty all day reconciling Julian's role in the entire affair. More perplexing was the fact that all the years they stood back to back in the most life-threatening situations, Julian never showed the least bit interest in God or any other spiritual enlightenment. Apparently, that was the way of Tarsusians.

He stepped across the hall and called out to Julian to join him. Julian and his two guards rose from the table. Hitch motioned to the guards to stay put, then nodded to Julian, who still wore the loose fitting clothes of his Indian disguise and fake arm. They confronted one another above the barge's wake, and Meta joined them seconds later.

"This is how you treat your friends? Jesus, I'd hate

to be your enemy," Hitch said without flinching.

"What?" Julian actually seemed surprised by Hitch's comment.

"Your buddy who saved you from bleeding to death in the desert. That would be me."

"Oliver…"

"I trusted you. A Tarsusian, no less."

"You want to bring down the Church."

"Bring down the Church? No, I want to save my grandson."

"It's always about you, Oliver. It's always been about you. You are the most narcissistic son of a bitch I…"

"It's the president of the United States who wants to bring down your fucking church, and for good reason, you bastard."

Julian reached up into the sleeve of his fake arm and stepped back from Hitch. The arm fell to the deck. His good hand came out gripping a small laser pistol. He pointed it at Hitch. "I won't allow it, my sacrilegious friend. Neither you nor your president will destroy us on such fallacious grounds. The Click is the work of God."

Hitch could not believe what he heard from someone with such high intellect. "Julian. The bastards have been lying their asses off. The Cūtocracy is a fraud. It's over."

Meta stepped between them. "We have proof."

"Proof! Ha! We took it from your safe. The document is a forgery. The so-called Smotecal Decretum. You can dip a pig in gold and it is still a smelly pig. Our experts…"

Meta laughed. "Fool! Do you think I would be

stupid enough to keep the original at home? We DanShebans are masters at forgery. Your president has the original, fingerprints and all, and she is ready to tell the world."

Julian, still gripping his laser gun, stared at her. "Tell the world what?"

"The truth. That the Click is manmade. That a deal was struck years ago between your Supreme Minister Innocent II and the Cūtocracy."

"Your high and mighty church knew what was going on all along," Hitch added.

"It watched the Cutocracy delay the vaccine until the Click was ready, causing millions of human beings to die in the meantime."

Julian began to shake. Hitch had never seen him look so conflicted. "No!" His head darted back and forth, first to Hitch, then Meta, and back again. He searched their eyes for a sign of the truth, then stepped back against the railing. He looked up for an answer.

As if God Almighty gave him his orders, he swung his pistol around and aimed it at the man who saved his life and fired. *Zing.* Meta jumped in front of Hitch and took it in the arm. Hitch lunged toward Julian and took him down. They wrestled for the pistol. *Zing.* Julian went limp in Hitch's arms.

Hitch was now conflicted. They were friends, comrades in the trenches. He had saved Julian's life and he knew well one doesn't take the life of a person he once saved. He gently set Julian down. "I'm sorry my friend, but on Edna's grave, they lied to you and the rest of the world. On my wife's grave I swear it."

"Edna's grave?" Julian gasped for air. He reached up and pulled Hitch down. "You need to know about

Elana. *She…*" A last gasp and Julian died as Meta stood over them holding her arm.

Hours later, in the middle of the night, after making sure Meta's arm was cleaned and bandaged, Hitch stood alone at the bow of the barge and peered out into the lightless future. He would make sure his friend was properly buried. As he wondered exactly what that entailed for a man of his extreme faith, he heard someone whispering out his name. He pivoted and smiled. Elana approached.

"If it weren't for Julian," she said taking his hand in hers.

"I know, but it wasn't exactly a benevolent act, at least not toward you."

He turned away from her. His gaze focused down, into the wake of the hull as it glided through the dark water. She moved close to his side. Their bodies brushed up against one another.

"Then why?" she asked.

"He really believed he was doing the work of God. Just the thought that his Church or even the Cūtocracy would betray God, he couldn't handle that."

"But he betrayed you. He was CIA and your friend."

"Friend? Maybe, maybe not. CIA. Tarsusian. Cūtocrat. Librarian for sure. What the hell else was he?" Hitch gripped the railing so tight he couldn't help but notice the pain across his knuckles. One of her hands covered his, warm, soft. He felt the other touch his thigh. He turned to her. She kissed him. He kissed back with such passion he felt dizzy. Their bodies came together; his groin pressed against hers. With their tongues clinched, his hand slipped under her blouse, up and down her braless back, into her bare buttocks. Her breathing became heavy.

"Shanghai women don't wear anything under…"

"In the rush when I changed, it seems I forgot."

Hitch moved her to the raised side of the hull and lifted her skirt. She unzipped him, then wrapped her legs around his thighs. As the barge skimmed across still water, Elana's muffled moans were swallowed up by the jungle's rhythmic heartbeats.

In the morning, everyone gathered on deck and were welcomed with coffee and rolls. They gazed ahead as the barge navigated the narrow river and multiple forks until a wharf with throngs of black people in colorful outfits burst into view. Reds and oranges, blues and greens, and yellows swirled among the crowd. Some waved bright purple handkerchiefs, others clapped. Meta nudged Hitch and pointed to a hill abutting a glassy multicolored mountain wall that reflected the sunrise. Hitch could hardly see beyond the wharf. It was as if the village itself had disappeared.

"Like you said, geography."

"And blackout shades at sunset come down automatically."

All of a sudden, something occurred to him. "Meta, Nagasi had a V-Mark."

"You mean like this?" She pulled up the sleeve of her good arm. The other arm was wrapped within a sling. "A tattoo so good even VAMA can't tell the difference."

Hitch was about to respond, clearly impressed, but just then spied his daughter tremble as she watched Dr. Ringthaller bend over Christopher with his stethoscope.

Meta reached over and gripped Hitch's shoulder.

"We dock in minutes. He'll be taken directly to the hospital, a hospital like you've never seen. I promise."

Hitch took a deep breath, held it for a moment, and let it out. He turned back to Meta and was about to respond when he heard Kathy call out to him. She was in tears.

"He's asking for you, Dad."

He rushed over only to see how pale his grandson was. Christopher opened his eyes. "Grandpa?"

"I'm right here."

"Grandpa, I…I don't want to die like OJ."

"We're here in DanSheba so don't you worry. Just be tough. That's important."

"Why?"

"Because you're a Hitchcock. You're…"

"No, I mean why me?"

Before Hitch could respond, the barge bumped against the wharf and a number of DanShebans rushed aboard to help dock it. At the same time, they carried Christopher away on his gurney down to the wharf. Kathy froze as she watched him go. She stepped closer to her father and whispered in his ear. "He's going to die in this jungle. I know it."

Before Hitch could even react, she was gone, following after her son. He stared after them for several moments, then at all the villagers crowded around the wharf. His eyes drifted to the highly polished mountain up the hill, the river that disappeared upstream and downstream, and the impenetrable jungle across the river. Jesus, he thought. She's right.

****

Rousseau went from the East Bombay Wharf to the Jewish School of Learning. She naively thought she could waltz right onto the grounds and cut Hitchcock's throat. The gate was chained shut and VAMA had it surrounded. When she attempted to climb the wall with the help of an old man's stool, one of the guards came running and grabbed her by the ankle. The stool toppled over, and she fell to the ground. Her instincts took over as one leg, then the other slammed into the guard's groin. By then, several other guards were on top of her.

"Get off my ass, you fuckers," Rousseau hollered. "Do you know who in the fuck I am?" She jumped up, pissed as hell, and showed them her credentials.

"Orders from above. No one comes or goes, ma'am," one of the guards insisted.

Upon returning to the East Bombay Wharf, still pissed at being treated like a private, she received a call from Rosewall. He instructed her to return to her hotel. McGivney was insisting on a conference call amongst the three of them. Getting to the hotel was as difficult as getting to the wharf in the first place, in fact more so. More cars, more people, more protesters. Something big was happening.

Shortly after reaching her room, Rousseau had both McGivney and Rosewall on her scud in split screen mode. Rosewall instructed her to set up the Blue Cube. She hesitated until the Minister assured her he knew all about it. In fact, he had a similar one operating in his office at that very moment.

Before long, she stood beyond her own huge HS-Screen. After some instruction from McGivney, she saw a protolyte view of India with a cross-hair pulsating over the jungle.

"Is that what I think it is?" she asked, astonished, baffled in fact. She heard McGivney hoot with gloating happiness.

"I told you both to have faith."

"I've had enough faith to last a lifetime," the general responded. "Now that I know it's real, I plan to blow that shitty village to bits."

"Just a bit longer, Rosewall. It would be better if we had the entire UN fleet on our side. In the meantime, I want you there to lead the charge."

****

By the time Hitch climbed down from the barge, Christopher and Kathy had disappeared. He hurried up the hill to the village square and past the tall flagless pole toward what clearly had to be the hospital, a one-story red brick building that seemed simple enough. He wasn't sure what Meta had been bragging about, until he arrived. Equipment everywhere, labs, offices, patient rooms seemingly placed everywhere at random. Research scientists and doctors, all DanShebans, filled those rooms. Several huddled with Elana and Barnaby when Hitch finally found them at the end of a narrow hall.

Meta stood by herself talking on her scud.

Hitch looked around for Kathy and wondered where Christopher had been taken. He started toward the huddled group when he heard Meta call out.

"Oliver, wait."

Hitch stopped and approached her as she clicked off.

"That was Yennie. The president says VAMA has our location. They're coming, the entire UN fleet, unless she can stop them."

"What? We searched Julian. He had no tracker."

Meta glanced over at Elana.

"Oh, Christ. The bastard planted a… Jesus, am I a dumb shit." Hitch wheeled around in Elana's direction.

Meta grabbed his arm. "Leave it. She doesn't have to know. We always knew the risk was there. Now, we must work that much faster."

"What else did your man Yennie say?"

"They hear the UN will invade DanSheba to vaccinate the population. But the president fears the Cūtocracy won't settle for that, and…"

"And…"

"And we have to prove scientifically the Click is a fraud before the president will expose the Smotecal Decretum and be able to convince the UN to turn back. Only independently validated proof will stop them."

Is that all, Hitch thought? No it was not all. They also had to make an antidote or Christopher would…

Chapter Thirty-One

The entire village, men, women, and children, dug ditches and built barricades under Hitch's direction. He was in his element and actually enjoying it, temporarily oblivious to the fact that Christopher was deteriorating rapidly at that moment. He would learn soon enough. In the meantime, he and the others watched an Indian helicopter and two from Israel land within the shadows of the mountain. According to Meta, the White House had leaned heavily on India's prime minister. As for as the Israeli helicopters were concerned, apparently no leaning was necessary. Many DanShebans secretly lived in Israel, as they did in most other areas of the world, but in Israel many of them occupied high positions in government and in the military.

While Hitch watched the Indian and Israeli troops unload weapons, he continued to dig trenches alongside the villagers. As he explained where to dig next, his scud *rang*. It was Barnaby. He had just left Christopher and Kathy and thought Oliver should get to the hospital right away.

With his shovel gripped in one hand, Hitch raced up the hill toward the square, trying to keep up with his beating heart. He passed dozens of DanShebans lined up in front of the hospital waiting to donate blood. As soon as he entered, Barnaby grabbed hold of his arm and led him into a large futuristic scientific lab where he and Elana were working with vials of blood and fancy equipment.

"Oliver, before you see them, you should know that Christopher is failing fast. The Clicks are increasing in both intensity and speed and Kathy's state of mind is hyperventilating at the same pace. You need to calm her down."

"Calm her down?" Hitch dropped the shovel. He was having trouble processing the words.

"And tell her we are still hopeful," Elana added. "No, tell her we will get him the antidote."

Hitch merely nodded then practically flew down the hall. Christopher was in the room on the right, and Kathy was standing vigil outside the opened door, biting her nails with chattering teeth. As he rushed over to her, she quickly shut the door behind her.

"No, I won't let you see him. We wouldn't be in this…this place if it weren't for… Damn it, Dad." She clutched on to him and bawled. "He's going to die just like OJ. He's going to…"

Hitch held her tight and whispered in her ear. "No, he's not. As God is my…"

She broke away and stepped back with pain oozing from her eyes. "You don't believe in God. How dare you." She left him standing there as she marched back into her son's room and slammed the door behind her.

For a moment he froze, then followed her in. The oxygen, the IV tubes, the monitors hit him even harder than the verbal slap across the face he had just received.

****

Yennie Tawahada sat in his office waiting to talk to Dillon Burber about scheduling a meeting between the Ecclesian ambassador to the United States and

President Wainwright. The president planned to show the ambassador the Smotecal Decretum before going public in hopes of thwarting an all-out invasion of DanSheba, but first she needed to know as a matter of fact that the Click was a fraud.

About the time he looked up at the clock wondering where Dillon was, he received a text message on his scud. Dillon was going to be late. The television had been on but muted all the time Yennie waited for his boss. What he observed was one pro-Cūtocracy march after another in Rome, Beijing, London, and right there in Washington, DC. He paid little attention to the orchestrated show of support until UN Secretary General Heinrich Flum of Germany filled the entire screen. Yennie knew him as a devout Ecclesian who managed somehow to stay loyal to both the Church and the Cūtocracy.

Yennie unmuted the TV and listened to the Secretary General blab about how the disillusioned left was attempting to destroy their beloved institutions using all types of baseless allegations. The member nations were united, he insisted, and ready to march into DanSheba and inoculate the heathens. He went on to describe what he claimed was a real-time buildup in troops on the east coast of Mumbai and then displayed camera shots from there. It surely looked to Yennie like a major invasion was eminent.

That was enough for one day. He turned the TV off altogether and began to think. At that moment he would have preferred more than anything else to be in DanSheba with his family and friends, with Meta and the others. Just as that yearning seemed to build, Dillon strolled in as if he had all the time in the world, as if the world weren't coming to an end.

"We're still waiting to hear from his Eminence, the ambassador, I'm afraid," Dillon said sarcastically. "Have we got the verification team lined up?"

"Yes, believe it or not. My contact at the UN told me they have selected three so-called experts that were blessed by the Secretary General himself, secretly."

"Do we know anything about them?"

"A young woman from Boston, no doubt tied to the Church there. From what I've been told she's about the same age as Elana Wu and may in fact know her. I'm not sure if that's good or bad. The second expert is from Frankfurt, in his late sixties, quite possibly a friend of Herr Flum, and that surely isn't good."

"And the third member?"

"The most problematic one if I had to guess. A Chinese man, also around Elana Wu's age, said to be brilliant, and highly conservative religiously, whatever that means in China."

Dillon shrugged. "Let's hope it all works out, and tell your people it has to be unanimous." He disappeared before Yennie could process that last comment or ask him anything else about the meeting with the ambassador.

****

General Rosewall arrived in Mumbai and convened a meeting in Rousseau's hotel room. He brought with him two of his trusted lieutenants, Grozier and Reebert, both younger than Rousseau and both highly unappealing. The four of them sat around the table in her suite. Grozier, sporting a beard without a mustache and dangling earrings in both ears, constantly chewed enough gum to glue an elephant to the floor. Reebert, who was cross-eyed and clearly didn't realize his fly was down, started to relight up a black-market cigar butt. That's when Rousseau put her foot down.

"You want to smoke that fucking phallus hang yourself out the balcony. And for Christ's sake zip up your fly. What you want to show off is probably smaller than your cigar butt."

"Enough," Rosewall snapped. "We have work to do."

He then proceeded to describe how they, a small band of carefully selected warriors, were to take a battle-ready barge and a small flatbed carrier to DanSheba in order to preempt McGivney and the UN. Grozier stopped chewing long enough to ask whether they had anyone inside in DanSheba. Rosewall nodded toward Rousseau, who smiled.

Chapter Thirty-Two

The Rose Garden cottage, where everything that was spiritual in DanSheba took place, sat up the hill at the foot of the mountain. It was surrounded by a fence so thick with red, white, and yellow roses one had to pass through the gate to see the front door. The cottage itself, constructed of shiny stone chipped away from the mountainside, seemed to pop out of a fairytale. Meta remembered thinking that when she saw it the first time she arrived in DanSheba with her mother. On Friday nights the cottage and backyard filled up with villagers who wanted to light Shabbat candles together. How she always loved the Rose Garden cottage, Meta said to herself as she and Oliver Hitchcock walked up the hill toward the large crowd gathering out front.

"How are they doing?" Meta asked.

"Christopher's in a coma but Elana says that's good. It slows down the progression." Hitch shrugged.

"And Kathy?"

"Ringthaller gave her a sedative and she's sleeping, finally."

"In that case, why don't you take a deep breath and relax. I think you need it. Hopefully your president will disclose the Smotecal Decretum to the world, DanSheba will live to see another day, and Christopher will grow older than we all could have imagined."

Hitch shrugged again. Then he stopped and looked

at Meta. "But how does this Decretum thing fit into the Click? I never did understand that from what you gave me."

"It both condemns and exonerates the Ecclesian Church. Once the Cūtocracy understood how bad the ERAM plague was, it spent months creating and producing a vaccine. As the plague intensified, Smotec Innocent urged the Cūtocracy to dispense the vaccine they had stored up—thanks in large part to my great, great granduncle Jonathan. The Cūtocracy wanted to wait until the Click was ready so they could incorporate it into the vaccine, apparently months and millions of deaths later. A vote by the Council was taken and everyone except Innocent's representative voted to wait. Innocent's Decretum instructed him to vote *No*, to dispense the Clickless serum immediately."

"So the Church was against geriatric euthanasia. How does that condemn it?"

Meta stopped, picked up a wildflower and smelled it, then turned back to Oliver. "Because Innocent knew about the Click from the beginning and the Cūtocracy's plan to delay the Clickless vaccine until they could incorporate the time bomb, knowing that millions would die needlessly. He and the Church chose to keep everything secret in the name of population control, and to weaken the arguments for birth control. After so many people died in the ERAM plague, the church needed more babies to shore up its following and the Cūtocracy needed to make sure the church coffers overflowed."

"And these Tarsusian extremists like Julian, were, are still part of the Church?"

Meta blew the petals from the wildflower as she

walked on toward the crowd waiting at the cottage, and Hitch followed her lead. "Yes, but apparently they were not aware of the conspiracy of silence between the Church and the Cūtocracy and tolerated the Cūtocrats only because they believed the Click was truly the work of God."

As they approached the cottage, a DanSheban videographer greeted them. "We're ready to go, if you are," she said to Meta.

Meta nodded then turned to Oliver. "In the end, because of your president the world will know the truth. And with God's help, ironically, both the Cūtocracy and the Church will be expunged from the Earth along with the Click."

Hitch stood there speechless. Meta recognized the look. He hadn't expected such vitriol. He'll get over it, she thought. After all he hasn't lived nearly as long as she knowing what the Church perpetuated in the name of their extreme dogma. With that, she allowed the videographer to escort her to the camera set up in front of the cottage and took a deep breath, taking in the mixed aroma of all the roses of different colors—reds and whites and yellows.

****

Rouseau watched Rosewall guide one of the barges and a small carrier from East Mumbai into the jungle thicket. They were going to survey the area he told the other fleet commanders. Once they were far enough away he had Rousseau turn on her Blue Cube, and the HS-Screen appeared. She was caught off guard when she realized that Elana Wu was no longer transmitting. "Damn. She probably flushed the bug down the toilet."

Rosewall laughed as he stepped up to the Blue

Cube and tapped away. "Not a problem. It automatically saved her location."

Sure enough, a dot over DanSheba began pulsating. They plugged that information into the navigation system on the carrier and it did all the work, that is, until it steered them into turbulent waters toward a magnificent waterfall.

"Holy shit!" Rousseau stood at the bow and gawked at God's creation in front of her.

Rosewall stood next to her and growled out orders into his ship phone to stop. He and Rousseau then ran below deck and gathered around a navigation screen with members of his crew.

"If we're going to get to DanSheba without circling around all of India we have to go through the falls," one of the crewmembers said. "According to this, it's hiding the entrance to a cavern of sorts which leads out here." He pointed to the river on the other side of the mountain.

After they double- and triple-checked that conclusion, Rosewall gave the orders to plunge through the center of the falls since they weren't sure how wide the opening was. First, they had to tie down and waterproof everything on deck that couldn't be carried below. That took them several hours.

Finally, they made the plunge and swiftly found themselves on the other side, in a cavern and water as calm as the waterfall was turbulent. By the time the sun set, they approached the DanSheban wharf and made no attempt to hide that fact. Twenty minutes later, Rousseau found herself looking down on the village from her seat in a VAMA helicopter chuckling. "This has to be a joke," she radioed back to Rosewall, then scurried over all parts of the village to make sure she was seen. She hoped that Hitchcock would get a glimpse of her. While she fondled the controls of a pair of stingray laser guns on opposite sides of the helicopter as if they were Oliver's private parts, she also hoped her bravado would wake up the Israelis. No such luck. Their fleet was sound asleep on a makeshift landing pad.

She returned to the carrier, jumped out, and strolled to Rosewall who stood on deck talking on his scud. As she approached, Rosewall turned it to speaker mode.

"It's smaller than a gnat's ass. We can level it in ten minutes," Rousseau insisted.

"No. Not until I say. The U.S. president has a meeting scheduled at the Ecclesian Embassy. Let her make a fool of herself, then I'll give you the go-ahead," High Minister McGivney demanded.

Rosewall clicked off and turned to Rousseau. "We'll see," he said as both gazed out into a void of blackness, in the direction of DanSheba. Not a flicker of light from the village could be seen, or from where Rousseau was sure the Israeli and Indian troops, and Hitchcock, stared back.

She had to laugh to herself. McGivney didn't seem surprised at all that they stole off to DanSheba and yet said he was. Something told her that she and Rosewall were doing his bidding whether they knew it or not. Christ! The fucking games that people play!

Chapter Thirty-Three

Hitch, Elana, Barnaby, and Meta sat together in front of an oversized hologram screen projecting up from a computation shell in the hospital conference room directly across from Christopher's room. Hitch purposely placed himself in clear view of his grandson's bed. Kathy sat next to Christopher, and Dr. Ringthaller seemed to come and go.

A conference with President Wainwright and Yennie, both in the Oval Office, was in progress. At that moment the president spoke directly to Hitch, who knew her quite well from her early days as head of the NSA before her reign as Governor of Florida.

"I have to admit, Oliver, I always worried someday you might start a world war."

"Now, Madam President, back then we were coconspirators most of the time. This time around you're the Queen Bee of this hornets' nest."

"Maybe so. But you need to know that this Queen Bee is looking at twenty-four, maybe forty-eight hours, before she has no control over the soldier bees that will swarm over DanSheba faster than you can open a jar of honey."

"Not much of a window. And let's hope that the VAMA contingency sitting within rock throwing distance from the wharf here in DanSheba doesn't go rogue. In the meantime, you better talk with Elana, Dr.

Wu," Hitch said. He moved to the next chair, allowing Elana to take his seat."

"Now then, Dr. Wu, the UN is flying in a team of experts to verify your results. It must be unanimous. Do you understand?"

"Yes, unanimous. I welcome their input, Madam President."

"How confident are you that the Click is in fact part of the ERAM-V vaccine? More important, can you prove it within the time frame you have?"

Elana hesitated and looked over at Barnaby, who gave her a questioning expression and then a nod. "I am one hundred percent confident. We will prove it. I would stake my life on it."

"Well, it may be your life and everyone there if you don't. Not only will DanSheba be invaded, but I will not go public with the Smotecal Decretum."

With that overt threat, the Oval Office closed communication. Elana glanced over at the other three in the room and insisted they follow her into the hall around the corner from Christopher's room. At the same time, Hitch noticed Dr. Ringthaller step into the hall but gave that little thought at the time.

As soon as Hitch, Meta, and Barnaby huddled around Elana, she started to speak but struggled to get the words out.

"What?" Hitch asked.

"I just lied to the president," she said, causing Meta to flinch.

"Lied? What do you…"

"We need the real thing. The synthetic version will work with unvaccinated blood to make a Click-free vaccine but will not prove the Click is part of the

ERAM vaccine. I was sure it would work but it doesn't."

Elana's pronouncement was lost on Hitch. "What do you mean the real thing? What the hell is she talking about, Barnaby?"

"She means the virus itself."

Elana was adamant. "Without the actual virus we can't prove a thing. We need it to infect some poor guinea pigs before we vaccinate them."

"Unless we find a carrier," Barnaby added.

"Of what?" Meta asked.

"Of the plague," Elana answered. "Someone who carries it but was not infected. But even if there are people like that, they would never know it. Besides, we don't have the time to find such a person and then extract the virus."

It was as if she dropped a bomb that exploded at Hitch's feet and blew him back to Ralph Delahunt's office. "Two Preemies in one family does not appear to be coincidental," Ralph said. "Are you saying it's because of…" Edna started to say but never finished her question. Hitch finished it. "Because I'm a carrier, carrier, carrier."

Hitch turned away from Elana, Meta, and Barnaby. He was the reason Christopher was dying. He was the reason OJ died. He was, was, was, was…

He heard Meta between the self-incriminating voices he knew so well. She asked if he was all right.

All right! No, damn it, I'm all wrong, he wanted to scream.

"I'm a carrier," he finally declared. He went weak at the knees but held himself up. Out of the corner of his eye he saw Christopher's doctor, Ringthaller, run down the hall and out of the hospital, but again didn't give that a thought.

An hour or so later, Hitch stood with Elana, Barnaby, and Kathy in Elana's lab staring at vials of blood. Elana and Barnaby explained exactly how they planned to extract the ERAM virus from his body. They were not talking about a normal blood donation. Elana made it clear that it was more akin to a chemically induced bilateral transfusion that sometimes causes the body's DNA to creep up or down its chain. That caused both Hitch and Kathy to recoil.

"We will inject you with a substance that isolates the virus without harming…" Elana started to explain but Barnaby interrupted.

"Enough! We will monitor all your critical organs, I promise, but we must move on."

"He needs to know the risk," Elana snapped. For a moment the room went silent, as if Barnaby didn't want to say what the risk was, as if Kathy didn't want to know. But Hitch wanted to know.

Elana finally spoke up. "It could trigger the onset of the Click."

"Jesus!" That wasn't something Hitch had expected. "What are the odds?"

"There's a twenty-five percent chance…"

"A pretty good bet then," Hitch said.

"That the Click won't trigger, but of course most of this is speculation since there's really no data to support any real prediction."

"There's something else," Barnaby said, almost in a whisper. "We suspect you may have a rare DNA mutation that somehow coupled itself with the virus you carry. Probably helped make you a Beater and pass it on. For sure it explains why you look decades younger than your actual age, and that could…"

"Kill me."

This time Elana recoiled. Hitch turned to her. "So, the odds of living through this at all are stacked against me. But if I make it, what? I'll look like I'm your grandfather?"

That was enough. Elana put a stop to the discussion. Hitch could only imagine how somber he looked. Elana reached for his hand. He sighed. Elana and Barnaby shared a look of concern. Kathy turned away from them, edged to the window.

"My God!"

Hitch walked out leaving all three to wallow in the wake of all the dire possibilities. He wasn't going to show weakness. He was after all Oliver Hitchcock, a Beater, a man with a body and mind of a much younger man. He kept repeating that as he marched down the hall, passing lab workers who greeted him kindly. He acknowledged them with a nod but his eyes never wavered from a blank straight-ahead stare.

He entered the restroom, where he was greeted by lines of white porcelain sinks under one continuous mirror and immediately lost his bravado. A DanSheban around sixty in a lab coat was washing his hands. Hitch slinked away to the furthest sink and bent over to grip the porcelain, as if its cold surface would somehow chill the anxiety that held captive all the muscles in his body.

The DanSheban looked over. "Are you okay, Mr. Hitchcock?"

Hitch started to nod when Kathy burst through the door.

"Dad?" She gestured for the DanSheban to go, and he quickly complied.

Hitch remained at the sink trying to ignore her. She approached and stood next to him. From the corner of one eye he could see her gaze fixed on his image in the mirror.

"My God! You're not going through with it!"

She might as well have been speaking in a language he was only slightly familiar with. He understood the tone of her accusations but couldn't quite process the words.

"I'm… I don't know…"

He felt her swing him around. *Slap*, across the face. He heard it. He saw it. But at that moment he felt nothing.

"How can you even look at yourself?"

Again, he couldn't process the accusation and didn't respond, causing her to stomp toward the door. She stopped and turned. "The invincible CIA spy and lady's man, adulterer I might add, too damn scared to save his daughter's son."

"And my grandson."

"By default, and that's the truth."

He turned away hoping she would leave, hoping he could be alone, wishing he was on another planet.

"I knew you were a carrier. Ralph Delahunt told me. So what?"

"So what! So what! First OJ, now Christopher." Hitch could hardly process those two words. He turned back to his daughter. "You have no idea what it's like to know."

"Well, you have the chance to make things right. If not for us, for Mother." Before that admonition had a chance to cut through him, she was gone.

Hitch turned back to the sink and focused hard on the man in the mirror.

Chapter Thirty-Four

Rousseau paced around the hologram projecting from her scud as Rosewall watched from a desk on the deck. Ringthaller stood within the hologram and scanned the area outside the hospital as if to make sure he wasn't being seen. "If I were that kind of a doctor, maybe I'd know. They need a carrier to make it work. He's it. That's all I do know."

"Just keep low and stay available. I expect you will be earning all that dough you demanded." Rousseau clicked off as she looked back at Rosewall. "So? Now what?"

"To hell with McGivney and his orders to wait. We have no choice. Eliminate Hitchcock. The United Nations will probably cave even if Wainwright proves nothing. We can't have that shithole in the jungle succeed. That is not an option. I have a reputation to maintain," Rosewall shouted, slamming his fist on the desk. "So, you have two choices. You stop them and Janine Rousseau becomes the new Director of VAMA International, or fail and…" He sneered.

"And what?"

"And you'll be back where I found you, on the streets of Paris. And that money laundering business of yours? It'll be history. I'm all you and your kid have left, I'm afraid."

Rousseau stiffened. She could feel her eyes harden.

****

Yennie stood in his office with Dillon Burber and President Wainwright in front of the TV as they watched Meta in the village square. *Recorded Earlier* flashed at the bottom of the screen.

"Hello. I'm Meta DeCarlo. Welcome to DanSheba. Allow me to give you a walking tour of this not so little village, this crown jewel created by God Almighty." She strolled through most of the village, pointing out the different landmarks that came into view.

She began at the rose garden cottage where a large group of DanShebans had gathered and then stood by the flagless pole in the town square. She explained how it had been built centuries earlier to receive the First Coming of the Messiah who was to talk to God right there, at that pole. To the present generation of DanShebans, including Yennie, it wasn't clear whether the Messiah actually came or was still coming. Most, especially the young DanShebans, looked upon the pole as a metaphor; the long arm of the village reaching up to the heavens declaring to God that they are the lost tribe of Israel. Declaring that they are the Chosen People according to the Old Testament, the true survivors according to a reasonable account of history's toll on human belief systems of the past.

Meta passed the only hotel and slowed down to explain that all those DanShebans who lived abroad had a very nice place to stay when they came back to visit. What she didn't say, Yennie knew, was that all DanShebans over twenty-one were urged to visit regularly and bring back with them needed supplies and the latest innovations.

By the time she finished the tour and returned to

the rose garden cottage and the crowd of DanShebans she had left earlier, Yennie beamed with pride. "My home," he announced.

President Wainwright smiled and held onto his arm with both her hands.

As the camera panned in on Meta and the group surrounding her, it became apparent that most of them, at least a hundred villagers, were octogenarians—if not in their nineties, or even older. One man stood out. Nagasi who smiled into the camera. Another man stepped forward and Meta introduced him.

"I would like everyone to meet Isaac Gardner. Isaac, please tell the audience how old you are."

"Today happens to be my birthday." Everyone *applauded*. "I am eighty-eight years young." More *applause*.

"Isaac, have you ever received the ERAM-V vaccine?"

"God forbid. Never! Or I wouldn't be here to tell about it."

Meta then turned to the crowd. "How many of you over seventy-five have not been vaccinated with the ERAM-V vaccine?"

Everyone in the crowd raised his or her hand.

"My Lord!" President Wainwright exclaimed and *clapped* her hands.

****

Rousseau stood on the bow of the barge this time, talking to Ringthaller on her scud. She saw a glimpse of him not far up the hill from the wharf. "I don't care if you have to use a butcher knife or a scalpel, Doctor. You grab the girl and take her to the wharf directly in front of you. And one other thing. I will be watching.

Later that night Rousseau, dressed in a wetsuit, took out the Blue Cube and a short time later she had Ringthaller practically floating within the greenish-blue haze of the HS-Screen. The volume was turned up and the infrared mode was operating. Scuba gear and a waterproof pouch sat on a table close by.

"Dis ting sure comes een andy," Oedipus said standing a short distance away. "Going to a masquerade ball?" He laughed.

Rousseau didn't. She remained focused on the doctor, who by now could barely be seen in the shadows of one of the buildings just off the town square. Then suddenly, Kathy Hitchcock came into view walking with someone else in the direction of Ringthaller. Rousseau frowned.

"No. I'm perfectly fine to walk back to the cottage alone. I'd rather you stay and keep an eye on Christopher and my father. Please. I was a bit rough on him I'm afraid." She took Barnaby by the shoulders and turned him around, then waited as he walked back to the hospital before she headed for the hotel. Rousseau couldn't help but smile.

As Kathy crossed into the shadows, Rousseau saw Ringthaller jump her from behind. A knife of some sort was at her throat.

A short time later, Rousseau connected up her scuba gear, tied the waterproof pouch to her waist, and moved swiftly through the murky water until she finally surfaced under the wharf. She removed her mask and whispered into a device on her wrist, then listened.

"The air cruiser at the far end. It's ready," Ringthaller said. His voice quivered like a child. Rousseau put her mask back on and cruised underneath the hulls of boat after boat until she reached the one she was looking for. She made her way to where its stern was tied to a post at the end of the wharf.

After surfacing, Ringthaller helped her on board. Kathy was already there, hogtied on the recessed hull, her mouth wrapped with medical gauze. Rousseau slipped off her gear, reached into her pouch, and offered Ringthaller a laser gun.

"I brought an extra. You'll need it," she told him.

Petrified, he shook her off. "I… No, not me. I don't…"

"I wasn't asking. Take it." Before he had a chance to respond, she shoved it into his ribcage. Rousseau then turned to Kathy and took a long look at her.

"You have your father's eyes."

Kathy stiffened and mumbled something inaudible. Rousseau scoffed and released the tether from the mooring. She used one arm as a paddle to maneuver the boat and sneak away from the dock. For a moment, the doctor just sat there until Rousseau demanded he give a hand, quite literally. Once they were far enough from shore, Rousseau moved to the bow and hot-wired the ignition. The boat's air-prop rotated without much of a sound and the hull elevated just above the surface. They whisked away down the river.

****

Hitchcock sat on the edge of his bed with his head in his hands. He felt Elana staring at him from the chair in the corner.

"I can't help you, Oliver."

Hitch knew she couldn't. There was no decision to be made. There were no options to choose from. He knew that, but his entire adult life had been predicated on a physical advantage he was blessed with. Even as early as junior high the boys his age were either in awe or scared of him, and the older girls flocked to him. How could he throw all that away?

Just then his scud *rang*. He looked at the clock on his nightstand, then at Elana. "It's Kathy." He clicked on.

"Dad, it's me. I'm…"

"Actually, it's me, Oliver."

Hitch punched his scud into visual mode. "Janine. What the…"

"No! I do the talking. You have thirty minutes to get to the VAMA carrier. Come alone and unarmed. And Kathy goes free. Otherwise…"

"You know I can't do that. I have Christopher…"

"Now, Oliver. Thirty minutes, and the clock is ticking."

She clicked off and Hitch stared at Elana. "Rousseau's kidnapped Kathy."

"What does she want?"

"Me."

"Oh my God! You can't go. You have to…"

"You don't have to tell me what's at stake."

"Not just Christopher, Oliver. We need you for the virus to prove…"

"I will be back with Kathy, I promise, and then I'm yours."

He rummaged through his things for a knife, then started for the door. Elana stepped into his path and they embraced, then kissed.

****

After she clicked off, Rousseau stuck her head out and found Oedipus standing outside her cabin. She ordered him in to keep watch on Kathy and on Ringthaller while she conducted a quick inspection. She found two VAMA guards pacing along the low-lying gunwales, port and starboard. Another stood ready at the stern near the helipad and Rousseau's helicopter. A female guard covered the bow. She warned each guard to be on the lookout for Hitchcock and bring him to her cabin unharmed.

Four were enough she thought. If they ran into a problem, which she doubted, there were many more troops asleep in their quarters.

She returned and ordered Oedipus to stand guard outside her door.

After making sure Kathy was tied to her chair, she wrapped the medical gauze around her mouth once again and tried to calm down the jittery doctor who mumbled under his breath in one corner. She then went back out and looked for Rosewall to settle him down. The general was heading her way.

"For your sake, this better work," he called out.

"My dear general, I know Oliver Hitchcock. He relishes any chance to be the hero. He'll show up." She then returned to her cabin, leaving both Rosewall and Oedipus just outside.

Rosewall approached Oedipus. "Look me in the eye and tell me you're satisfied working for that bitch."

Oedipus said nothing.

"Didn't think so," the general said and walked away. "Stay with me and I'll make it worth your while."

Rousseau shook her head as she listened with her ear cupped to the other side of the door.

****

It didn't take long for Hitch to find scuba gear. They had enough in DanSheba to outfit a swimming team. In no time, he was in the water heading for the carrier. Fifteen minutes later he found its submerged hull, portside. He removed his scuba gear, let it drop, then slid out a knife from a sheath on his belt and rose to the surface. He could hear two people above him talking.

"But, general, she told us to take Hitchcock to her cabin."

"To hell with Rousseau, private. Your orders are shoot to kill if you see him. Do you understand?"

"Yes, sir."

"And nobody in that cabin comes out alive, including Rousseau if need be. You have a problem with that, private?"

"No. I mean no, sir."

"Do this right, son, and you will be promoted. That's a promise."

Hitch heard enough. He headed aft along the gunwale. After reaching the stern he peeked up, looking for a guard. After several moves to the right and left, he was successful. Directly above him the barrel of a laser rifle came into view. Hitch made a small splash and quickly submerged. The guard above leaned over the edge, ready to fire. By that time, Hitch had jumped aboard and wrapped his arm around the guard's throat. In a single, swift motion, he hammered his free thumb into the young man's vagus nerve. The guard was rendered unconscious and lowered to the deck quietly. After taking the guard's handgun from his holster, he pulled his own knife from its sheath and headed starboard looking for another guard but kept a careful eye out for the general.

On his way, he heard the general's voice. Rosewall was telling a female guard to position herself in front of Rousseau's cabin and shoot to kill on sight. It seems I'm a popular guy, Hitch thought.

At first, Hitch couldn't find another guard. But suddenly there he was, a fat kid, sitting down as if he had nowhere else to be, nothing else to do. He leaned his rifle against the gunwale and as best as Hitch could tell began dozing. But then the fat kid pulled out a candy bar.

Hitch, now behind him, whispered, "That shit can kill you," then looked at his knife. *Christ! I can't do that.* As he made that decision, the guard turned toward him. Two quick raps to the temples just above the outer edges of the eyebrows, and the kid went quickly back to sleep.

Now he had to find the guard he first heard talking to the general. Just then came the rustle of foot steps behind him. With a quick turnaround, he let the knife fly. It cut through the belly of the first guard before the poor kid had time to pull the trigger. Hitch wasn't happy about killing someone so young. That wasn't his plan.

****

Rousseau sat directly in front of Kathy and looked her up and down. Kathy's glare as she was unable to respond made Rousseau laugh. "Not only do you have your father's eyes, I believe you have his defiant disposition."

Thump, thump, thump, rattled across the top of the cabin. Rousseau pulled out her gun. She stepped to one side of Kathy and shoved the barrel against her temple.

Oedipus, now in the room, stood behind the door with his gun raised upward.

****

Hitch rolled across the roof of Rousseau's cabin and spied the female guard standing firm, armed and ready, in front of her door. He threw a stone over her head. *Clink*. She turned. He lunged for her. She reacted in time to dodge his grasp. They hit the deck together. He jumped up ready to lunge again. She was out cold. He was relieved.

****

Rousseau recoiled when the commotion outside the cabin suddenly stopped, but she held steady with her gun aimed at Kathy's temple. Her eyes focused on the closed door. The doctor cowered in the corner. Oedipus took a position where he could see the door and Rousseau.

The door opened. No one entered.

Rousseau heard Hitch's voice. "Let her go."

"We need to talk. Come inside," she demanded.

"Suicide's not my thing, Janine."

Rousseau ripped off the gauze from Kathy's mouth, pressed the gun barrel hard against her temple, and suggested she call out to her father.

"Dad."

"See, Oliver. She's fine. I gave strict orders. Neither of you are to be harmed."

"Got news for you. Rosewall has other ideas."

"Dad, please."

With his laser gun in one hand and the knife in the other, Hitch stepped inside and swung his laser gun at Oedipus's head. Oedipus returned the favor. Each stared at the other, both ready to shoot.

"Oedipus! Back off," Rousseau shouted.

Oedipus hesitated, but she knew him well. She watched his gaze dart back and forth between her and Hitchcock. Oedipus lowered his gun a bit. Oliver stepped toward her and Kathy. Rousseau caught Oedipus's eye and knew. As he raised his gun, she jumped in front of Oliver. *Zing*. She took the hit and fired back before she fell. *Zing. Zing.* Oedipus fell to the floor. Rousseau fell into Hitch's arms.

****

Rosewall was at the stern looking across the river at DanSheba, anxious to invade. Fuck McGivney and those meddlesome Ecclesians. Now was the time, he was sure. As Rosewall was about to make the final decision, he heard foot steps behind him and turned quickly. It was his female guard holding her head.

"The others are dead or unconscious, I'm not sure which," she yelled. "Hitchcock is in Rousseau's cabin. There was shooting inside."

"Sound the alarm, for Christ's sake," he yelled back and raced to the weapons room.

****

Hitch laid Rousseau down. Her eyes opened. For him it was as if they were alone, if only for a minute. All the good times raced through his thoughts, including the time he thought he would leave Edna for her. She coaxed him to reach in her pocket and pull out a set of keys.

"Take them," Rousseau whispered. "In my safe, a letter." Her eyes closed.

Ringthaller, who had remained in the corner the entire time, jumped up and untied Kathy. All the time, Hitch merely stared at the keys in his hand. Suddenly he heard an *alarm* on deck.

Hitch grabbed Kathy and Rousseau's rifle. They started for the door as Ringthaller slinked back into the corner. Once outside the cabin, he looked for Rousseau's helicopter. He pointed to it, making sure Kathy knew where they were going. While Rosewall's troops stormed onto the deck, they raced for the helipad. All the time Hitch had the rifle on automatic mode. *Zing, zing, zing.* By the time the troops knew what was happening, Htich and Kathy were at the helicopter. Hitch pushed Kathy up. Just as he began hearing return fire, he had the bird well above the carrier. He glanced back down and caught Rosewall racing toward him with rifles in both hands. *Zing, zing.*

Hitch wound around and swooped back down, took aim and *zing*, he caught the general between the eyes. *Whoosh*, the helicopter shot away like a rocket toward DanSheba.

Chapter Thirty-Five

Before the helicopter blades stopped rotating, Kathy and Hitch reached Christopher's room. Except for Elana and Nigel Quicksilver, one of the DanSheban doctors who had been watching over him since the early hours, the village was still asleep. Elana looked up as Kathy and Hitch raced in.

Hitch could see from Elana's forced smile that things were not good. Before he could say anything, he heard Kathy scream out.

"How is…"

Hitch knew without her asking. Christopher's breathing was shallow, his face pale blue, his V-Mark… Hitch could hardly look at it.

"This doesn't mean anything. He's been up and down all morning," Elana said. "We'll have him stabilized shortly."

As she made that promise, Barnaby walked in, trying to make himself presentable, and looked around. "Where's Ringthaller?" He looked at Elana, then Hitch.

"That's a long story for later. For now, I don't believe we have to worry about our enemies on the river. We've got to get that fucking virus out of me so Elana can get on with her antidote." Hitch turned back to Kathy, who tried to smile through the tears.

Minutes later, Meta rushed in. "I just got off with Yennie at the White House. The verification team is on the way. We have to convince all of them and we have to do it quickly. They can't hold off the smotec or the UN much longer."

Hitch groaned. The others just stared at her, as if her news was anticlimactic.

"What?" she responded. Hitch chortled. He would tell her later about his latest escapades.

****

High Minister McGivney stood before the Supreme Minister, listening on his scud. "I see. Thank you for the update." He clicked off and looked at the smotec.

"Well?"

As you requested, Your Sacredness, I let Rosewall and Rousseau go rogue, and I'm afraid they failed. You must insist the whole fleet go in."

"I don't think that's possible now. The UN appears to be breaking from the Cūtocracy and demands that we wait." The smotec looked at his watch and grumbled. "Let's hope the American president is bluffing."

****

The cold room kept everyone alert. The whiteness of the walls and cabinets made that much more effective for the magnetic triadic arcs under translucent domes that filled the ceiling. Hitch could almost feel his own *clicking* in unison with Christopher's, with Edna's…with OJ's, and they hadn't started the procedure yet. Technicians in light yellow surgical gowns stood over him. He followed the tube taped to his left arm. It hung down and into an empty glass container that spun at high speed. A second tube dropped down from a container filled with a violet liquid into his right arm. The way he was oriented, he could see a heart monitor and a monitor displaying brain waves. Nigel Quicksilver watched both as he stood behind Elana. Nigel was Meta's first cousin and closest confidant, Hitch knew from conversations he had with Meta. Behind them, Hitch saw Kathy peering through a viewing window.

He looked up at Barnaby, who smiled from behind his mask, then to Elana, who winked above hers. He felt her fingers squeeze his hand as Nigel injected a sedative in the second line.

Seconds later, or so he thought, Hitch heard a voice, hollow, strange, call out.

"Grandpa, Grandpa."

He opened his eyes and saw OJ standing over him, smiling. "We won, Grandpa. We won, three to two."

Hitch smiled back, then closed his eyes. He hadn't recalled being this relaxed. He took in the euphoria, not recalling why he was there or who had just called out to him.

Again, seconds later, it seemed, his eyes opened. He watched Kathy jump up from his bedside. Barnaby stood behind her.

Kathy took his hand. "Hi." She smiled. "You did it!"

"How's OJ?"

Kathy turned to Barnaby, then back to her father.

"I mean Christopher."

"We gave him a nap around the same time you went down," Barnaby said.

"I want to see him when he wakes up. Can I see what I look like?"

"You look the same, Dad," Kathy was quick to say, followed by Barnaby's words of caution.

"Oliver, the process is slow. We won't know for

twenty-four to forty-eight hours, or even longer, whether…"

"That's okay, Barnaby." Hitch held up his hand and stopped him. "It's enough to know you got what you needed. Did you?"

"More than enough. We're meeting with the verification team tomorrow and Elana is busy preparing."

****

Long before going through the gruesome process they had just completed, Elana discovered something VAMA learned early on when they began vaccinating people with the ERAM-V vaccine containing the Click. It appeared in a single footnote somewhere in the middle of an old textbook written by the Nobel Laureate Sivle Melasurej right after the ERAM plague. The footnote took up many pages and for all but truly sophisticated immunology experts willing to spend weeks and possibly months analyzing it, the words and equations amounted to nothing more than gibberish hallucinations intended to hide their true meaning. Otherwise, the Cūtocracy would never have allowed it to reach the light of day.

Dr. An Wu, Elana's father, was a physical chemistry professor at the University of Beijing. He gave Elana that old text book and dared her to read that footnote. The dare was enough for her to do more than just read it. She was determined to make sense of all the gibberish and wound up spending a good part of her adult life to that end. During all that time, she hadn't realized how important the footnote would be to her and quite possibly to humanity until the moment she fully understood it. That moment happened to coincide with her introduction into the Cause.

As she explained to Barnaby at the time, all that gibberish including made up equations, processes, and theorems camouflaged what Nobel Laureate Sivle Melasurej was attempting to disclose. When a person who had already contracted the ERAM virus was immunized with the vaccine containing the Click, according to the hidden meaning in the Melasurej footnote, their V-Mark appeared unchanged at first, but then turned black within minutes. Their viral symptoms were exacerbated, in most instances causing death. As a result, during the initial introduction of the ERAM-V vaccine, at the tail end of the ERAM plague, there were many black V-Marks, all of which remained purposely undisclosed and undocumented. The science was lost to future generations of vaccine research scientists.

A vaccine free of the Click had no adverse effect on the same person, or so the footnote postulated. All that gibberish also explained how the Click was made "invisible" within the vaccine and exactly what it was chemically speaking. All that eventually made it possible for Elana to make a Clickless vaccine. Unfortunately, the gibberish did not provide an analytical technique or even a clue to actually determine the presence of the Click within the vaccine. That had to be done clinically—that is, by injecting the vaccine into a person or some poor guinea pig with the virus, and observing his or her or its V-Mark. That was the reason Elana desperately needed the real virus to begin with.

Most of Elana's secret research after joining Barnaby Bloom's Cause was devoted to fully understanding the Melasurej footnote. She spent the time working to confirm the basic difference between the ERAM-V vaccine containing the Click and the Clickless vaccine. Unfortunately, the two vaccines appeared identical down to their genetic makeup. Their DNA lined up as if they were twins split from the same egg. And yet she knew from the footnote and all her subsequent research that the thing responsible for geriatric euthanasia was present in the vaccine containing the Click. Even if the difference was invisible under the most powerful microscope and most sophisticated spectrometer.

The problem Elana had to solve was how to prove to three hopefully brilliant scientists that the ERAM-V vaccine contained the Click. Obviously, she couldn't purposely inject one of the villagers with Oliver Hitchcock's virus and then the vaccine she knew contained the Click. They began testing different animals, a true guinea pig. The only animal they had access to that replicated the human reaction was a white tail rhesus monkey. They were not rare but not readily available either. She used one of the three she had to test a current "official" vial of ERAM-V vaccine supplied by the UN, one she knew contained the Click, before the verification team arrived. Elana injected the monkey with the virus collected from Oliver and then vaccinated it with the UN supplied vaccine. Sure enough, the monkey's V-Mark turned black, and it got deathly ill and died. She only had two monkeys left, along with several vials of vaccine she was saving for the verification team. Once she knew the clinical test worked, she made sure each member of the team received the Melasurej footnote, along with her thirty-page white paper on it and the results she achieved with the first rhesus monkey.

All three members arrived on schedule and Elana was prepared. She already knew something about the team thanks to Yennie Tawahada. Elizabeth Hightower, the American, was from Boston and member of the Ecclesian Church there. Elana had met her once at a conference. They had a drink together, but that was all. Rudolph Holtorf was from Berlin, and a Dr. Zedong— his first name hadn't been listed—was from Beijing. Apparently, he was the most conservative of the three, or so she was told. All three had prepared for this meeting and could follow Elana's white paper and the Melasurej footnote. Whether that was true Elana didn't know, but they more or less blessed her interpretation of the footnote if for no other reason than pride. Elana also provided them with a video of their experiment on the first rhesus monkey.

The next morning, Elana found herself holding up a hypodermic needle filled with another sample of the ERAM vaccine supplied by the UN and authenticated by the three members of the team. Each of the members had also authenticated the virus taken from Oliver after they arrived the day before. The two remaining rhesus monkeys were injected with it. Now it was time to inject one of the monkeys, a female, with the vaccine.

"As you well know, she will react the same way as a human who has contracted the virus and is subsequently vaccinated according to the Melasurej footnote. If the vaccine contains the Click the monkeys will develop V-Marks, which will eventually turn black. Then within hours each will more than likely die. If the vaccine does not contain the Click, the V-Marks will not turn black and the monkeys will be fine." Elana repeated what the three team members already knew but she was taking no chances.

All three nodded and Elana injected the female monkey now tied down on the table. All four of them plus Barnaby and Meta, who were also in the room, watched the monkey squeal in pain then relax.

Elana repeated the process on the other monkey, a male this time, and when she had finished, she placed both monkeys in separate cages and suggested they have lunch in the cafeteria while the vaccine took effect.

"No!" Dr. Zedong blurted out. "I will stay and watch."

"That's really not necessary," Elana said. "Two of our technicians will stand guard and tell us as soon as the V-Marks appear."

"No! I am not hungry. I will stay and watch," Zedong persisted.

Elana shrugged. "Suit yourself. You are welcome to keep our technicians company. In the meantime, I will have some lunch sent over."

During lunch, both Drs. Hightower and Holtorf were quite engaging and inquisitive. However, neither of them made any reference to the reason they were there, either because they still didn't believe the Click was a fraud or because they did. In either case, Elana and the others knew not to raise the issue.

Just as Dr. Hightower began talking about her beloved Boston baseball team, Elana's scud *rang*. "Yes. Thank you." She clicked off and turned to the others. "The female is showing. By the time we get there, my guess is the male will also be showing."

All five of them marched back to the lab—Elana

taking the lead, Barnaby walking with the American, and Meta trailing behind with the German.

The first thing Elana noticed was Dr. Zedong's lunch, untouched. Each of the monkeys sat in its cage looking somewhat docile. Their hair had been shaved where Elana had expected the V-Marks to appear, and there they were, a light Indian red.

Within minutes, both V-Marks turned black and both monkeys began to squeal. It took Dr. Zedong time to respond. "Two monkeys prove nothing. I need more."

"I'm sorry, Dr. Zedong but those were the last two we have," Elana said. "Besides, you saw the video of the first one.

Zedong kept shaking his head. "No! Two tests are not enough."

****

Yennie stood in front of a large TV at his apartment watching a series of split screens. He had muted the TV and was on his scud with Meta when she asked him to hold on. He stared at the screens. Pro-Cūtocracy rallies were taking place in Rome, Beijing, and Berlin. The screens went black just as Meta returned, then they turned dark green with bluish strings running through them.

"Yennie…"

"One moment Meta." Yennie stared in disbelief as the image zoomed in. What he saw was an aerial view of the Jungle east of Mumbai. He observed strings of rivers, like interconnecting veins, and a flotilla snaking slowly toward DanSheba. He quickly unmuted the TV.

"Meta, one more second."

"And so fellow Ecclesians around the world, and

Cūtocrats, we are told that the UN has not made a decision but plans to be ready to inoculate that tiny village in the Jungles of India. Our sources tell us they are just waiting for further information from…from the United States is what we are being told. Stay tuned."

Yennie turned the TV off and returned to Meta. "Have you been watching TV?"

"Yes, I'm afraid what you were watching was a recording. We saw it earlier."

"So, where are you with the verification team?

"Close."

"What does that mean?"

"The Chinese expert. He's a problem. You were right."

"Meta, the president needs all three to agree. And she needs it in writing by this evening your time."

"Or what?"

"She has a meeting at the Ecclesian Embassy, finally. We show up empty handed, or don't show, the invasion goes forward and the Smotecal Decretum goes up in smoke."

****

Hitch caught Elana pacing in her lab talking to herself in Chinese while Meta and Barnaby looked on worried. Meta had just finished telling Elana and Barnaby about her discussion with Yennie.

"What's the problem?" Hitch asked.

"That…that jerk from Beijing. He insists on a third test," Barnaby volunteered.

"And?"

"We don't have another damn monkey and he knows it. I've spent the last hour trying to find a way around this. We need another rhesus monkey or we need to wring that little bastard's Chinese neck," Elana shouted.

"He won't budge, Oliver. We tried everything short of a three-million-dollar bag of Ethiopian diamonds," Barnaby added.

Hitch stiffened. "Meta, get me the documents."

"What?"

"Your copies of the Decretum and Diary. Now! Then find Zedong and drag his ass into the conference room."

Within minutes Hitch found himself sitting across from the Chinese holdout, disheveled and sleepy-eyed, but as defiant as he was earlier.

"Kid, you look like shit. Seriously, a good night's rest would go a long way."

"I demand to know why I was brought here by force."

Hitch leaned across the table and got into Zedong's face. "Really? Problem is, you see, I do the demanding around here. And I'm really tired of you holding up the show. Time for you to accept the idea that the scheduled death of a human being might have been incorporated into the vaccine."

"We don't deal with ideas. We deal with science. You might as well ask me to accept Darwin's theory of Evolution based on the first chapter."

"Oh, in that case, let me show you the entire book, ours." Hitch slid the documents over to him along with the verification form signed by the others. "This is all the proof you need. Study them, and then sign this fucking form, and you aren't leaving this room until you do."

Zedong, still defiant, slid the documents and

verification form back to Hitch. "I will do no such thing. I am not afraid of you, old man."

Old man! Hitch reached up and touched his cheek, saw wrinkles beginning to form on his arm. That and Zedong were more than he could take. He reached across the table and grabbed the bastard by the collar. "You have no idea what I'm capable of, you little shit. If my grandson dies…"

Zedong held his ground. "I am not responsible for the death of anyone. I do the work of God and the Ecclesian Church. God is great. The church is honorable."

"Great? Honorable? Good for you. Now, read these and you'll find out what's so fucking wonderful about your church. I'll be right outside that door." He let go and marched through the door, slammed it behind him, then stomped into the lobby where Elana, Barnaby, and Meta waited.

"He'll come around," he barked to their awaiting ears.

"From what I've just learned, there is a Tarsusian connection between Zedong and Julian," Meta barked back, as if to question Hitch's optimism. "Apparently Tarsusians would rather lose their lives than their faith."

That bit of information did not make Hitch happy. Just as he was about to say something, Meta's scud *rang* and she listened.

"Of course I know what time it is there, Yennie. Twenty more minutes, maybe. I'll call you."

Minutes after Meta clicked off and began pacing, they all heard a *zing* from inside the conference room. Hitch was the first to reach the conference room door.

He grabbed the doorknob. The door was locked. Elana fumbled for her keys but couldn't find the right one fast enough. Hitch *kicked* the door in. The smell of burned flesh filled the conference room but there was no Zedong.

"Here, under the table," Meta yelled.

The gun was still in his hand, his head and the floor covered with blood. The verification form sat on the table, his signature added to those of the American and the German. Meta grabbed it and rushed out. Hitch fell to his knees and watched Zedong's stillness. First Julian, now this shit, he thought. What ever happened to the old adage that the truth will free you?

****

The president's limo moved slowly out of the White House onto Pennsylvania Avenue. Yennie sat next to President Wainwright. He was nervous, she was agitated. It took less than fifteen minutes to reach the Ecclesian embassy.

"I can't wait much longer, Yennie."

Yennie was holding his breath. It had already been twenty minutes since he last talked to Meta. Suddenly, he felt his scud vibrate. He reached for it and saw Meta's text and attachment. "It's here."

They both stared down as Yennie opened the Verification form. Seconds later his scud *rang*. It was Meta.

"Did you get it?"

"Yes. We're set."

"Yennie, everyone here is expecting the president to take down the church. Please do it for DanSheba."

Yennie looked over at President Wainwright. "We'll do our best."

****

While Elana and Barnaby were busy producing an antidote, Hitch sat at Christopher's bedside, stroking his hair. Kathy watched from the other side.

"Why couldn't they have done this first?" Kathy said, not accusingly it seemed to Hitch, but rather choking with fear that they would be too late. The president couldn't wait, he guessed. Or maybe Elana needed some type of validation before experimenting on a Preemie. He kept all that to himself.

Christopher's eyes opened. He looked up. "Grandpa? He reached up with one hand and touched his grandfather's face.

Hitch bent down and kissed him on the forehead. "I know, a little bit older since the last time you saw me."

Kathy smiled. "It suits you dad, more mature."

He laughed. She laughed. Even Christopher laughed.

Minutes later Elana and Barnaby came in with Nigel Quicksilver.

"Well, Christopher, it's time we make you well," Elana said as she hid a hypodermic needle behind her back.

Kathy took her son's hand. Elana explained to him what she planned to do. Christopher grimaced but only for a second.

"I'll be brave, like Grandpa."

Hitch felt a tear drop from one eye as he watched Elana save his only grandchild. He looked at Elana. She nodded. Her only concern, she told Hitch earlier, had been that Christopher was a Preemie, but it was only a small concern.

"We need an hour or so before we can test his

blood," Elana said then approached Kathy and kissed her on the cheek. "I'm sure he will be fine."

In disbelief, Hitch watched the two women left in his life hug one another, a sight he could not have imagined just days earlier.

Grandfather and daughter stayed with Christopher and played cards—war, the youngest Hitchcock insisted. The deck was divided into thirds. Christopher started by turning up a jack, Hitch a nine, Kathy a ten. Christopher took the three cards and neatly stacked them next to him. He turned over a three, Hitch a two, Kathy an ace. Christopher groaned. This went on forever it seemed to Hitch as he kept one eye on the door and the clock above it. *Click, click, click.* Hitch blinked. *Tick, tick.* He tried his best to stay cool.

In the meantime, Christopher chortled as he won and groaned continuously louder each time he lost. He moaned when it came to war and he lost four additional cards.

"My God, Christopher, I never realized how competitive you were. Just like your grandfather," Kathy said with a smile Hitch knew was forced.

Christopher smiled back. Hitch smiled even wider. But then suddenly Christopher's V-Mark began darkening. Kathy gulped. Hitch ran out looking for Elana. He found her watching Christopher's tube of blood vibrating in what looked to be a device for shaking a paint can.

Elana looked over. "What?"

"It's…" He could hardly even get that out. He grabbed her by the hand and started back to Christopher's room. Kathy was leaning over her son. The cards were spread across the floor.

Elana took Christopher's pulse, felt his forehead, then ran her fingers over his V-Mark. She looked up at the clock. *Tick, tick.* "He has no fever. His pulse is normal, and the V-Mark feels fine. Let's give it a bit more time. I will be back in a moment with the blood test results." She hurried out.

"But what does it mean?" By then, Kathy was back to her old self, worried sick and spiraling downward.

Hitch looked at her, then stepped to the edge of Christopher's bed and held his hand. "You'll be fine, son," he said with a smile, then turned to Kathy. "Won't he, Sweetheart?"

He watched Kathy gulp, then smile. "Yes, my darling, you will be fine."

Within minutes Barnaby and Elana marched in, all smiles.

"He's fine," both said in unison as Christopher's V-Mark began to lighten.

Chapter Thirty-Six

It spread across the Net as fast as digital data could travel. The Spider rooms around the world generated the news and the protolytes circling the Earth could hardly keep up. The president of the United States was to speak to the United Nation's General Assembly. Any possible invasion of the tiny village in the jungles of India had been terminated.

The lobby at Hotel DanSheba was filling up fast with villagers and guests, all sitting or standing in front of a big screen brought in especially for the occasion. Barnaby, Elana, Meta, Hitch, Kathy, and Christopher were given the front row of honor.

President Wainwright was to enter the UN from the east side of the public lobby and cross in front of an enormous stained-glass window donated to the UN by French artist Marc Chagall hundreds of years earlier. According to the commentator, she would walk from there to the lobby of the General Assembly where its amazing Foucault pendulum prominently hung.

"Meta, what do we hear from Yennie?" Barnaby asked. "Do we know exactly what the president's going to say?"

"I haven't heard from him since I sent back the executed verification. I only know they were on their way to see the Ecclesian Ambassador."

"She does plan to divulge the Smotecal Decretum,

doesn't she?" This came from Nigel Quicksilver.

"Of course," Meta responded. "And I can't wait."

The presidential caravan could be seen on the big screen pulling into United Nations Plaza as Secretary General Heinrich Flum stood at attention waiting to greet the American president. No doubt he wasn't happy, Hitch thought. He and everyone else in the hotel lobby watched the president and secretary general as they walked through the public lobby and eventually into the General Assembly Hall. It was similar to the way she entered congress at the beginning of a State of the Union—the greetings, the handshakes, the kisses on the cheek. And like the State of the Union, there were many who stayed back, who refused to even acknowledge her presence. After all, she was in the den of the world's real governing body—the Cūtocracy, and everyone knew she was there to do battle.

It took at least a half hour for the formalities to conclude and the president of the United States to approach the podium at the bottom of the steeply rising auditorium. She stood directly below the UN emblem. The insignia consisted of a map of the world, as seen from the North Pole, flanked by olive wreaths as a symbol of peace. On the walls to her left and right were large abstract murals designed by French artist Fernand Leger. Hitch could only imagine the history that took place in that auditorium.

"Ladies and gentlemen of this august body, fellow citizens of the world, I stand before you not as a politician but rather as an aging member of society. As such, I will come to the point and not mince words. Time is running out for many of us. I am here to talk about what we all know as the Click and I do so with heightened emotions. You are all aware of the age-old controversy between those who believe the Click is God's way of protecting the Earth and those who prefer to give credit to the natural order of things—Darwin, Mother Nature, call it what you wish. In either case, heretofore, the Click has always been viewed as a phenomenon beyond human hands. However, more recently there has been controversy surrounding the ERAM-V vaccine and whether or not it contains the Click." Hitch saw the president take a breath and scan the assembly hall. She was greeted with dead silence there and also in the lobby where he sat amongst the people he loved most.

"Of course, the idea that the Click is manmade has always been considered outrageous conjecture. That is, until the people of DanSheba leaped onto the world stage and into our living rooms. The DanShebans comprise an entire population of unvaccinated citizens in the tens of thousands now residing all over the world. Many of them are living healthy lives into their eighties, nineties, and well past one hundred years old." Once again Andrea Wainwright hesitated. Hichcock had to laugh to himself. She sure knew how to work a crowd, especially a crowd of cameras.

"So where is the Smotecal Decretum?" Nigel Quicksilver asked.

"Be patient and shush up," Meta scolded her cousin. "It's coming."

The president continued. "Because of that jewel in the jungles of India, the United States Government created a commission including the world's best minds in immunological science to study the DanSheban people as well as the ERAM-V vaccine. Its objective was to determine whether or not there was any truth to the conjecture. The commission, sanctioned by this body, also included three of the most brilliant scientists from Boston, Massachusetts, Frankfurt Germany, and Beijing, China, respectively, to determine the truth about the Click. It should be noted that those three scientists were independently selected by Secretary General Flum." The president stopped and turned to her host. "Mr. Secretary General, would you please join me at the podium and read the commission's conclusion as unanimously verified by your scientists from Boston, Frankfurt, and Beijing."

"She is one cool son of a gun," Barnaby piped in.

"And she sure knows how to take credit," Hitch added looking at Elana.

"The world's watching; don't knock it," Elana pointed out.

"Thank you, President Wainwright," Secretary General Flum said and slowly put on his glasses. As he did, the camera closed in on the tightness around his eyelids. Clearly a difficult moment for him, Hitch thought.

"I have in this envelope the commission's report unanimously verified by the scientists selected by this body, by me personally." He took a red-covered report from the envelope. Everyone in the room at the Hotel knew it to be thirty-two pages. The secretary general began reading the first page, the Summary/Conclusion. "We the undersigned scientists on the day indicated above completed a detailed evaluation of the vaccine used to immunize against the triple-stranded RNAx3 virus Tricaudovirales, more commonly known as the ERAM virus. Our evaluation focused specifically on the following question. Is the ERAM-V vaccine in any way responsible for what had always been considered the natural demise of human beings, what we refer to as the Click? Our conclusion is set forth below followed by the details describing our analysis."

Secretary General Flum took a deep breath and continued without looking up from the report. "It is an undeniable fact, the undersigns have unanimously concluded, that the ERAM-V vaccine contains the necessary formulation to and indeed does initiate the programmed demise of any person injected with the vaccine."

Most everyone in the hall had to know that would be the conclusion. Why else would the president of the United States be there. And yet a shocking wave of silence filled the enormous hall. It was as if someone had muted the TV at the hotel. Andrea Wainwright was brilliant. How she got the secretary general of the United Nations to utter those words was something Hitch could not fathom. The very organization that had been ever-vigilant in its enforcement of the vaccination program for the Cūtocracy was now pronouncing its demise in front of the entire world. The moment of silence seemed appropriate. Let the dead be buried with dignity, Hitch said to himself, then watched the president take center stage once again.

"So this is where she exposes the Ecclesian Church?" Nigel uttered once again.

Before anyone could respond, President Wainwright's voice filled the lobby at the DanSheban Hotel. "Thank you Secretary General Flum for agreeing to personally disclose such devastating information. I know it was not an easy undertaking." The Secretary

General stepped back allowing his guest to continue.

"Here it comes!" This time it was Barnaby.

"Fellow citizens of the world, history teaches us there are times when the phoenix indeed rises from its own ashes. At this very moment, that golden firebird circles above this great institution heralding a new age of enlightenment, an age when the wisest of our society, our senior citizens, will live longer. When secular principles in government will be protected and all religious values in homes respected. When no single theocratic dogma will be allowed to flourish like ivy strangling controversial thought, poisoning individual belief, sucking the oxygen out of the very air we breathe." Andrea Wainwright paused and stood erect as if she were a statue, as if she were the symbol of a new world order, then continued.

"And yet, fellow citizens, it won't be easy to champion the cause, to keep the phoenix flying high in our hearts. There will be resistance, winds from the east and the west, attempting to bring down the great bird whose plumage glistens with a thousand shades of gold as the French author, Voltaire, once noted. The old order will fight to maintain the status quo, and it will do so knowing that much of humanity has died prematurely on its watch. No more, I tell you, not so long as I am still a leader of the free world. Every person on Earth who has been vaccinated against the ERAM virus will receive free the antidote against the Click, and we will start with our oldest citizens and our youngest Preemies."

With that pronouncement, half those in attendance within the great hall of the General Assembly stood and applauded the president of the United States. The other half remained seated and could be seen cowering under the thunderous acceptance echoing overhead.

Once the hall quieted down, the president continued. "In order to accomplish our objective, to create a Clickless society, a herculean effort that cannot possibly be achieved by government alone will be required. All the people must become involved, in both the public and private sectors. To that end, I have been in consultation with Supreme Minister Pius, who has graciously agreed to the following on behalf of the Ecclesian Church. Pastors of all parishes throughout the world will be ordered to make available their churches as places to administer the antidote, without charge, and their parishioners will be encouraged to volunteer their manual labor as best they can. The High Ministers of all dioceses will supervise the effort and the ArchMinisters of each province will report back to the Supreme Minister any and all breaches in his commitment. In addition, on behalf of the Ecclesian Church as a whole, the smotec has agreed to sever all ties, financial and otherwise, with the Cūtocracy in regard to its active and/or passive legislative roles in government." The president paused once again as a good part of the hall erupted in standing applause.

By then Barnaby, Meta, and Nigel Quicksilver expected to hear about the Smotecal Decretum, no doubt, but not Hitch. He knew what was coming or more accurately what was not coming.

President Wainwright continued. "I have also consulted with the heads of state throughout the world and they have agreed to make available their government facilities and to call out their respective military reservists to staff those facilities. They have also agreed to make their scientific laboratories available for the manufacture of the Click antidote, following our lead here in the United States of America."

Still another standing ovation. In the meantime, the room at the Hotel remained silent. Everyone seemed to be wondering.

"Finally, citizens of the world, you must be patient. I am told it will take weeks before the antidote will be in full production across the globe. And when it is, we plan to devote the first two months, or however long it takes, to inoculate the elderly, those individuals who are at least seventy years old and—most important—the Preemies who deserve to experience not only childhood but old age. In order to coordinate this extraordinary effort, the Secretary General and Supreme Minister Pius have agreed to co-chair a United Nations Click antidote team, CAT, along with me. Thank you and God bless this fine institution, the nations of the world, and all the people on Earth."

Those final words brought the president's backers to their feet for an applause that seemed to last forever. They also caused Meta, Barnaby, and Nigel to look at one another in silence. No one appeared to know what to say. Meta pulled out her scud and began tapping away at its keys. "Yennie," she finally said and then just listened. Less than a minute later she clicked off and told everyone in the room to keep watching. The president would be giving a news conference outside the UN shortly.

Nigel couldn't wait. "I don't get it. I thought the whole idea was to crucify the Ecclesian Church," he hollered out causing many in the room to grumble in agreement. Many of the others knew about the Smotecal Decretum and were also expecting it to be exposed.

"Just wait," Meta snapped. "We will have plenty of time to talk after the president's news conference, which should be any moment according to Yennie."

"I agree," Hitch said. He then walked across the lobby to see how Christopher was doing during a commercial break.

Others visited the restroom or merely stretched. The room was quiet but seemingly filled with confusion and exasperation, Hitch thought as he considered everyone there. A few minutes later, the president entered the main lobby of the UN. The media all but surrounded her as she stood before a portable podium that had been brought in for the occasion.

President Wainwright took questions for a full forty-five minutes, answering each with a great deal of deliberation. Surprisingly, not one reporter questioned the truthfulness of her assertion that the Click was manmade. Mostly, the press corps was interested in knowing how the Click antidote team, CAT, was going to be administered, in detail, and how long she thought it would take to inoculate the entire population. And what about those individuals already in the throes of the Click, one reporter asked. She didn't have the answer to that and would have to defer to the experts. Another reporter asked how the nations in a Clickless world were going to manage population growth.

In response to that last question, Andrea Wainwright reached for her glasses and glanced at a note. "His Sacredness, Smotec Pius, has assured me he will be issuing a proclamation that church followers are no longer to be excommunicated for practicing birth control or participating in abortions, although any and all such acts will continue to be considered a sin against God. In the meantime, I will work diligently with the political leaders worldwide to cause their governments, and ours here in the United States, to stand aside and let women and families in general decide what is best for them when it comes to both birth control and abortion—and I might add, the smotec has given his pledge not to interfere."

After several follow-up questions to her last answer, which clearly stunned everyone listening and watching, the president was about to end the press conference when one of the reporters in the back could be heard. "Madam President, can you tell us what you know about a Smotecal Decretum having to do with the Click?"

"Okay!" Nigel said, jumping up from his chair. "It's about time."

"I'm sorry sir," the president said, "I know nothing about a Smotecal Decretum." She then ended the press conference, leaving the world to wonder what the reporter was referring to—everyone, that is, except the crowd in the lobby of the DanSheban Hotel and certain others, including the Supreme Minister of the Church of the Ecclesia.

"I think we've been double-crossed," Nigel pronounced as everyone else sat in silence.

It was Hitch who finally responded. "Nigel, you're wrong. What the president of the United States did was nothing less than brilliant. She used the Smotecal Decretum to move a colossal mountain in a way that its exposure would never have accomplished—could never have accomplished. It certainly is true that public knowledge of the Church's complicity in the history of the Click would have been damaging, but not lasting. Andrea Wainwright used that document to extract important concessions from the smotec, concessions that are needed now. Concessions she would have never obtained by exposing the Church to ridicule."

Hitch looked around to see if his words were sinking in. "And should the smotec, or a future smotec, consider reneging on those concessions, the Decretum will always be a robust reminder not to," he added and then focused his attention on Elana. "Are you confident the antidote will be effective on people in the throes of the Click?"

"It will be once we tweak the formula some, and yes I am confident of that."

"In that case, I believe our work is just about done here," Hitched announced as he took his daughter and grandson in his arms. "I may have a head start, but let's all go home and grow old together."

Epilogue

Spider rooms around the world were all but overheating with information on the Click antidote program worldwide. All one had to do was turn on his or her computation shell or TV or scud. The streets of New York, San Francisco, London, Rome, and others exemplified what was happening across the Earth. Lines of people, the Ecclesian clergy, government officials, and volunteers from their various communities were brought together to eradicate the Click.

Oliver Hitchcock was happily watching his computation shell when the keys, Janine Rousseau's keys on the dining room table, caught his eye. He had been putting that off but couldn't do so any longer.

Twenty minutes later he was at Janine's front door. He opened it with one of the keys she gave him and entered. Everything seemed different, familiar but different, since Rousseau was no longer... Hitch quickly shook himself out of that thought and immediately went to the safe and opened it with two other keys. He stared at the photo next to the safe, the one of Rousseau and a little girl hanging on the wall, then looked in the safe. He pulled out a satchel, opened it, and thumbed through at least a million dollars in cash and credit notes. "Oh, Janine." He couldn't help but laugh.

He then pulled out an envelope. It read on the front—*Dearest Oliver*. He opened the envelope, took out a formal document and note. He studied both. He read them again and moved in front of a mirror. He looked at himself and touched the wrinkles that weren't there a month ago. He looked at the note again. "I can do this. I want to do this."

Two days later he was in a rented convertible on the outskirts of Paris, France, approaching the gated entrance and lush grounds of Bouchaur Academy, a private school. Classical music streaming from Radio-USA was interrupted by an announcement. "Today, the Israeli Institute of Science has confirmed the validity of the recently published findings by geneticists from the tiny village of DanSheba and a consortium of secret labs around the world. Together they have unlocked the secret of aging, making it possible for people to live well beyond one hundred years of age. Reaction from the UN has…"

"Jesus, not again!" He shook his head. "Please, no more plagues!"

Hitch turned off the radio as he pulled up to a white building and focused on its magnificent Eighteenth Century Gothic architecture. He turned off the engine and got out. As he did, he watched the doorman watch him. He climbed the steps and showed the man the formal document he had been given. The doorman merely nodded without saying a word and went inside with the document.

Hitch paced along the grounds in front until he heard his name called out.

"Mr. Hitchcock, I am Andre Roue, director of

Bouchaur Academy. We have been expecting you. We just didn't know when. And this here is Olivia Rousseau."

"Bonjour, Papa."

Hitch smiled, then crouched. They hugged, then walked along the beautiful grounds hand in hand toward a bench where they sat and talked, where he told her how his mother saved his life, how she would meet Kathy and Christopher, how they all planned to live together. No more boarding schools. He reached over and kissed her on the forehead.

A word about the author…

The Trials of Adrian Wheeler was my first published novel (L&L Dreamspell, 2011). It was awarded runner-up in the San Francisco Book Festival 2015. It has also been optioned as a movie by EVW Entertainment (producer of the movie Break the Stage), and the screenplay has been written by Erik Wolter and me. EVWE is presently looking for partners to produce the movie.

The Wild Rose Press published The Fountain of Youth, my second novel, in May of 2017. It has received exceptional reviews, some of which appear on Amazon and Goodreads.

My wife, Susan, and I collaborated on The State vs. Max Cooper and The Steele Deal (published by ArtAge Publications), courtroom plays in which the audience serves as the jury. Both are being produced around the country.

In addition to those recited above and The Click, presently being published by The Wild Rose Press, I have three novels that have recently been completed: The First Coming, An Eye for an Eye, Black Hearts and Hungry Bears (a trilogy).

I have been writing poetry for over fifteen years (some of which have been published) and am also a portrait and figure artist and sculptor, having been represented by a number of galleries in Denver and Boulder, Colorado. I am presently represented by the Delta Gallery in Brentwood, California and on line by Vango Art. My work can be seen at my website, http://www.steveshear.net.

Thank you for purchasing
this publication of The Wild Rose Press, Inc.

For questions or more information
contact us at
info@thewildrosepress.com.

The Wild Rose Press, Inc.
www.thewildrosepress.com

To visit with authors of
The Wild Rose Press, Inc.
join our yahoo loop at
http://groups.yahoo.com/group/thewildrosepress/